D0971667

COMING HOME

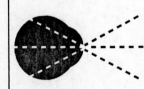

This Large Print Book carries the
Seal of Approval of N.A.V.H.

COMING HOME

STACY HAWKINS ADAMS

THORNDIKE PRESS
A part of Gale, Cengage Learning

Detroit • New York • San Francisco • New Haven, Conn • Waterville, Maine • London

GALE
CENGAGE Learning®

Thorndike Press, a part of Gale, Cengage Learning.

Thorndike Press® Large Print African-American.
The text of this Large Print edition is unabridged.
Other aspects of the book may vary from the original edition.
Set in 16 pt. Plantin.

LIBRARY OF CONGRESS CATALOGING-IN-PUBLICATION DATA

Adams, Stacy Hawkins, 1971–
    Coming home / by Stacy Hawkins Adams.
      pages ; cm. — (The winds of change series #1) (Thorndike Press large print African-American)
    ISBN 978-1-4104-5086-9 (hardcover) — ISBN 1-4104-5086-4 (hardcover) 1. Terminally ill—Fiction. 2. African Americans—Fiction. 3. Married people—Fiction. 4. Large type books. I. Title.
PS3601.D396C66 2012b
813'.6—dc23   2012024590

Published in 2012 by arrangement with The Zondervan Corporation LLC.

Printed in Mexico
1 2 3 4 5 6 7 16 15 14 13 12

*This book is dedicated to
my friend and mentor,
Dr. Bobbie Walker Trussell,
and to women everywhere
who seek to gift themselves, and others,
with deeper levels of unconditional love.*

When a gentle south wind began to blow, they saw their opportunity; so they weighed anchor and sailed along the shore. . . . Before very long, a wind of hurricane force, called the Northeaster, swept down from the island. The ship was caught by the storm and could not head into the wind; so we gave way to it and were driven along.

Acts 27:13–15 (NIV)

ONE

Dancing alone hadn't been an issue for Dayna Wilson in recent years, and tonight was no exception.

The habit marked her choice to live again, and on evenings like this, a sense of delicious freedom and rightness with the world returned. She two-stepped around her bedroom in her purple silk robe to the up-tempo melody pouring from her surround-sound speakers, singing along to the chorus of a Tina Turner classic: "What's Love Got to Do with It."

Ms. Tina's career had peaked well before Dayna's birth, but this song revived it during Dayna's early teen years, so she considered herself as big a fan of the ageless rock star as her mother and grandmother had been.

Dayna sashayed to her sitting area and sank into the caramel-colored leather loveseat. She closed her eyes and mentally rehearsed her speech for tonight's benefit gala.

Introducing Spencer wouldn't be a big deal; she could recite his credentials as easily as her own. Plus, this would be a friendly crowd. Most of the guests would write checks because he had personally invited them. Few business leaders and socialites in this community would snub the CEO of Chesdin Medical Center. Not only was their attendance a networking and power-play obligation, it was an informal insurance policy. Many of them surmised they'd eventually need the medical care Chesdin Medical provided, and when their turn came, they wanted to be treated like VIPs.

Dayna visualized herself introducing her boss, then opened her eyes and stretched. Time to get up and get to work. That meant sliding into her Spanx without breaking a sweat, and stepping into her dress before Warren arrived. He would be ready to go the minute he showed up, but she was certain he'd pause when he saw her in the apple-red, floor-length gown. Shoot — looking at the formal and accepting that she, the always-wear-black, stay-on-the-safe-side executive, had ignored her comfort zone and bought the dress, made *her* pause. She had come a long way, thank God.

Dayna chuckled. Between being more daring with her wardrobe and dating a man like Warren, she was on the verge of becoming unpredictable, and it was fun. What wouldn't be out of the norm were the questions she and Warren would receive from colleagues tonight about the status of their relationship. As usual, they would share very little in an effort to maintain the fine line between their professional and personal lives; but whenever they showed up as a pair for a work-related event or social gathering in the community, speculation over when they would tie the knot raced through the hospital with virus-like speed. So far everyone had lost the bet.

Dayna wondered when he'd ask her too, but she could be patient. With what he'd been through, Warren couldn't, and shouldn't, be rushed. He was wise to take his time, and so was she, for that matter. Half the battle of winning his heart and getting the ring would be making it obvious that choosing her was his decision, and his alone. The way he gazed at her when he thought she wasn't looking told her it wouldn't be much longer.

The thought of walking down the aisle to become Mrs. Avery didn't fill her with the youthful excitement she'd exuded the first time she'd wed; she knew now how much work marriage was. But after all these years of being single, she craved the daily companionship that marriage offered, and Warren was someone she could see herself working with through the thick and thin times. Her desire to be a mother hadn't waned, but having a baby was no longer a must. She loved Warren's boys and would be happy helping raise them.

Dayna's sound system looped to another CD. This time the melodies of Ben Tankard filled the air, and she thought of Daddy, who was probably at home this evening, getting ready for tomorrow's worship service. His "preacher rule" called for low-key Saturday nights, spent at home with no TV or movies, so he'd be ready to deliver the Word during two services on Sunday.

One of his regular means of relaxation was gospel jazz, and Ben Tankard ranked among Daddy's favorite artists. Funny how she didn't feel connected to him or Mama in most other ways, but she shared their taste in music.

The sweet, soothing sounds of the saxophone lulled Dayna into a relaxed state, and she reclined on the sofa again, telling herself it was just for a few minutes. They couldn't be late tonight. Spencer was counting on her and Warren to help greet guests.

She lay there, though, through another full song. When the opening melody of a fourth instrumental tune began, she leapt up and trotted across the carpet to her walk-in closet. The red dress was waiting for her on an outside door hanger. After wrestling into the girdle that made her thighs thinner and her mid-section pouch disappear, she tugged the gown free and stepped into it with the ease of a model. She straightened to her full height and felt the dress hug every curve.

"Girl, you look good!" Dayna struck several poses in front of the mirror above her dresser and marveled at how comfortable she felt in both the dress and in boasting about herself. Her girlfriends had assured her she would change in exciting ways when she turned forty. Still two years shy of that milestone birthday, she could already appreciate the new level of self-confidence they told her to anticipate.

On a practical note, she had selected the red dress because February was Heart Disease Awareness Month, and the hospital's efforts to combat this serious health issue would be recognized tonight at the gala. Yet as she turned this way and that in the mirror, she decided she didn't need a reason to be daring; this was her color and she would own it.

Minutes later her earrings, necklace, and diamond bracelet were in place. She slid into her silver heels and bathed in a spritz of the perfume Warren had given her for Christmas. A light dusting of loose powder removed the shine from her forehead and cheeks, and she looked picture perfect. The doorbell rang just as she applied her final stroke of lipstick, and she glanced at the grandfather clock in the corner.

Was Warren really here at 5:45? He'd be bragging about this all night.

She strode to the door as quickly as her flowing dress and stilettos allowed and swung it open, preparing to tease Warren before thanking him with a kiss for being on time. "Hey, babe —"

The bouquet of red roses that greeted her, and the man holding them, snatched away the rest of her words. He was much thinner than she remembered, but it had to be him.

"Brent?"

TWO

Dayna and Brent held their doorway poses like statues, frozen in place and time.

"Wow," he said, taking in her outfit. "Yes, Dayna, it's me. How are you?"

How was she? That was the best he could come up with?

In those few seconds of recognition, all of the hurt, shame, rejection, and anger she'd worked so hard to escape over the past seven years coursed through her.

"Why — what are you doing here?"

He shrugged and seemed embarrassed. "Let's just say I had to come. I want to fill you in on everything."

Somehow she couldn't form full sentences. "Your wife?"

"Tamara knows I'm here. She helped me find you."

His baritone was as rich as Dayna remembered, and his ebony eyes as deep. He stared

15

into hers, and extended the flowers toward her.

Dayna wasn't sure whether to slam the door in his face or invite him in. She knew what shock felt like — it was weightless and numbing, yet caused the heart to race like an out-of-control freight train, unable to anticipate the next curve. The last time she had felt unnerved to this degree, it had been due to Brent. Ironic how his leaving her and his finding her again stirred the exact same emotions.

She tried to process what he'd just said.

What wife in her right mind would help her husband search for his ex-wife? And allow him to show up at that woman's house alone, with the former wife's favorite flowers? Dayna wasn't sure she wanted to know, but what she couldn't deny was that after all of these years, looking into the eyes of the man who had once been her life still took her breath away.

She fixed her eyes on the roses Brent clutched and tried to steady herself. Whatever happened, she'd never let him know what she was feeling, regardless of why he had come or what he had come bearing.

Brent shifted from one foot to the other and cleared his throat. "May I come in?"

"Are you serious?"

Her curiosity wanted to let him in, to find out why he had come, but her rational side stood fast. She had become much stronger since their divorce. He couldn't sway her with fanciful words or a tender look like he had once been able to do, even when he was cheating on her.

This was her turf and her decision.

Brent seemed to have read that declaration in her eyes. His shoulders slumped. "Look, I know this is crazy, me showing up on your doorstep unannounced and —"

"Uninvited," Dayna said.

His eyes took another head-to-toe tour. "Obviously you're getting ready to go out. But may I come in for just a few minutes? I drove up from Cocoa Beach because I had to see you. I need to talk to you. Please."

How convenient to let it slip that he was staying just forty-five minutes away, Dayna thought. Did he live there, or was he in the area vacationing?

She looked past Brent, toward her driveway, hoping Warren would pull up, step out of his SUV, and save the day. Based on his track record, he probably wouldn't be here for another half hour — just in enough time to scoop her into the vehicle and make it to the reception minutes before special guests began arriving.

Dayna glared at Brent. No matter how sad and handsome he looked as he pleaded his case, she couldn't forget those same eyes holding contempt and coldness when he told her it was over and that he had fallen in love with someone she had considered a friend. How could Tamara really have sent him here today?

She wanted answers, but then again, she had learned to live without understanding Brent or what had happened between them to cause their split. So how would having some resolution now improve her life? Besides, she knew whatever he had to say would justify his and Tamara's choices. Dayna couldn't imagine how this out-of-the-blue visit and gift of roses could benefit her.

The Tina Turner song she'd been jamming to less than an hour earlier began playing in her mind. Brent reached for her hand and broke her reverie.

"Please, Dayna —"

Dayna stepped back, out of his reach. She recognized the desperation in his eyes and tone. Was he pleading with her the same way she had begged him not to leave, to give their marriage a chance? Really?

Brent tried again. "I know I don't deserve your time or have the right to enter your home, but can I please just talk with you for five minutes? Or, if you don't want me to come inside, would you step outside?"

He was persistent, but there was no way she was crossing the doorstep in her fabulous red dress before Warren arrived. Dayna sighed. Maybe if she heard him out, he'd leave her alone for good. She opened the oak door wider and motioned with her head for Brent to come in.

She left the door ajar and strode to the opposite wall to switch on the chandeliered light. They stood across the foyer from each other with what seemed like an ocean between them. Every second he spent surveying the spacious entrance made her heart beat faster.

But now she understood why, without hesitation, she had written "Return to Sender" in bold, black ink on each envelope when it arrived. Brent's presence today confirmed that opening his recent correspondences would have been akin to stepping into quicksand. She had blossomed when she'd made the decision to leave Brent in her past, and that was where she intended for him to stay.

"You've done well for yourself, Dayna," he said.

Should she tell him that had been part of

her revenge — to thrive without him? She held her tongue and refused to reciprocate his smile. Dayna turned to lead him to the living room so they could sit and talk, but paused midstep. Why make him comfortable?

She faced him again and folded her arms. "Tell me why you're here."

"Want me to throw you these flowers in a touchdown pass?" Brent chuckled at his own humor and extended the bouquet toward her, with a "please?" in his eyes.

"Still the comedian," she said, mindful that he had avoided answering her question. She approached Brent to take the bouquet by its cellophane-wrapped stem and laid it on a side table.

"Thanks for accepting them."

"You're welcome." She folded her arms again. "What's up?"

He took a step toward her, and she took a step back after catching a whiff of the cologne he'd always worn and she'd always appreciated. "Just answer the question, Brent: enough of the melodramatics."

"I'm here because. . . . I need to share something important with you, Dayna. It's long overdue, but I need to do this. I sent three letters, and each was returned unopened, even after I verified your address.

So I thought I'd come in person and —"

"And force me to hear you out? Is that it?"

He seemed hurt when she laughed.

"How dare you just show up out of the blue," she said. "Please tell me we're on candid camera or that the MTV crew is lurking and I'm being punked. This has got to be some kind of joke."

The pain sizzling in his eyes surprised Dayna. It was clear that her response had doused him like a bucket of cold water.

"Did you know I never stopped loving you?" Brent's soft question was delivered like a declaration. "I came to apologize for hurting you and tearing apart our marriage."

Dayna's knees turned to jelly. She fought to keep her composure.

"The apology I halfway understand — it is *long* overdue," she said. "But did you just stand here in my house, wearing your wedding ring, and tell me you've always loved me? Please."

Brent crossed the room, and before she could react, he grasped her hands.

"This isn't funny," she said. She tugged her hands out of his and hugged herself. The temperature was the usual February, seventy-ish, central-Florida degrees, so why was she shivering?

In the seven years since their divorce, they hadn't talked or crossed paths. On rare occasions their once-mutual friends would let it slip that he was still working in IT, or that he and Tamara were still together. Someone must have been giving him crumbs about her life too. How else had he managed to find out where she lived and be confident enough that the address was correct to show up with roses?

The more she thought about his surprise appearance this evening, the more questions surfaced. She wanted answers, but she also wanted him to leave.

"Brent, really, what do you want from me? You couldn't have possibly sent me letters and shown up at my home just to say you're sorry. I returned your letters without opening them, so obviously I didn't want to be bothered. And what did you mean when you insinuated that Tamara sent you here? Do you know how crazy that sounds? Come on, how —"

Brent silenced her chatter by placing a forefinger on her lips.

Dayna's eyes widened. This man was bold! In a split second, she raised her palm and slapped him hard across his cheek. "You need to go," she said, her voice shaking. "Now."

Brent parted his lips to speak, but hesitated when she shook her head. "Go, Brent. You are out of line, and I can't do this."

His face fell. He pulled a business card from the pocket of his khaki slacks and leaned past Dayna to place it on the side table next to the roses. "I know my coming here seems stupid, if not insane," he said. "But I didn't want to miss an opportunity to make things right if I could. I came to tell you how sorry I am for hurting you and to ask you to forgive me. I don't deserve it, but I had to ask. My cell and home numbers are on the card. Would you please consider having dinner with Tamara and me? We have something to share with you, and today doesn't seem as appropriate as I thought it might be."

Brent's brief touch had upset Dayna's internal equilibrium. She inhaled and struggled to hold at bay a volcano of emotions, including tears. There was no time to redo her makeup before tonight's fundraiser, and Brent didn't deserve to see the effect he still had on her.

Get it together, girl.

"Dinner with you and Tamara?" The laugh that escaped resembled a bark. "Just as you

23

moved on years ago, Brent, I've moved on. I heard what you had to say today and that's enough apology for me. I think you should go."

Before Brent could respond, Warren's shadow filled the doorway. He stood just behind Brent, but seemed to engulf him.

Dayna watched the two men size up each other. Both were tall, but Warren's long, lanky frame towered above Brent's shorter, now thinner one. Both wore well-trimmed mustaches and goatees, a commonality that Dayna hadn't picked up on before now.

"My knight has arrived," she said. She strode toward Warren and bypassed Brent to hug him.

The shock on Brent's face was priceless. If he hadn't been born cocoa brown, he might've turned three different shades of red — a feat Warren could actually manage.

Yes, she wanted to tell him. She had moved on, and race didn't matter. Warren's heritage might not make him a brother, but in many ways, he was more loyal and loving to her than Brent had been throughout their seven-year marriage.

"Sounds like you were leaving, Mr. . . . ?" Warren wrapped an arm around Dayna's waist and stepped inside, giving Brent the doorway to make an exit. Dayna wondered what he was thinking as she watched his eyes scan the foyer and land on the roses.

Brent cleared his throat and stepped outside, onto the stone porch. He turned back toward Warren and extended his hand.

"Just call me Brent, man. Dayna can tell you the rest."

Warren's jaw locked into the position that signaled he was ticked off or frustrated. He felt like Brent was disrespecting him, Dayna realized, but she knew he'd keep his cool.

He nodded at Brent but didn't shake his hand.

"I'm Warren . . . man," he said. "Dayna can tell you all about me too. Or, too bad if you've missed that opportunity."

He turned toward her. "You ready for the gala, my lady? Your carriage awaits."

Dayna summoned a smile. "I'm ready. Give me a second to get my purse and shawl."

Brent watched their interaction like a little boy passed over for the dodge ball team at recess. Her heart was still racing because of what had transpired between them, in just those few moments. She could tell he wanted to say more; instead, he turned to leave.

"Thanks for your time, Dayna. Hope we can get together soon." He struggled to smile at Warren. "You take good care of her, all right? That's something I didn't do."

Dayna and Warren watched him approach his black Mercedes Coupe, which was parked on the street in front of Dayna's house.

Warren turned to her. "You okay, babe? Looks like I got here just in time. Was that *the* Brent — your ex?"

Dayna hugged him again and pressed her cheek against his. "That was *the* Brent, and that was an interesting visit. I'm glad you showed up when you did. Let me get my things, and I'll tell you about it on the way to the benefit."

She released him and headed to the rear of the house, toward her bedroom. She'd have to take a few extra minutes to compose herself and clear her mind before they left. Brent's surprise visit, plea for forgiveness, and dinner invitation had unsettled her. Warren would hear some of the highlights about what happened before he showed up, but it would be wiser not to mention the rush of old feelings that engulfed her when her eyes had met her ex-husband's. She couldn't believe her heart had tried to betray her, and Warren wouldn't either.

THREE

Dayna waited until she and Warren were two blocks from the gala hotel to slice the thick silence that had settled between them.

"So, what do you want to know? Aren't you curious about why Brent was there?"

"What do you want to tell me?"

Dayna tried to quell her frustration. Did he have to answer a question by posing a question? She knew he wanted answers — why didn't he just admit it?

"I'm not one of your marketing staff or one of the reporters who routinely interview you, Mr. Avery. You don't have to play cat and mouse with me."

Warren glanced at her. "You're the one holding out on me. I just happened to show up before 'brother man' left. Last I heard, you hadn't seen or talked to the dude in years, and he just shows up at your house?"

The use of slang by some other forty-something white man might come across as forced or awkward, but the words rolled off Warren's lips with ease. His three-year stint just out of college with a black-owned East Coast marketing firm where, for all intents and purposes, he was the minority employee had yielded friendships and experiences that ingrained the lingo into him as easily as the West Coast surfer lingo he'd adopted in his teens had been ingrained.

Serving as vice president of marketing for Chesdin Medical Center, on the ritzy outskirts of Calero, hadn't changed him. He used the same laid-back, keeping-it-real candor with hospital executives, the media, and his staff, and it was one of the things Chesdin's CEO (and Dayna) loved about him.

Warren sighed and rested one hand on Dayna's thigh while keeping the other on the steering wheel and his eyes on the road.

"Look, it's not cool to show up for a date with your lady and find another man there, plain and simple. I know he's been long gone from your life, but this man came with flowers, and he looked like he wasn't ready to leave."

Dayna squeezed Warren's hand. She appreciated how, despite his efforts to appear nonchalant, he wore his heart on his sleeve.

"Yeah, I guess that did look a little crazy.

It was a strange visit, and I agree — he wasn't ready to leave."

"What did he want?"

"He wanted to tell me he's sorry for how our marriage ended, and he wants me to forgive him. He and his wife, Tamara, want to take me to dinner so he can explain what happened and why he now wants to make amends. Can you believe that?"

Warren shrugged. "Seems strange, out of the blue. How did he find you, anyway?"

Dayna shook her head. "Don't know. My number is unlisted as it always has been, but these days you can find just about anybody on the Internet. I *am* curious about how he got my address, which brings me to something else I haven't mentioned — he's been trying to contact me for a while."

Warren turned into the hotel parking garage and Dayna waited while he pressed the button to receive a parking deck claim ticket. When he had maneuvered his Range Rover into a corner spot near the elevators, he turned off the metallic-blue SUV and faced her.

"This isn't the first time you've heard from him, but it's the first time I'm hearing about it?"

An edge crept into Warren's voice and his jaw set again.

"I should have mentioned it — I'm sorry. He started sending me letters about three months ago, to my home address. At first I was stunned that he'd found me, but even with that first letter, I decided not to go there. I didn't care what he wanted after all this time. I made peace a long time ago with what happened between us — at least I moved on. I returned the letter unopened; and I did that again, two more times."

Warren frowned. "He wrote you three times?"

Dayna nodded. "And each time I sent the letters back, unopened. That's why he showed up today, to talk to me in person."

Warren smirked. "And to ask you to dinner, huh?"

Dayna shook her head. "I don't get that, either. He wants me to join him for dinner — with Tamara."

"Didn't you tell me he married the woman he cheated on you with?"

Dayna flinched at Warren's matter-of-fact mention of an experience that had left her with scars. With as much work as she'd done to get past it, her reaction surprised her.

"Yeah, that's Tamara. And apparently they're still together. He said she knew he was visiting me today. Wonder if she knew he brought flowers."

Warren unbuckled and climbed out of the SUV. He grabbed his tux jacket from its hanger on the rack just above the seat behind him and slid into it. Seconds later, he was opening Dayna's door.

"Doesn't matter what this Tamara knows or doesn't know, right? Did you absolve him of his guilt today? If so, you don't need to see him again."

Dayna unfolded her long legs and stepped out of the SUV with Warren's help. He surveyed the floor-length red dress, her short layered hairdo, and flawless makeup, and smiled.

"Perfect, babe. You're stunning."

She thanked him with a kiss, then wiped her red lipstick from his lips. His compliment pleased her, but it didn't prevent the questions that had once tormented her from surfacing. Her physical beauty had landed her a man before, but it hadn't been enough to keep him.

"I don't plan to see Brent again," she told Warren, "but why do I feel like you're issuing an ultimatum? What's with the attitude?"

Warren closed the door behind her and embraced her around the waist to guide her toward the parking garage elevators.

"I don't know Brent's current wife, but

the one he was stupid enough to leave isn't hard on the eyes or difficult to fall for," Warren said. "And guess what? She's taken. You don't want me to dictate whether you can see him again? Fine. But if you decide to accept that dinner offer, tell him he's paying for four, 'cause I'm coming too."

FOUR

The alarm clock chimed and Dayna hit the snooze button for a third time.

This was ridiculous. How many Sunday mornings would she play this game with herself? Either she was getting up and going to church or not. In another fifteen minutes, the decision in favor of the pillow she was hugging would be obvious. She'd been making a concerted effort lately to prioritize church again; but at times like this, when she'd only had an hour or two of solid sleep, it was easy to talk herself into staying home.

She had stopped attending church altogether after the breakup of her marriage, but she'd never lost her preacher's daughter guilt about it. Never mind that her reasons felt legitimate at the time and had, in some ways, been validated by her divorce recovery therapist; what should have been a temporary break from organized worship had morphed into a way of life she still struggled

33

to feel okay about.

Dayna rolled onto her back and stared at the ceiling. Her thoughts turned to the issue she had fallen asleep fretting over: Brent's reappearance. What kind of person showed up at your door after treating you like a dog, marrying the woman he cheated with, and never giving you a decent explanation for why your relationship hadn't been worth saving? Every time that question and its accompanying indignation surfaced, Dayna summoned the truth her therapist had urged her to accept: she might never get an answer.

Dayna couldn't help but smile, though, when she replayed Brent's brief visit in her mind and how, in an instant, she had slapped him. She had been just as surprised as he was, but reminiscing about it now, she decided it was a blow she should have delivered seven years earlier. Her actions yesterday were warranted, as far as she was concerned, and even after all this time, it had felt good. What would God, or even Daddy, the good preacher, have to say about that? Daddy's track record told her that he would chalk her actions up to being MIA from church for too long and the lack of spiritual discipline that fostered. Would God understand and cut her some slack, or would he also chastise her?

She lay there, wishing a heavenly response would thunder down, then admitted that if one did, she might not recognize it. She struggled to a sitting position and released the pillow she'd been clutching. The only way her relationship with God was going to improve was if she put some effort into making that happen.

Yes, Warren, you are now officially living inside my head.

Dayna glanced at the bedside clock. Warren was probably leaving his house right now with his sons to attend service at the Presbyterian church a few blocks from his house. Why hadn't she called him when her alarm first woke her? She could have gone with them instead of waffling about whether to race to Rock Hill Ministries where she'd have to reassure the usher who offered her a visitor's card that she was indeed a member.

Dayna sighed and climbed out of bed. Maybe she'd slip into Warren's church and surprise him.

On her way to the bathroom she passed her red dress, once again hanging outside the closet door. She'd received more compliments last night than she had her entire adult life. The dress would go to the cleaners tomorrow and then be tucked in the back of the closet, but her memories of how she had felt in it would be permanent — including the look on Mr. Brent's face.

She stepped into the shower and mentally ran down a list of potential outfits for the worship service while the warm water soothed her. Jeans and other casual wear were always welcome at Warren's church, but since he never dressed less than business casual, she would follow his lead.

She wasn't sure what God would say through the minister today, but she had a few questions for him, including wanting to know why Brent had to show up when everything in her life finally seemed to be going well. If nothing else, his appearance had taken her back in time, to a place she had no desire to revisit. Brent and his flowers and his pleas to reconnect could undo the hard work and emotional energy she'd invested in letting go of her anger, boosting her self-worth, and creating a full and satisfying life without a mate. Just as she had mastered those goals, Warren had finessed his way into her life at her first-ever visit to a salsa dancing class. The timing had been impeccable, because in her head and in her heart, she'd been ready to live again, on her own terms. No way was she going to

36

let Brent interfere with the eighteen months and counting of magic that she and Warren were nurturing. If Brent thought he could take up space in her world again, he had another think coming.

FIVE

Thank goodness Dayna texted before leaving home.

Minutes after sending Warren the message to let him know she was on the way to his church, he replied for her to stay put. Dayna frowned at her iPhone and checked the clock on the dashboard of her car. Service started in five minutes, and he wasn't there?

Before she could text him again, he pulled into her driveway. Mason jumped out of the SUV and ran into the garage, where she still sat in her Lexus.

"Hey, Dayna, we're not going to our church today. Dad's friend from work has a child getting baptized, so we're visiting their church instead. Want to come with us?"

Dayna unbuckled and followed Mason. She settled into the front passenger seat and waved at Mason's twin, Michael, who sat behind Warren playing a video game.

Warren leaned over and hugged her.

"Good morning, babe. With all the hustle and bustle at the gala last night I forgot to mention on the ride home that Stephanie stopped by our table while you were mingling with guests. She invited me to her son's baptism today. I didn't promise to come, but seems like I caught your sleepy bug this morning and couldn't get up in time for service at Calero Presbyterian, so I thought the boys and I would go to the baptism instead."

Dayna swatted his hand. "But you were going to let me stay in bed and be a heathen, huh? Why didn't you call?"

"I did, and when you didn't answer, I let it go. I was a block from the interstate ramp when I got your text."

Dayna checked her phone. "My ringer is turned off, and it looks like I might have been in the shower when you called. Talk about missed signals. Glad it worked out. This means I'm not late for church after all."

Warren shook his head. "Nope. Stephanie's church starts at 10:30. I'm impressed you were even interested in going. All dressed and in the car . . . wonderful."

Dayna narrowed her eyes. "You're supposed to be encouraging me."

"Let me rephrase that," Warren said. "I'm

glad you wanted to come to church with me and the boys."

If Michael and Mason weren't right behind them, she would have kissed him; but she was always mindful that while their mom had been gone for four years, they still missed her. She couldn't imagine how hard it was to see their dad with someone else, even though she hoped they liked her.

"That was nice of Stephanie to invite her boss to witness her son's special day," Dayna said. "She must think a lot of you."

Warren was far from hard on the eyes, and she knew his name ranked high, right behind a few doctors, on the Hottest Hospital Catches list that circulated every few months around Chesdin Medical. Because of her newfound self-confidence, and because of the man Warren was, instead of fretting, she felt honored to be dating the "cream of the crop." Stephanie might be among the women who swooned over him, but Dayna's radar hadn't detected any overt flirting. Stephanie appeared to be a single mom who appreciated having a boss who allowed a flexible schedule in a busy hospital marketing department.

They pulled in front of a red-brick church with white columns. People of all ages and in all forms of dress, from Sunday best to shorts and sneakers, were streaming inside. Michael and Mason spotted a few kids they knew from school. "Dad, can we sit with them?"

Warren hesitated, but relented when Dayna winked at him.

"As long as you behave and don't talk the entire service," Warren said. "Leave the DS game in the car, and I'm gonna quiz you on the sermon later, so you better pay attention."

The boys rolled their eyes and climbed out of the SUV to catch up with their friends.

Dayna grinned at Warren and accepted the soft kiss he planted on her lips. "Good morning again, babe."

"You silly man," she teased, even though she loved this more-romantic greeting. "Let's go inside."

"I'm just glad to be spending the morning with you," he said when he reached her side of the Range Rover and opened her door. "I know Sunday mornings can be a struggle for you, but I appreciate it when we worship together."

She peered at him. Warren had been nudging her for a while to spend more time studying the Bible and attending church, but this was the first time he'd articulated how much it meant for her to accompany him. She'd have to do better.

Once inside the sanctuary, an usher escorted them to the front center section to sit with Stephanie and her guests. Stephanie beamed when she looked up from her program and saw Warren.

"You came!" She stood and gave him a hug, then leaned past him to hug Dayna.

Dayna and Warren settled in the pew just behind her, and Dayna feared that Stephanie's cloud of strawberry-blonde hair might block her view throughout the baptism and sermon. She was contemplating whether to trade places with Warren when Stephanie turned and motioned for her to lean forward. She cupped her hand around Dayna's ear. "I hope you're going to be okay being the only . . . person of color here. I didn't know Warren was bringing you."

Dayna decided to be appreciative rather than offended. She knew Stephanie meant well. Day in and day out, she served as one of a few minorities on the hospital's executive staff, a reality that mirrored her days in advanced placement high school classes and throughout college and grad school. Though she had struggled with feeling good enough while in her marriage, coping as a minority wasn't one of her issues.

"It's okay," she whispered and patted Stephanie's arm. "This is God's house, and we're all created in his image. I may learn a few new songs or rituals today, but that's a good thing."

Stephanie blushed. "Just wanted to make sure. I'm glad you're here. You and Warren are so good together."

Dayna sat back and Warren reached for her hand. He questioned with his eyes what the exchange had been about, and Dayna shook her head and mouthed, "No worries."

Organ music filled the sanctuary, and the pastor and associate pastor entered the pulpit. After a few pleasantries and the reading of Scriptural passages, they prepared to baptize three adults and five children, including Stephanie's son.

Dayna's thoughts wandered to her own baptism, at age twelve, and how afraid, yet obligated, she had felt. Daddy had been hounding her for waiting so long. "No preacher's daughter should enter their teen years without knowing the Lord," he'd said repeatedly as her thirteenth birthday approached. When he'd threatened not to let her have a birthday sleepover if she hadn't "gotten right with God" before the time came, Dayna knew what she had to do.

Six weeks before her birthday, she wrote

and memorized what she'd say when she stood before the church to give her life to Christ. The next Sunday, when both sets of grandparents happened to be visiting River-view Baptist, she ran to the altar and fell into her father's arms when he asked if anyone wanted to accept Jesus.

Daddy had clung to her that Sunday and shouted praises. She remembered praying for God to really come into her heart and to help her daddy love her since she had taken this big step. After she'd been dipped in water a few Sundays later, Dayna had marveled that she felt like the same girl, and she'd been saddened that Daddy's affection had ended with that one-time public display.

Warren insisted that baptism was merely a public symbol of one's changed heart and acceptance into God's family; the true change occurred gradually, as one grew to know God on a personal level and followed the principles he outlined in the Bible. Dayna wondered whether someone had taken the time to explain this to Stephanie's adorable son and to the others who seemed so excited to be initiated into God's kingdom this morning. Or would they, too, spend years wondering what was different now and why the process of baptism hadn't literally changed everything?

Dayna's thoughts skated around again as she held a hymnal and stood next to Warren singing "Amazing Grace." This time they landed on Brent and how his abandonment had led her to defiantly stop "playing" church. If her church service and religious obedience had been worth something, why had God allowed her to lose everything that mattered?

During those numb years, the only emotion she'd truly felt was anger. It bubbled forth when she sat in church next to so-called friends who gossiped about her circumstances instead of extending kindness and concern, and when members of her family — the Christians who knew her best — accused her of losing a good husband because she'd been a poor wife. When she listened to other parishioners shout for joy during sermons about God's grace and healing power, she sat stone faced, because none of that seemed evident in her life. Eventually, it had been easier to stay away, and when the craving for inspiration arose, to turn on one of the popular TV ministries and get her fill for an hour.

Usually these memories were accompanied by resentment, but this morning, standing next to Warren, she felt okay.

Warren believed in God's Word, and he sought to live by it, and while he wasn't perfect, his relationships with his boys, his parents, his employees, and even with her, proved he was succeeding.

His routine, gentle suggestions that she dig deeper, beyond the surface requirements of what it meant to live for God, intrigued her, but also made her uncomfortable. The wonderful thing about Warren, though, was that he loved her unconditionally. She didn't have to move at his pace to make things right between them and that made all the difference.

She glanced at the church program and saw that today's sermon title was "Letting God Lead — No Matter What, When, Where, or How." Whoa. This was deep.

Unbidden, an unsettling question filled Dayna's spirit: What if the unexpected encounter with her former husband this weekend was a test? What if God wanted her to go to dinner with Brent and Tamara? Not so much for Brent's sake, but for hers? What if her former husband's return meant she really hadn't forgiven and forgotten, as she had worked so hard to do since their divorce?

Her prayer skills were rusty, but in recent months, she'd been trying to simply talk to

God — something she'd never done before. Growing up, her prayers and blessings over meals had always been formal. Warren kept urging her to just have a conversation, and right now, with the minister preparing to speak, she did just that.

Lord, sometimes I think too much. Don't let me read too much into Brent's return, or too little. Show me whether to ignore him or take him up on his offer for dinner so I can resolve my lingering questions. For me to get it, make it really clear, will you? Either way, please help me go back to life as it was two days ago — pre-Brent — when my past wasn't taunting or haunting me. Thank you, and amen.

Dayna realized she'd done more request-making of God than surrendering to him, but a lot was at stake. Didn't she have a right to preserve her peace of mind?

Six

Dayna sat at her desk on Monday morning preparing for the executive team's weekly meeting and weekend fundraiser debriefing when a new-message alert popped up on her computer screen.

She did a double take when she saw Brent's name. First he tracked down her home address, now he was emailing her at work. Was the man stalking her?

She took several deep breaths to calm herself, then opened the email. His message seemed harmless.

Dayna, what a blessing it was to see on you Saturday, after all of these years. I apologize for showing up at your home unannounced, but thanks for talking to me. I wish we'd had more time, because there are some things I need to tell you, and I think face-to-face would be best. Would you bear with me again and allow Tamara and me to treat you to dinner? I promise to leave you alone after that. This is just something I really need to do. Feel free to email me back. Or better yet, here are my phone numbers again.

Dayna glanced at the numbers and realized she'd misplaced the business card he'd given her on Saturday. She didn't remember him being this persistent when they were married, but she had changed a lot too.

Sometimes the best way to get the message across that one didn't want to be bothered was to ignore the "bother-ee." Her computer pointer was hovering over the delete key when her cell phone rang. She released the mouse to answer the call.

"I'm about to go into a meeting shortly," she said, without first saying hello to her girlfriend Vanora, "but boy, did you call at the perfect time. I hope all is well in Chicago."

She quickly filled in Vanora, who had been her college roommate and maid of honor, about Brent's appearance and persistence.

"What do you want to do?" Vanora asked.

"I don't know if I can tell a good Christian girl like you," Dayna said. "Let's just say I'm more into slapping the other cheek, rather than turning it."

Vanora remained silent for a few minutes, and Dayna knew her friend was trying to find a nice way to share her point of view.

"Dayna, I thought you'd worked through the pain and anger from this relationship. What is this I'm hearing? One visit and an email can throw you that much off course? Makes me think you've got more work to do, my friend."

Dayna felt her anger rising. "Van, this isn't about me."

Vanora sighed. "Look, I know exactly where you're coming from, and you have every right to think and feel what you're experiencing. But in the broad scheme of things, Dayna, this *is* about you. You want to move forward with Warren without any baggage from Brent. Maybe you should meet with him, hear what he says, and let him know how you've felt all these years about what he did. That might move you a step closer to really letting go, regardless of what Brent is saying or doing."

Dayna considered how thoughts of Brent had consumed her the past few days and how along with those memories had come negative emotions.

"So maybe I should meet with him on my

terms to say what I need to say, huh?" Dayna said. "I can't think of a thing that I'd want to say to him, though. Nothing that would matter. He wants to meet to get something off his chest, it sounds like. How is that fair to me?"

Dayna could imagine Vanora nodding on the other end of the line.

"I hear you, Dayna. But the fairest thing you can do for yourself is to take care of you — emotionally, physically, and spiritually — and it just so happens that each of those areas is intertwined. If you're weak in one, it prevents you from performing your best in the other two. Meet him for dinner, and if you don't like what he has to say, you can always get up and leave. But if he has something to say that's worth hearing, listen, and try to make peace with him, with yourself, and even with his wife. This is all about *you*. If they happen to get some perk out of it too, you can't be concerned about that."

Dayna's long-time assistant Monica rapped on the office door and stuck her head in to remind Dayna that her meeting would start in fifteen minutes. Dayna gave her a thumbs-up.

"Okay, okay, I hear you, Van," Dayna said. "I've got to run, but thanks for your advice.

I'll keep you posted. Love you."

She tucked her cell phone in her briefcase and read through Brent's message for the tenth time.

She hit reply and started typing, then deleted her message.

"Forget that," she said and picked up the phone on her desk.

She read Brent's email again and decided to try the cell number. He answered on the third ring.

"Brent speaking."

"Why do you want to treat me to dinner so badly?"

A brief silence hung in the air. "Dayna?"

"Yes."

"Thank you for calling. Why dinner? I don't know. I figured that would be the least awkward way for us to get together. I just really want to clear up some things, so we both can move on."

"What makes you think I haven't moved on? It's been seven years. You don't think the personal apology and the roses you gave me on Saturday were enough? Come on, Brent. What's up?"

He was silent for so long that Dayna thought the call had dropped. She glanced at the clock. She needed to leave in five minutes or she'd be late for the meeting.

"That's a fair question," he finally said. "What's up is that I don't deserve any of your time, and here I am pleading for it and telling you in what package to give it. Look, if you don't want to go to dinner with Tamara and me, I'll understand. But I would like to finish our conversation and at least put some things to rest between us."

Dayna gripped the phone and let the movie in her mind replay several pivotal incidents from their marriage and breakup. She sat there wrestling with herself over the longing that just wouldn't go away: the need to know what she had done to lose Brent to another woman. At least that was the way Mama always phrased the question.

Maybe this was an opportunity she shouldn't ignore. Maybe it would help her recognize some detrimental habits that she should avoid in her relationship with Warren. She sat back in her leather chair.

"I'll join you for dinner, Brent. Where do you want to meet?"

"Really?" His joy was palpable. "Thank you, Dayna. You pick the place and the time."

She didn't want to think about this any longer than she had to, so she mentioned what came to mind first. "Wharfside Restaurant on Pelican Drive. Seven o'clock tonight. And Warren's coming with me."

"That's cool, Dayna. Tamara and I will see you two then."

She hung up without saying good-bye and tried to squash the knot of fear growing inside her belly. She had chosen a tasty restaurant, but something told her she'd better eat a solid lunch, because seeing Brent and Tamara together might be more than she could stomach.

SEVEN

After all of his insistence, Warren couldn't come. "Why'd you set the date and time without checking my schedule?"

She leaned against the door to his office and pouted.

"I don't know, Warren. It was impulsive. He emailed me first thing this morning, and I called him to get it over with so he'll go away. I didn't even think to ask if you had to work tonight. You can't get away?"

Warren stood up and walked around the desk. He pulled her into the office and closed the door behind her before resting his hands on her shoulders.

"Sorry, babe. The title VP of marketing comes with official and unofficial duties I can't change. I came in early for the morning meeting, then went to lunch with Spencer and a few other folks from the executive team. That's when he asked me to join him for dinner tonight with several of the hospital's board members. They want to explore using some of the funds raised at Saturday's gala to expand Chesdin Medical's hospice program."

Dayna rested her head on his shoulder and hugged him. "That's important; we've wanted to add more beds and nurses to that program for a while," she said. "I'm a big girl; I can handle tonight by myself."

Warren stepped back and looked her in the eye. "Are you sure you're up to sitting across from this Tamara person? Why don't you reschedule to tomorrow or later in the week? They're doing this on your terms, right?"

Dayna considered Warren's advice. He was right; she didn't have to go tonight. She could change their dinner meeting to an evening when he could be there with her.

"Yeah, I could reschedule . . ." she said, but stopped herself. "I could, but I don't think I will. I need to face the two of them on my own, I guess. Whatever he, or they, want to say, I need to hear it and get it over with. Just pray that I don't do or say anything I'll have to apologize for later."

Warren chuckled. "I know you better than that. Even in this situation, you'll be a lady."

She wanted to tell Warren she'd slapped Brent on Saturday, but then she'd have to share that Brent had invaded her personal space, and Warren would have a fit.

Dayna embraced him again and stared over his shoulder at a newly framed picture on the bookshelf behind his desk. It was a candid shot of the two of them at a recent holiday party thrown by friends. She was sitting on Warren's lap, smiling and hugging his neck. He looked happy, and she did too. Whatever tonight might bring, her goal was to make sure she and Warren stayed like that — forever.

EIGHT

The hands on the grandfather clock in the corner of Dayna's bedroom ticked so slowly she was convinced they had been submerged in ice and needed to thaw.

Of course, the clock wasn't the problem, she was. She'd left work promptly at five to dash home and change into something less businesslike. Half an hour later, she wanted the minutes ticking by to both speed up and slow down. The faster time went, the sooner this dinner would be over; the slower it went, the longer she'd have to stress about what to wear and how to style her hair as fabulously as she could. She hadn't seen Tamara in years and didn't know what to expect from the former beauty queen; she just knew she needed to step into the room ready to turn heads. It was shallow, she knew, especially since Brent was part of her past, but she was human. She had just the

58

right outfit, still bearing tags, hanging in her closet.

As six-fifteen approached, Dayna donned a cranberry wrap dress and a pair of black slingback sandals with a slight heel. She wore a diamond pendant necklace and diamond stud earrings. She also wore her favorite piece of jewelry, the sterling silver charm bracelet Brent's mother had given her on their wedding day.

To this day, Dayna hadn't added any additional charms. The three Mama Davidson had presented with the bracelet — one bearing the word *Faith*, the second the word *Hope*, and the third the word *Love* — were representative all on their own of how Dayna sought to live and love others. After Brent left, wearing the bracelet had comforted her and served as a reminder of who and what she was called to honor, no matter the circumstances. Even when she'd found herself frustrated with God, somehow the words on these charms still resonated in her spirit. She wore the bracelet tonight, not to send a message to Brent, but to center herself.

With every hair in place and her bright smile ready, Dayna took one last look in the mirror before stepping into her garage and sliding behind the wheel of her car.

She closed her eyes and sat in silence for several minutes, summoning the courage to do what the minister at Stephanie's church had admonished every person present yesterday to do: STG — his acronym for Simply Trust God.

The idea felt foreign for someone who had picked up the pieces of her life and transformed herself into a top-notch corporate executive. But if she couldn't let go with God, how would she ever manage to do so with anyone else? That was the question of the century, at least from her perspective. Trusting in small things was a good place to start, she supposed, along with talking to him like a friend.

"I need you tonight, God, if you don't mind showing up," Dayna finally said aloud. "Give me the words to speak or not to speak, and somehow let this night bring peace to us all."

She already felt better after uttering that prayer. Warren would be proud.

In quick calls to Vanora and to her friend Audrey on the way to the restaurant, they reassured her she was doing the right thing.

"You've been waiting for years to get some of your questions answered," Vanora said. "Don't get caught up in the emotions of the past; just try to get at the truth. I'll be praying on this end. Call me as soon as it's over."

BeBe and CeCe Winans' song "Still" filled the Lexus as she drove. This meeting with Brent felt like a reunion of sorts. Time would tell what kind.

NINE

"I must love this man."

Tamara Davidson couldn't stop muttering those words to herself or to her mother, who had come by to help her get ready for the dinner with Brent and Dayna this evening.

Her mother nodded. "You do, Tam, you do. 'Cause not many women would take what you're going to endure tonight."

Endure. What a strong word Mom had chosen. But the past three months had felt like a race of endurance, perseverance, and whatever else she could summon, to keep her sanity and remain loving and patient. Brent understandably had things he wanted to take care of sooner rather than later, but tracking down and reconnecting with Dayna was almost too much.

How in the world was Tamara supposed to sit across a table from that woman for an hour or more and look her in the eye? Brent felt the need to apologize to Dayna, but

Tamara didn't have any interest in revisiting the past. Brent had insisted that the only way he could go through with the meeting with Dayna was if Tamara came along. She had talked her way out of showing up at Dayna's house with him, but tonight had been unavoidable.

Tamara wrestled with the two emotions seesawing through her spirit — wanting to support her husband on one hand, and wanting to jack him up on the other.

Who wanted to have dinner with her husband's ex-wife, no matter how honest and sincere his motives? Yet who in her right mind would leave the two of them alone? Brent had dated Dayna six years and had been married to her an additional seven, and the history the college sweethearts shared never seemed fully part of his past.

Calls and visits from college buddies always led to trips down memory lane that ultimately included experiences with Dayna. Hours spent reminiscing about his career-ending knee injury during a college football game weren't complete without details about how he had been nurtured back to health by his college sweetheart Dayna, who happened to be one of the top nursing students on campus. Recollections of his first job out of college and the first home he owned included memories created with Dayna and a funny incident or two about how she had handled being a new wife and homeowner.

Over the years, Tamara had learned to cope with the stories from his past by leaving the room or pretending to listen while allowing her mind to wander. And with Mom's help, she had accepted that his occasional reference to experiences that included Dayna didn't mean he didn't love her; it just meant he had a past. Lately, however, Tamara needed Mom's encouragement more frequently.

"I wish you could come to dinner with us," she told her mother tonight. "I would feel so much better."

Tamara's mother left her seat at the dining room table and strolled into the living room through a shared doorway. She stood behind her daughter, who was peering at herself in the mirror that hung on the wall above the sofa.

"You don't need me, baby. Brent will be there, and he will be there with you. He needs to do this, for whatever reason, but he asked you to come along and support him. This is his way of showing how much he loves you, Tami. He's not trying to hurt you or disrespect you. He wants Dayna to know that you two are solid."

"I hope he doesn't expect me to go groveling to her and asking for her forgiveness," Tamara said. "The past is the past. I repented for my part in what happened a long time ago, and I made peace with God. I've been forgiven and I've moved on. That's enough for me."

Mom gazed at her, then began stroking the soft, sandy brown hair that flowed past Tamara's shoulders.

"Just take a few deep breaths now — and when you get there — and you'll be all right, baby. Everything happens for a reason, even this meeting tonight."

The two women turned toward the foyer when they heard Brent trotting down the stairs. He stopped when he reached the landing and his eyes grew wide. Seconds later, so did his smile.

"You look wonderful, baby."

He walked over to his wife and surprised her with a deep kiss. Tamara smiled. She had purposely worn one of his favorite dresses — the coral sheath with the spaghetti straps and a length that stopped just above her knee. She had straightened her naturally wavy hair and draped it behind her ears, tucking a coral flower behind the left one, and she was wearing the perfume that stopped him in his tracks.

Mom had taught her well — she knew that all she had done to get him were the same things she needed to do to keep him, especially this evening. "Sorry, Mom," he said to Tamara's mother after surfacing from the provocative kiss. "Couldn't help myself."

Tamara's mother beamed and looked from Brent to her daughter with an I-told-you-so smugness.

"You two have a good time tonight, okay? Be good to each other."

Brent smiled at Mom and grabbed Tamara's hand. He intertwined his fingers with hers. She appreciated the strong and reassuring grip and kissed him again.

"I love you, Brent."

"Right back at ya. Come on, let's go."

The tension in Tamara's shoulders eased, and the vise of stress around her heart loosened its grip. Brent had calmed her once again. Tonight wasn't about dredging up the past; it was about helping him release his long-held guilt so he could move forward with peace.

If doing it in this fashion meant that much to him, she needed to be supportive. When he was happy, she would be too.

Please God, let it go smoothly and quickly, and let Brent's heart be settled.

Funny how years ago, when she had met Dayna, the ever-faithful and optimistic preacher's daughter, she had dismissed the value of having a connection to God and the power in prayer. In recent years, however, she had reached a point where prayer and her relationship with God were her primary sources of strength and peace.

Tamara wouldn't share any of that with Dayna tonight, because Dayna probably wouldn't care. But it was her secret weapon, and she planned to use it to extend grace to this woman who had once hated her, and likely still did.

TEN

The second Wharfside Restaurant came into view, Dayna's internal "danger alert" signal veered to extreme. Every fiber of her being screamed, "Drive away!"

Instead, she cruised deeper into the restaurant's parking lot and found a spot a few yards from the front door. A text popped up on her cell phone just as she turned off the ignition.

I am with u in spirit. U can do this.
Tell Brent u have a man waiting at home . . . I mean at work. ☺

She laughed out loud and responded out loud.

"You're right, Warren. I can do this. I will do this."

Dayna took a deep breath before strolling toward the veranda that covered the restaurant entrance. A suited gentleman greeted her with a gracious smile, swung open the door, and ushered her inside where a hostess picked up by welcoming her warmly.

"I'm here to meet the Davidson party."

The young woman led her around a corner to a quiet spot in the spacious, mostly empty dining area. Dayna was grateful in that moment that she had chosen to do this on a Monday night when the place wouldn't be full.

The hostess moved swiftly through the dining room, leading Dayna to Brent and Tamara's table, but when Dayna spotted them in a far corner of the restaurant, she hesitated.

There they were, Mr. and Mrs. Davidson, sitting next to each other looking like a spread in either *Ebony* or *Jet* magazine's hottest couples issue. He, with his dark chocolate, clean-cut good looks and she with her naturally long hair, honey complexion, and a beauty that gave her the aura of a TV star. They looked good together, and they looked happy.

Dayna's stomach quivered. Before she could turn and flee, the hostess motioned for her to join them.

Time to put on your game face, she told herself. *You agreed to this.*

Dayna squared her shoulders and lifted

her head. She caught up with the waiting hostess and was soon standing next to the table, peering down at the couple.

Brent rose from his seat. He pulled out a chair for Dayna across from Tamara, who gave her a strained smile.

"Dayna."

Dayna returned the greeting with the same reserve. "Tamara."

Brent looked from one woman to the other and sat down next to his wife. "Um, ma'am, can you have our waiter take our drink order?" he asked the hostess. "We're ready now."

An awkward silence filled the space as they waited. Minutes later, a young man who introduced himself as Austin appeared to serve them. He took their beverage orders and shared the dinner specials for the night.

He could have been speaking Greek for all Dayna comprehended. Her mind drifted, and she felt like she was having an out-of-body experience as he ran down the list of choices. She wanted to pinch herself to make sure she was really here, and that this was really happening.

No one could have convinced her when she was Brent's wife that their marriage wouldn't last, or that she would someday join Brent at a restaurant with another Mrs.

Davidson at his side. Who knew she'd summon enough strength to sit across the table from the woman who had cheated with and stolen her husband, without wanting to strangle her? She didn't want to choke Tamara anymore, but Dayna sat there wishing this woman wasn't so pretty or so seemingly content.

The three of them eased into conversation by discussing the menu options and choosing their meals. Dayna ordered shrimp and mussels over pasta, Tamara chose salmon, and Brent settled on soup and a house salad. He looked into Dayna's questioning eyes after handing Austin his menu and chuckled. "Watching my diet these days. It's okay if you ladies eat more than I do."

He and Tamara exchanged a knowing glance that Dayna pretended to ignore. As they waited for their food to be served, they chatted about the central Florida humidity, the latest news with Congress, and a couple of Hollywood scandals. The fact that Warren didn't come up until half an hour into the dinner meeting clued Dayna in that despite his confident demeanor, Brent found this nerve-racking too.

"By the way, where is he this evening? I was expecting him."

"He's the marketing director for Chesdin

Medical and had a dinner meeting with the CEO. He sends his regards."

Brent chuckled. "I bet he does. I could see all over his face on Saturday what those regards entail." He cocked his head to one side. "I wouldn't have pegged you as one to date interracially."

Dayna shrugged. "I wouldn't have either. But as Warren always says, color is just skin deep — he's more concerned about his faith than his ethnicity, and since we're both Christians, we're part of the same family."

Brent laughed. "Amen, then. That's a good thing. I wish you both well."

"Thank you, Brent."

Austin and another waiter arrived with their piping-hot dishes, and the table fell silent while each of them tasted their selections. Dayna was finally able to enjoy the restaurant's live pianist, but before long, Brent had more questions.

"So tell me about your work," he said to Dayna between bites. "I read in the Alabama U alumni magazine a few years ago that you'd left nursing for the administrative side of hospital care. To discover that you were living in Florida was amazing, since we also live here."

Dayna didn't think their winding up in the same state was "amazing" — just ironic.

She took a sip of water to quell the urge to speak. Now it was beginning to make sense how he'd been able to find her. She received that same magazine every quarter, and each issue included news about graduates' promotions, job changes, and personal accomplishments.

"Yep," she finally responded. "I decided to go back to school to get my master's in health administration. Being an RN and knowing how to better help patients and keep good nurses on staff left me frustrated when none of those things were happening. By bringing my nursing background and perspective to the administrative side of health care, I'm in a position to make a difference for patients and for the health care providers. I love it."

"What's your official title?" Brent asked. "All I can remember is that it's long!"

Brent seemed to have researched her like a job applicant trying to impress an employer. She wasn't.

"I'm Vice President of Patient Care/Chief Nursing Executive."

Dayna glanced at Tamara, who was toying with her hoop earrings and seemed to be struggling to maintain an interest in the conversation. She wondered how Tamara felt about the effort Brent had put into finding her.

"So you read about my career change in the alumni mag, but how did you get my home address?" Dayna asked Brent.

He shrugged. "Your address and phone number weren't listed in any online public information directories, but the more I searched your name, the more I was able to track down charitable donations and other information for which your address is recorded. You know you can pay for some of this information too, right? And I have to be honest . . . the Alabama U alumni association helped. I called and reminded them who I was, and you know, they helped me find you through their database."

Dayna frowned. "I may have to reduce my alumni contribution this year." She made a mental note to use her work address in the alumni directory going forward.

Brent grew concerned. "I shouldn't have told you that. Don't take it out on the school. I had to do a lot of arm twisting. It wasn't easy information to get. Promise."

Dayna pursed her lips. She'd address that issue later. At this point, she was reaching her limit on politeness. She didn't know if she'd be able to sit through dessert; Brent needed to get to the point.

"Tell me what brought you . . . and Tamara, to Florida, and how long you've been here."

"I got a great offer five years ago to work for a company that has a contract with Kennedy Space Center, similar to the company I worked for when you and I were in Alabama. This job actually allows me to work on-site, at Cape Canaveral."

Dayna nodded, but inside, she was yelling, "And?"

Maybe if she diverted the conversation to Tamara this would end sooner.

"And you?" She looked at Tamara, who had begun to squirm.

"Me? I'm a teller for a local branch of BankOne. I've been doing that since we've been here. It gives me steady hours and allows me to be home when Brent's there."

Aha. Though he had denied it all those years ago when she asked, maybe Dayna's inability to be readily available to meet Brent's needs had been the issue all along. The realization that he had married a woman who was doing just that unsettled her. Her nursing career required long hours and odd shifts; she couldn't be the happy homemaker to accommodate Brent's nine-to-five schedule. Sometimes he'd had to cook his own meals or meet her for dinner out. Sometimes she'd worked twelve-hours shifts and he'd had to occupy himself.

Dayna had always thought that was a good thing. It gave him space to spend time with his friends or to give attention to his hobbies without her being underfoot, but maybe he had felt differently.

"I'm proud of her," Brent said. He reached for Tamara's hand under the table. "She has been taking college classes off and on for years and will get her bachelor's degree in business administration from the University of Central Florida in May."

"That's great, Tamara," Dayna said and smiled at her. "You should be proud." She was surprised that she really meant it. It didn't hurt to offer the compliment.

Tamara seemed relieved. "Thanks, Dayna. I appreciate that."

With Dayna wondering where this conversation was going and for how much longer, Brent launched into more details about their respective jobs and hobbies, and about how Tamara's widowed mother had moved from Michigan to Florida last year after visiting in January and deciding she could no longer endure arctic-cold winters.

"We don't have kids, so she takes care of us like we're her babies," Brent said and grinned.

Was she imagining it, or did Tamara flinch?

It struck Dayna that Tamara must feel as much "on stage" as she did this evening, with Brent going on and on like this was a happy high school reunion.

"So," Dayna said, changing the subject from children, just in case her eyes hadn't betrayed her, "you guys live about forty minutes from here. How do you know this part of central Florida so well?"

"I'm taking classes at UCF's Cocoa campus, not far from where we live," Tamara said, "but every now and then I need to come up here to the main campus for a class, so I know my way around pretty well. Plus, we travel as much as we can, even within the state. On weekends, we'll just get in the car and go find a new beach or restaurant or place to shop."

Brent chimed in. "It's been fun, and even though we've lived here five years, we haven't run out of cities to explore. We've got some favorite spots, like South Beach, but there are still new areas to discover."

Dayna was surprised that learning about the life they had settled into didn't faze her.

When Austin returned and offered to present the dessert cart for their viewing, Dayna and Tamara simultaneously declined. Dayna pondered whether she and Tamara shared the same reason — they'd gotten along well so far, but it was time to go.

"The ladies win, I guess," Brent told him. "You can bring the check whenever you're ready."

Tamara glanced at Brent. "I'm going to the ladies room, okay?"

Dayna read between the lines. With Tamara gone, Brent could now render the big apology he had in mind.

When his wife was out of sight, he cleared his throat and leaned toward Dayna. "I really want to thank you for taking time to join us tonight, Dayna. You didn't have to do this, and I know you probably didn't want to."

Dayna raised an eyebrow. "How did you know?"

Brent chuckled. "Let's see . . . the three returned letters, the cold shoulder when I dropped off the roses, and the slap across the face said it pretty clearly."

What could she say? "At least I came," she finally mustered.

"Well, I won't hold you much longer. There is a specific reason I asked you to meet with me."

The sentence hung in the air like a drumroll. Brent leaned forward. "Dayna, sometimes things happen in life and we realize we need to take a good look at ourselves and take responsibility for the choices we've made and how we've treated people; give thanks for the good stuff . . ."

"Say sorry for the bad stuff." Dayna completed his sentence with a wry smile.

Brent smiled too. "We used to finish each other's sentences like that all the time, didn't we?" he said. "Yes, you're right — say sorry for the bad stuff. And I've done some bad stuff to you that I need to apologize for."

He reached for her hand and Dayna hesitated. He noticed and withdrew. "That's okay. I just wanted to take your hand and formally say I'm sorry. You were a good wife. You didn't do anything to push me away. I was young and arrogant, and I just got caught up with the flattery and attention offered by someone else. I was wrong."

Before she could help herself, Dayna rattled off a comeback. "But you not only cheated, Brent. You left me for her. You married her. You're still married to her."

Brent nodded and glanced toward the bathroom. Dayna knew he was wondering how soon Tamara would return. She was curious too.

"Yes, I'm still married to her. I love her, Dayna. But I loved you too, and I was wrong in the way I went about it all. You and I . . . we were college kids when we got together. We were still finding our way. I think I got too comfortable, and when Tamara came along, she was new and different and exciting. No excuses for my behavior. I was wrong, and I guess I really didn't deserve you. Or, better put, you deserved better than me."

Dayna nodded. "I did, didn't I?"

Still, she felt relieved to hear that she hadn't done anything to push him away. Instead, it sounded like her error had been in not fighting harder to keep him. Maybe she had handed him over to Tamara too quickly.

She leaned back in her chair and crossed her arms. "Brent, I accept your apology tonight, since it means so much to you, but I want you to know that I forgave you a long time ago. I had to if I was going to move forward with my life. I was angry and bitter at you and at Tamara for a long, long time. Here she was, a new friend to both of us, and she betrayed me. And you allowed her to. I just couldn't believe it. I trusted you completely. I mean, you didn't cheat on me when you were the college jock — at least I never got wind of it — but six years into our marriage, when I thought we were solid, you stepped out just because the opportunity presented itself?"

Brent's eyes reflected a sea of regret. "You're right. But I can't turn back time. I know I did wrong by you, and in some ways, I've done wrong by Tamara, because she deserved to be married to someone who wasn't coming out of another relationship."

Dayna was intrigued by what he was hinting at regarding his marriage, but decided not to go there.

Brent continued. "We're here now because I don't want to die with any more regrets, without saying all the things I need to say, especially to you."

Dayna's heart hopscotched. "What are you saying, Brent?"

He leaned forward and exhaled. "Two years ago I went into the hospital for an appendectomy, of all things. While I was there, they did a full checkup and discovered that I had prostate cancer. It had gone undetected for quite a while. I started treatments right away, but they told me last November that my outlook is bleak. The cancer has progressed to stage four."

Dayna's head was spinning. "What are you saying, Brent? Prostate cancer is curable, especially in a man your age. Aren't you in treatment?"

Her nursing stats ran through her mind. Yes, more and more African American men were being diagnosed, and the earlier they caught it, the better. Remission was probable more often than not. But Brent was saying his was too far gone. This couldn't be right; he was way younger than most terminal patients.

"I'm not in treatment, Dayna. The cancer has spread to my bones, and I'm dying. In November they declared that I have six to nine months to live, but it could be longer, depending on how fast-growing my cancer is. That's why I had to see you. To tell you I'm sorry and that you'll always mean a lot to me. Yes, I'm married to Tamara, and I love my wife. But you were my first love, and I shouldn't have shattered you the way I did. Lots of people don't get a chance to ask for forgiveness. This is one of the things I needed to do before it was too late. So thank you."

Tears streamed from Dayna's eyes before she could stop them. She used the linen napkin in her lap to staunch the flow. "Brent . . ."

Her thoughts were racing. She had returned all of his letters unopened. What if he hadn't been bold enough to show up at her house? What if she had refused to join him for this dinner?

Yes, he had been wrong, but had she not given him this chance, he wouldn't have been able to tell her that she'd done nothing to hurt him in their marriage.

"I'm so sorry, Brent. Tamara . . . ?" She looked toward the bathroom and saw that Tamara had emerged and had purposely wandered over to a bank of windows to take in the view so they could finish their conversation. When she turned toward the table and saw Dayna's tear-streaked face, she strolled toward them.

Dayna didn't know what to say or do when Tamara reached the table. Tamara stood awkwardly next to Brent, then leaned forward and grasped Dayna's hand.

"You okay?" Tamara asked.

Dayna nodded. "The news just caught me off guard. Are you okay? You and Brent?"

Instead of answering, Tamara gazed at her husband.

Brent looked from one woman to the other. "We take each day as it comes, you know," he said. "Some days I'm fine and it's hard to believe; other days I'm doubled over in pain, wondering if I need to give the chemo and radiation a try."

"Why don't you?" Dayna asked. "You're a young man. It may work better than they anticipate. You can't give up!"

Brent shook his head, and Tamara slid into her chair next to him and draped her arm across his shoulder.

"I'm with you, Dayna. I don't want to lose him. But we've gotten a second, third, and even a fourth opinion. The cancer is so advanced and so aggressive, the treatment would make him sick and he'd still have a short life span."

Brent continued. "I've decided to spend my final days doing what I want to do, rather than recovering from medicine that's only prolonging the inevitable and making my time here miserable. If there were a shred of hope that the treatments would make a difference, I'd give it a try, even for just a few more months with Tamara. But right now, that doesn't seem to be God's will."

Dayna was reeling. Now Brent's persistence made sense. And Tamara's understanding.

"I don't know what to say, other than I'm so sorry."

"I am too," Brent said. His eyes softened. "I've been furious, in denial, and everything in between. But now I'm at the point of accepting that I have a lot to be thankful for, and tonight is one of the major things on that list."

Dayna fell silent, wishing Austin would interrupt them with the dessert cart despite their begging off. How did you carry on a conversation with someone who was dying and planning his final days? She had helped quite a few patients transition during her years as a nurse, but this was the man she had once planned on spending her life with — until death do them part. It was unsettling to realize how soon that time would have come to an end for them had she been sitting in Tamara's seat.

She had grieved over losing Brent in a different way seven years earlier; now it looked like Tamara would have her turn.

Dayna continued to sit in silence, and Brent seemed prepared for that. He kept up small talk and tried to put her at ease. The more he chatted, the more she felt ready to leave so she could have some time to herself to let it all sink in. But this was Brent's party and she wasn't going to rush him. At his prompting, she was soon filling him in on what her mom and dad and the rest of her family were up to.

"I don't see them regularly, but when I do, they are well."

Brent seemed surprised. "You and your parents were so close back then. You don't see them as much now? Is it because of the move to Florida?"

She wasn't going to add guilt to his plate by sharing that the rift with her family had been due in large part to her split with him, so she nodded.

He filled her in on what his brothers, James and Winston, had been up to, and how his sister, Natalie, was now married with four children.

"Tamara and I weren't blessed with any, so Natalie, James, and Winston had enough for themselves and us," he joked.

Tamara looked away, and once again, Dayna could tell that his words stung.

"If you don't mind sharing, what are some of the other things you're planning to do before . . ." She couldn't bring herself to say the words *die, pass away,* or *leave* and kicked herself for bringing up the subject again.

But Brent seemed comfortable with his reality. "You know what's next on my list? Remember back in college, after I got hurt during my sophomore year and struggled to find meaning when I couldn't play football anymore?"

"How could I forget?" Dayna shook her head as the memories engulfed her. "That was a rough time. You were as mean as a snake, but I knew it was because you were scared and lost. Thankfully you had a great GPA, so they let you keep your football scholarship."

"But remember my two teammates who didn't have a support system after they suffered injuries?" Brent asked. "They lost their focus and eventually dropped out of college. Remember my great idea?"

Dayna's thoughts wandered back to those days at Alabama U, and she tried to focus on where Brent was steering her, instead of how their romance had blossomed. "You said you wanted to someday start a foundation to offer mentoring to college athletes who get injured and need academic and career-planning assistance."

"Bingo."

Dayna's eyes widened. "You've actually done that?"

"Not yet," Brent said. "We've got a nice-sized savings, but I'm also well insured. After I'm gone, there will be enough left for Tamara to live comfortably, without working if she wants, and to establish the foundation I dreamed of back then. There will be five million available to get started."

"Wow," said Dayna. "Will it be public or private?"

"What's the difference?" Tamara asked.

Drawing on her work experience, Dayna launched into a mini-lesson on the benefits of being a public foundation, monitored by the federal government with oversight from board members chosen by the creator of the foundation, versus a private foundation, which has more leeway with who makes decisions but requires more administrative legwork. Questions and answers flew back and forth between the three of them until Brent paused and gently grabbed Dayna's wrist as she was mid-motion into rendering another answer.

His touch startled her, but she felt too uncomfortable to wrest herself from his light grip. Brent seemed oblivious.

"You know what? Your executive training has given you the knowledge I need to get this thing off the ground. I need your help to figure out whether to go public or private, or whether I need a community foundation or some other vehicle to manage the funds. Will you do it?"

ELEVEN

The short, shallow breaths she couldn't control convinced Tamara a panic attack would overtake her any second now.

Had she heard her husband correctly? She had purposely left Brent alone with this woman for fifteen minutes so he could explain his terminal illness and say anything else he felt was necessary to be at peace, and now Brent had come up with another reason to keep Dayna in their lives. Had he taken too much pain medicine before leaving home?

She couldn't breathe *and* she felt like throwing up. Tamara fought those physical sensations by inhaling deeply over and over again as Brent paid the check and bade Dayna good-bye.

Now well into their forty-five-minute drive home, Brent didn't appear to notice her silence or anxiety. He was so excited about how his foundation idea was unfolding that he seemed to have found a second wind. She hadn't seen him this energized or focused in months.

"Thank you for doing this, baby." He reached for Tamara's hand while keeping his eyes on the road. "I know it wasn't easy to spend that time with Dayna, but I thought it went well. And not only did I get a chance to apologize and explain what's next for me, tonight's meeting may lead to the next step in creating my foundation. Can you believe it?"

He glanced at her when she didn't respond. "What?"

Tamara shrugged. "Nothing."

In the silence that followed, she wrestled, as usual, with just how much to say. Was he really that oblivious to how uncomfortable tonight's "reunion" had been for her, and possibly for Dayna? Did he really think the three of them could work together in harmony as he grew sicker and sicker?

Lord, how do I tell him I can't do this?

"What is it, Tami?"

She sighed and rummaged through her hand-sized purse. "I don't know, Brent. It just seems like too much to have Dayna involved in the foundation. I thought we were going to have dinner with her and move on, baby. I know you needed to ask her forgiveness and all, but I'm not comfortable with seeing her on a regular basis. I can't do it; I'm sorry."

Brent kept his eyes on the cars zigzagging in front of him without responding. This stretch of State Road 520 was infamous for deadly crashes, and he routinely maneuvered with laser focus during this section of the drive, but Tamara knew that wasn't why his chatter had ceased.

She didn't want him to be angry with her, and she didn't want to hamper his progress, but this was asking too much.

"What are you thinking?" she asked after the third song on his favorite jazz CD began and ended with no conversation between them.

"I guess I went too far, huh?" Brent asked.

A sigh escaped like pressure released from a valve before Tamara could contain it. "I think so," she said. "I know Dayna is knowledgeable about what you need done, but can't you get help from someone else? What were you planning to do if you hadn't had that conversation with her tonight? I'm sure there are tons of organizations that help people set up foundations. I can probably get some contacts through the bank."

"To be honest, I guess I hadn't thought it through," Brent said. "Talking to her showed me there's more to getting this done the right way than I realized. I need someone to guide me and to help you make sure everything is handled correctly when . . . I'm gone."

He paused for a long time and kept his eyes on the road. "I don't know who else that could be," he finally said.

Tamara prayed for strength to keep from saying something rash. What he really meant was he didn't know who else he could trust — including her — to oversee the project like he wanted it done. Was he playing her emotions like a violin because he was dying? Did he realize that by bringing Dayna into the planning process he was asking Tamara to maintain a relationship with his ex-wife indefinitely? Was he crazy?

She placed a hand on his shoulder and squeezed it. "We'll figure this out together, okay? Let's just give it more thought."

That was the kindest way she could say no, and this request definitely deserved a no, cancer or not.

TWELVE

Dayna was a block from home when her cell phone began chiming. It was the ringtone for her friend and coworker Audrey, whom Dayna had filled in on her dinner plans over lunch today.

"Well?"

"Well, I survived," Dayna said. She pulled into her garage and cradled the phone between her jaw and shoulder so she could grab her bags and continue the conversation on her way inside. The minute she entered her kitchen, she laid her cell on the granite island countertop and tapped the speakerphone button to keep chatting with Audrey while she stepped out of her heels and prepared a cup of tea.

"What are you doing?" Audrey asked.

"Making you tea and scones," Dayna teased. "What are you doing?"

She turned on the faucet near where the phone lay and let water stream into her stovetop tea kettle. The roses Brent had delivered on Saturday caught her eye. Their stems pointed out of the trash bin she had tossed them into Sunday morning. Now that she knew his circumstances, she felt a wave of guilt for being so dismissive.

"I'm on my way home. Had a late meeting," Audrey said.

Dayna paused. "What late meeting did you have on Monday? Hospital accountants don't meet after hours. Aren't you guys too anal retentive for that?"

"Very funny," Audrey said. "Can we turn this conversation back to the reason I called? How on earth did the dinner go with Brent and his wife? Why are you dragging this out?"

Dayna placed the teapot on the stovetop and turned on the flame. "The dinner went fine, Audrey. It's what happened near the end that left me reeling."

"What?" Audrey asked the question in a hushed tone.

"Brent is sick. He has terminal cancer and maybe only a few more months to live."

Saying the words aloud made them real. What she was describing, about a man who used to be her world, sounded like something straight out of a soap opera.

"What? He's just forty. What kind of

cancer does he have?"

"Prostate. He says it spread before doctors discovered it. Now the cancer is in his bones. I don't know much more than that, Audrey, only that he wanted to meet with me to apologize for ruining our marriage and hurting me."

"Wow, Dayna. I don't know what to say."

"I didn't either. I think I accepted his apology; I really can't remember now."

"Was his wife with him?"

Dayna poured her tea into the oversized mug with the jewel-toned pattern she always used and reached for the jar of honey she kept in the cupboard. "Yeah, Tamara was with him, hanging onto his every word, except for the brief period when she left the table so he could share his diagnosis with me. Can you believe it?"

Dayna grabbed the mug and cell phone and headed toward the brown leather recliner in the corner of her family room. The room's wall of windows provided natural light during the day, but tonight the space was pitch black. Dayna stepped into the room, and a sensor-controlled table lamp switched on, filling the room with a warm glow. She closed the draperies on either side of the floor-to-ceiling windows before curling up in the chair with her tea and placing the cell phone on its arm, still in speaker-phone mode.

"Now it all makes sense," Audrey said. "Why else would he work so hard to find you to say he's sorry, and why else would his wife go along with all of this? What was she like, anyway?"

"What was she like?" Dayna said. "She was like . . . Tamara. Pretty. Catering to his every need, it seemed. Letting him do most of the talking. They seem happy."

"How did you feel being there with them? How do you feel now, since it's all over?" Audrey said. "I have too many questions, don't I? Want me to come over?"

Dayna shook her head, even though Audrey couldn't see. "Where did you say you were coming from? You live twenty minutes away. It wouldn't make sense for you to come by here on a Monday night. Besides, I'm gonna have to get off the phone with you shortly and give Warren a call. He'll have a fit if I don't let him know how tonight went."

"Yeah, you definitely have to update your man. Too bad he couldn't go with you. But at least you've gotten this all behind you now. I'm sorry to hear that your ex is dying, really, but now you can focus your attention on that fine man who loves you in the here and now."

Dayna rolled her eyes. That comment reminded her, though, that Brent had tried to hand her a new dilemma.

"I guess I should be celebrating, but I can't."

A full minutes passed before Audrey spoke. "I'm not sure where you're going with this one, friend."

Dayna released a nervous laugh. "I don't know either, Audrey. Brent started talking about a charitable foundation he wants to establish with proceeds from his life insurance policy, and all of a sudden he decided he needs my help in setting it up."

Audrey gasped. "You are joking."

"Nope."

"How did you tell him no?"

"The man is dying, so I tried to let him down easy. I told him I was flattered, but I wasn't the right person to help with something this important. How could I just come out and say no?"

"One word — Warren!"

Dayna frowned at the mention of his name. She sat upright in the chair and clutched the mug. "I know, Audrey, I know. I didn't say yes, but I didn't say no. So Brent took my 'I'm not sure' as a yes. The minute I didn't correct him, he ran with it. Now

I've got to figure out how to really tell Brent I can't help him, before he starts making big plans. And I guess I need to tell Warren how badly I handled it."

"I'm coming over," Audrey said. "We've got to figure out how to get you out of this one, and fast, so you don't have to tell Warren anything."

THIRTEEN

Instead of resolving how and when to share the latest developments with Warren, Dayna spent the next five minutes convincing Audrey to go home rather than drive to the southern end of Calero. "I've got this," Dayna told her. "Warren and I will talk it through and work it out, okay?"

"Don't jeopardize your relationship over some tug at your heartstrings, Dayna. It's not worth it, especially for an ex-husband who has a wife."

"Thank you, 'Dr. Phil-lis,' " Dayna said and laughed. "Please don't worry. I'm going to hang up now so I can give Warren a call."

"I wouldn't tell him, if I were you," Audrey said again. "Just plan on calling Brent tomorrow and telling him to back off."

"Your check is in the mail, doc!" Dayna said. "Now go home and get some rest. Good night!"

She ended the call and curled up in the

chair, thankful that she was now free to bring Warren up to speed. What Audrey didn't know was that she had to tell him. When they began dating exclusively twelve months ago, they made a pact to keep no secrets from each other and to mutually handle challenges, no matter how uncomfortable or unpleasant they might be. She'd already broken that promise once by not telling Warren right away about the letters Brent had sent. He hadn't called her on it, but she was determined to honor their agreement from now on. She would own up to being wishy-washy with Brent about his great idea, and maybe together they could come up with a plan for steering Brent elsewhere.

They weren't married, but Warren loved Dayna and he was good to her. He deserved her loyalty.

She sighed and picked up the cell. She punched the contact list and brought up Warren's picture in her favorites section. His tousled jet-black hair and goateed grin greeted her. It was just a photo, but the sapphire-blue eyes that peered into hers made her heart flutter. If he'd been with her tonight, telling Brent no would have been so much easier.

Dayna glanced at the clock. It was nine-thirty. She felt like crawling into bed and dealing with this tomorrow, but if she didn't call Warren, he'd call her.

"Let me put my big-girl pants on and deal," she said.

Her ringing cell bought her more time. Vanora's face popped up on the screen.

"Talk about perfect timing," Dayna said when she answered her college roommate's call.

"You knew I was going to call for details. How did it go? Does Tamara still have hair? You didn't yank it all out, did you?"

Dayna chuckled. "You are so silly! There was no catfight. Brent is her man now. We were civil to each other, pleasant even. It was a little awkward, but it went fine."

"But you still picked up on the first ring when I called; something went down. Spill it," Vanora said.

"Girl, you are in the wrong line of work," Dayna told her friend. "You need to give up teaching and become a private detective."

Vanora laughed. "In this economy, and with these gas prices, don't think I won't consider it! Back to you and Brent. What happened?"

Dayna filled Vanora in on Brent's apology, his revelations about what had ended their marriage, and the shocking news of his terminal illness.

"Brent? Our health fanatic football star? Dear Lord, be with him," Vanora said.

"Prostate cancer, of all things," Dayna said. "I just can't believe that a man as young as he won't survive it. But there's more. You remember those conversations we used to have over our potluck Sunday dinners about his dream of someday helping other college athletes thrive after a career-ending injury?"

"Yeah?"

"He actually wants to do that, Van. Can you believe it?"

"But he's dying. How is he going to pull that off with supposedly less than a year to live?"

"He thinks with my help."

"Excuse me?"

"Over dinner we got to talking about how he'll start with some savings and use about five million from life insurance to set up a foundation after his death, and I started giving him the pros and cons of each option. Before I knew it, he was trying to convince me to help him get everything established. He wants me to guide him through the process."

"Wow. What did Tamara have to say about this?"

"She didn't look happy, but she played the ever-faithful wife and didn't say anything."

"What are you going to do?"

"I told him I wasn't sure I could do it well, but he insisted," Dayna said. "I let it be, but I can't do this, Van. I'm sorry that he's dying, but I can't devote my life to him. That's Tamara's job now."

"What is your heart telling you to do?" Vanora asked.

Dayna frowned. "Call Warren and see what he says? I can tell you now his answer will be no."

Vanora chuckled. "I'm not thinking about Warren, or even Brent, right now. I'm asking you what feels like the right thing to do, when you think about *what* he's asking, not about *who's* doing the asking."

Dayna shook her head as if Vanora could see her. "Come on, friend. You know this is a case where I can't separate the two," she said. "If it were anyone else, I probably would do something to help, even if I didn't take on the whole project. With Brent, I'm inclined to wish him well and let him figure it out on his own."

"But Brent is dying, and the clock is ticking," Vanora said. "That's what his asking you seems to be about. Maybe you can at least steer him in the right direction without constant personal contact. That's the right thing to do."

It was easy for Vanora to declare what was right and wrong from the safety of her Midwest apartment and her husband's loving arms. But she had no right to judge how Dayna should deal with her ex-husband, even though Dayna had invited the commentary.

Dayna recalled how Brent had pleaded with her for help tonight and how thrilled he had seemed when she didn't say no. But how had she felt? Not good, uneasy even, and manipulated. Her thoughts turned to how angry she had been at him for years, before mustering the courage to forgive him. Tonight she was being put to the test, but in her opinion, it didn't mean she had to yield to all that he was asking. Vanora was right; she could steer Brent and Tamara in the right direction and be done with it. Warren might even have some ideas.

"I know you mean well, Van," Dayna said. "But my heart is saying move on and put the experiences with Brent in the past, where I had them nicely tucked away until two days ago. I'm also wondering what your aunt would tell me if I were sitting across from her at Sunday dinner."

Vanora laughed. "Mary 'Duchess' Miller has a ready answer for everything, doesn't she? I should have warned you about that when I introduced you two. Funny thing is, she's usually right, because she's operating in God's wisdom. I think she'd tell you to help Brent too. You're not trying to rekindle your relationship, you'll just be helping him fulfill part of his purpose — a part that you knew about and encouraged from its idea stage, back at Alabama U. That's all. What happened in the past is in the past. He's asked for forgiveness, and you have to move forward. How could Warren have a problem with that? Have you asked him yet?"

The tension in Dayna's chest eased. Here she was, getting all worked up about Warren's reaction without giving him the benefit of the doubt. Once he knew all of the facts, maybe he wouldn't have a problem. Maybe he'd encourage her to do this and then move on. There was only one way to find out.

"I love ya, Van," Dayna said. "I needed to hear what you just shared. I'm gonna hang up and call Warren now and fill him in. Who knows? He may agree with you."

In her heart of hearts, though, she knew Warren well enough to suspect he wouldn't be pleased. This might be asking for too much understanding, and something told her that Tamara was feeling the same way.

FOURTEEN

Dayna didn't want to fret, but this was the second time her call to Warren had gone straight into voicemail.

As head of the hospital's marketing division, his cell needed to be on 24-7, no exceptions. That realization had come just a few weeks after they began dating, when intimate conversations were interrupted by calls from reporters or hospital executives who needed immediate help with couching a particular message.

Surely Warren's dinner with their boss and members of the hospital board wasn't going on this long; it was now past ten. Then again, maybe discussions about the hospice expansion had taken on a life of their own. She started to speed-dial him for a third time, but decided against it. Warren knew where she was; he'd call when he was available.

She tidied up the kitchen and headed for

the bedroom, where she quickly shed her clothes and stepped into the shower. Every muscle relaxed for the first time that evening, and she was able to process what had transpired.

Dinner with Brent and Tamara. She had done it and lived to talk about it.

As the water soothed her tense body, she longed for something to soothe her mind. Why was she feeling guilty about not wanting to help Brent with his project? He had been out of his mind to think she'd agree. Now he'd occupy her thoughts for the next few days as she figured out where to send him for help when she told him no.

She emerged from the shower and slid a nightshirt over her head before sauntering into her bedroom to check her cell phone. Just as she'd expected, Warren had called while she was inaccessible.

She pressed redial, and he answered right away. She was surprised to hear chatter in the background this time of night, including a woman's voice.

"Hey babe, where are you?" Dayna climbed under the covers and lay back on her pillow.

"I'm on the way back to Lily's house to drop her off," he said. "She picked the boys up from basketball practice this afternoon since I had to work late, and when they got to her house, Michael started complaining about his thumb. Lily called as my dinner with Spencer was wrapping up and asked me to come get him and take him to the doctor, because the thumb was swelling and he was in tremendous pain. Turns out it's broken."

"Oh, no!" Dayna said. "Poor Michael. Is it a bad break? Will he be able to finish the season?"

Warren's twin sons were his spitting image, and Dayna loved them. So did Lily, his deceased wife's best friend, who had served as their paid caretaker/nanny and surrogate mom of sorts since April's death four years earlier.

"It's a pretty bad break," Warren said. "He'll be out for the rest of the season and will probably need surgery. But he's a tough guy; he'll be okay."

"Good, I'm glad to hear it. I guess that's why I couldn't reach you, huh?"

"Yep, that's why."

Dayna's green-eyed monster awakened. "So Lily went with you to the emergency room?"

What she really wanted to ask was why Lily couldn't have driven the seventh grader to the hospital or Patient First herself, and then called Warren. But this was characteristic damsel-in-distress behavior.

"Yeeees." Warren's carefully drawn-out response cued her that she was being rude.

"I see," she said. "Well, I'm glad she called you."

Dayna hated how guarded his conversation became around Lily, but decided not to pick a fight about that tonight.

While Warren was grateful for the support Lily had provided the family after April's sudden death — agreeing to leave her secretarial job and care for the boys, who were just nine when their mom suffered an aneurysm — Warren insisted that he'd never seen her as more than a family friend. Yet Lily took every opportunity to prove to the twins that she was a much better partner for their father than Dayna, and as a result, much better for them. At least that's how Dayna saw it. Warren stayed out of the fray by never agreeing or disagreeing, and while his maneuvering annoyed her, Dayna knew his goal was to avoid alienating Lily, because the boys loved and needed her.

Dayna sighed. She certainly couldn't fill him in on her dinner with Brent now; he had his hands full. But maybe this was for the best.

"Meet me for breakfast in the morning, in

110

the hospital café?"

"First floor, eight a.m. sharp," Warren responded. "Deal?"

Dayna smiled. "Deal, babe. Get your son home safely, then call me back if you want."

"It's already ten fifteen and we just left Patient First. Don't stay up. We'll catch up in the morning."

Dayna knew he wouldn't tell her he loved her with his sons and Lily in the car, so she made a kissing sound. "Take that, then. See you in the morning."

"Ditto."

When the lights were out, however, she couldn't sleep. The revelations shared over dinner looped through her mind again and again, specifically Brent's diagnosis and his efforts to convince her to help with the foundation. She thought about how years ago the sight of Tamara, or even the mention of the woman's name, had caused her to weep or rage with anger, and how tonight she had been able to hold a conversation with her. They would never be friends again, but they had both matured and found a way to leave the past in the past.

Dayna's thoughts turned to Warren and why she hadn't been able to reach him — because Lily couldn't deal with reality. Despite Warren's repeated reminders to Lily that he was in a committed relationship with Dayna, she clearly hadn't given up the fantasy of herself, Warren, and the twins someday becoming a family.

Michael's injury seemed to have given her a convenient opportunity today to show how she, and the boys, needed Warren. Dayna closed her eyes and rolled onto her side with Lily on her mind. Her green eyes, petite frame, and soft voice cast a spell on men and women, but Dayna had managed long ago to see through Lily's Southern-belle charm into the soul of a woman who did whatever was needed to get what she wanted.

Lily's wish list clearly included Warren, and if Dayna needed to put her boxing gloves on this time around, so be it.

FIFTEEN

"What time did you get home last night?" Dayna asked.

Warren grinned at Dayna before taking a swig of coffee. The tiny hospital café, with mint green and chocolate walls, was bustling this morning. She and Warren sat in a corner opposite the door and waved as colleagues entered and approached the counter.

"You checking up on me?" he asked. "You had a date with your ex last night; why couldn't I hang out too?"

"Ha ha — very funny."

He pinched her cheek. "You're cute when you're annoyed, you know."

She rolled her eyes. "Stop trying to butter me up and answer my questions. What time did Lily release you? Did you have to tuck the thirteen-year-old twins in bed?"

Warren laughed. "They wouldn't want to call it that, but yes, I got them settled into bed. Michael will be okay, but he was in a lot of pain last night. I called this morning on the way here, and he was getting ready to go to school."

"Poor thing. I know he's disappointed about having to sit out the rest of the season."

Warren cocked his head. "You know boys. More than anything he's embarrassed that he caught the ball the wrong way. Getting injured in a game might have been worth it, for the cool points he would have scored with sympathetic girls."

Dayna laughed. "That sounds about right for middle-school logic."

"Now, tell me about your night."

Dayna suddenly felt queasy. "It was surprising and interesting," she said. "I guess those are the best words to describe it."

Warren raised an eyebrow. There was no reason to give him the long version; he'd just want the facts.

"Brent's dying, Warren. He has end-stage prostate cancer. Apparently by the time it was caught, it had already spread, so they've told him there's little they can do."

Warren sat back in the café chair. "Whoa. Didn't see that coming. How old is he?"

"He'll be forty-one in August," Dayna said, remembering that he shared a birthday month with her mom.

"Is he doing okay? I mean, is he in pain? Getting treatments?"

Dayna shook her head. "Apparently not. He says it's too far gone for the treatments to do any good, so he'd rather spend this time clear-headed, doing what he wants, instead of sick from chemo or radiation, or foggy from too many pain meds. I don't know how much pain he's in, but he seemed okay last night at dinner."

"It may come and go," Warren said. "My dad died of prostate cancer, remember?"

Dayna reached for his hand. "I remember."

"Guess that's why Mr. Brent wanted to make amends so badly, huh?" Warren said.

Dayna nodded. "Guess so. And there's more."

"Yeah?"

"The longer we talked, the more he started sharing his plans for the time he has left. He wants to establish a foundation to help injured college athletes regroup, maintain their grades, and formulate a career plan so they won't drop out and miss the great opportunities that college offers. He's had the idea since his Alabama U days, when he was injured and unable to play."

"That means you were part of the dream-

115

ing process," Warren said.

Dayna nodded. "I was."

"Did he lose his way after his injury?"

"Obviously not — he's working for NASA," Dayna said and smiled. "Fortunately he was academically strong and a great athlete. Brent graduated with honors and a computer engineering degree. But a few of his buddies found themselves injured, out of athletic scholarships, and on academic probation because their grades weren't up to snuff. That hurt Brent to his core, and he always vowed that he'd make a difference someday."

"I guess someday has come, huh?"

"Looks that way," Dayna said, and gripped Warren's hand tighter. "And he wants me to help him."

"Come again?" Warren remained expressionless but pulled his hand away.

"He asked me to help him figure out the best way to set up the foundation and get it off the ground, so that when he's gone, it will be ready to roll."

"Why? You're a hospital executive."

Dayna shrugged. "I started rattling off all I know about how foundations work based on what Carmen shares in our weekly executive meetings, and before I knew it, he was begging for my help."

Warren took another swig of coffee. "And you couldn't say no."

Dayna hoped her puppy-dog expression would help.

"He's your ex-husband, Dayna, come on."

"He's dying, Warren. What was I supposed to do?"

"Where was his wife when all of this was going on?"

"She was sitting right there. She didn't say much, but she looked uncomfortable with the idea."

"I bet she did," Warren said. His jaw clenched and Dayna wanted to stroke it, but she was mindful that they had an audience.

"Actually, I didn't say yes, either. I told him I wasn't sure, and he took that as an open door. Don't be mad, babe," she said softly. "I'm going to ask Carmen to give me some websites and other information to share with him, so that I can at least give him some resources before sending him on his way."

Warren looked skeptical. "I'm not mad that you feel compelled to help him, Dayna," he said. "I'm just wondering if this is about more than wanting to create a foundation for him."

"Brent is married, Warren. And he's dying."

"Do you still love him, Dayna?"

Now it was her turn to be flabbergasted. She sat back in the chair and stared at him. "Where did that come from?"

"I'm just asking."

"Why? Have I given you any reason to think I have feelings for him?"

"You haven't given me any reason to think you don't. First you accept his invitation to dinner after much protesting, now you're talking about 'semi' helping him with a special project, even as you say you don't want to. I've never seen you quite this wishy-washy about anything in the time I've known you."

Dayna stood up and pushed her chair under the table. "Let's discuss this later, when we have more privacy." She gathered her paper coffee cup and the plate that held her bagel. "Want me to take your trash?"

"No, thanks. I've got it."

Warren looked like he wanted to say more, but he didn't. He stood and grabbed his coffee cup and headed out of the café. He turned and waved at her before walking to the bank of elevators that led to his seventh-floor office, but the faint smile on his lips didn't reach his eyes.

Sixteen

Tamara kept vigil in the doorway of her tan stucco home until Brent's car was out of view.

He usually worked from home but had insisted on driving himself to Cape Canaveral this morning to attend a quarterly Tuesday staff meeting. She had taken the day off to have some time to herself and wrap her brain around all that had happened over the weekend and last night. Dinner with Dayna hadn't been as strained as she anticipated, but she still was emotionally drained.

She strolled into her family room and found Mom glued to the TV, watching the last half hour of *Good Morning America*. Mom had stopped by just before Brent left to lure Tamara into a shopping spree. Tamara checked the clock on the DVD player. It was 8:40. Her massage and manicure were booked for eleven, which gave her just enough time to catch up on laundry and relax.

"I know the mall is open early today for some reason, but I don't think I'm up for it, Mom," Tamara said, and plopped on the sofa next to her. "Thanks for coming by, but I'm really tired."

Her mother put a hand on her plump hip. "I move all the way to Florida and don't get to spend any more time with my baby girl than when I lived in Michigan."

Tamara couldn't contain her frustration. "If you were still in Michigan, Mom, you wouldn't be sitting here on my sofa watching TV, now would you? We see each other just about every day. Besides, what special event at the mall has you all excited? You don't need another thing."

What Tamara didn't have the strength to articulate this morning was that spending time together didn't require them to spend money. Brent's medicine and doctor visit co-pays kept her mindful of their budget. Plus, she would have appreciated some motherly concern about how she'd survived the meeting with Dayna rather than this oblivious eagerness to catch the next big sale.

Tamara eased off the sofa and headed to the adjacent laundry room to sort clothes.

Mom joined her.

"I'm talking about the early-bird specials that started in January," Mom said. "Millcrest Mall opens an hour early on Mondays and Tuesdays so shoppers can take advantage of extra discounts in every store. Come on, let's go have some fun. You need to take your mind off everything."

"So in other words, today's sale isn't a one-time event? I'm going to the spa in two hours, Mom. How about you join me? I'll call now to book your appointment."

Mom plopped her petite, pudgy frame in the cushioned chair near the laundry room entrance and pouted. "I've been wanting a new purse . . ."

Tamara chuckled in exasperation. "Mom, please. I have a lot on my mind and on my plate right now. I'm just not up to shopping today. I'm not in the mood."

Her mother's face contorted into a familiar frown. "But —"

Before she could continue, a Holmes Regional Medical Center commercial filled the TV screen, assuring Space Coast residents that state-of-the-art care was available, specifically in the newly renovated cancer unit. Mom paused and looked at Tamara.

She left her seat and encircled Tamara in

a hug. "It's going to be okay, baby. I heard you and Brent talking this morning about Dayna helping with the foundation, and he said he understood your concerns. What's the problem?"

Tamara sighed for what felt like the hundredth time since the dinner with Dayna last night. What was the problem? Other than the fact that the love of her life was dying? Or that he wanted her to "bond" with his former wife?

Tamara wished she could express what she was going through, but Mom usually heard only what she wanted to hear — much like Brent these days. He told her last night, and again this morning, that he would explore other avenues to launch the foundation. But she knew Brent. When his mind was made up, he couldn't be deterred.

He would formulate a plan to turn her no into a yes. That was his pattern, and Tamara felt like a kettle about to blow. Had it been for any reason other than one that would require her to work with Dayna, she might agree. This time, she wasn't sure she'd budge.

Tamara leaned into Mom's embrace and closed her eyes. Trying to explain her husband to her mother would give her a headache. It was easier to relent.

"Give me twenty minutes, Mom, and I'll be ready to go."

Mom grinned and planted a wet kiss on Tamara's cheek. "Thank you, baby," she said. "You'll see — once we get there, you'll feel better. Go ahead and book my spa appointment. We'll leave my outing and wrap up the day at yours."

Tamara peered out of a window, in the direction Brent had driven a short while ago. One day he might drive down that palm tree-lined street and never come back. Shopping wasn't going to heal the dull ache that had become as familiar as breathing, and with Brent now longing to spend more time with his former wife, the ache was only growing sharper.

Seventeen

By the end of the business day, Dayna had collected a volume of helpful information to appease Brent when she backed out of his project.

She filled a Word document with website links, important terms and their definitions, and information about the pros and cons of public foundations versus private foundations. She also called Carmen Vargas, head of Chesdin Medical Center's foundation, to ask if she'd be willing to talk by phone or over lunch with Brent about his plans — her treat. Carmen had agreed.

Now all Dayna had to do was send the file to Brent. She'd email it, then work late to catch up on the tasks she'd set aside to do all of this research.

Her first call was to Warren.

"I'll be here 'til 7 or so tonight. We'll miss salsa, but want to join me for dinner?"

"Sure," he said, with no hint of lingering

frustration from their chat this morning. "Where are you taking me?"

"Your favorite place," she said and smiled.

Since his first visit to Bennie's Rib Shack, Warren had been hooked. They only went occasionally, and every time was a special treat.

"Good thing I had a light lunch. I'll meet you at your office when you're ready."

"See ya then," Dayna said.

"See ya, babe."

Dayna fingered the business card Brent had pressed into her hand last night and scanned it for information. He probably wouldn't want her sending the foundation correspondence to NASA; she needed a personal email address.

She grabbed her office phone and tapped the digits of his cell.

"Brent Davidson."

His silky smooth voice still impressed her.

"Dayna Wilson here," she said. It felt awkward using her maiden name with the man whose surname she had once assumed and uttered with great pride.

"Hi, Brent," she continued. "I'm calling because I've done some research on the foundation idea we discussed last night, and I wanted to email it to you. It should help you figure out how you want to move forward. What's the best email address to use?"

When he didn't respond, she called his name again. "Hello? You there?"

"I'm here," he said.

"Did you hear my question?"

"I heard you, Dayna," Brent said. "Does this mean you've decided not to help set up the foundation?"

She sighed. He wasn't going to let her off the hook. "Brent, I'm so sorry about your illness. But I'm extremely busy with work right now and with . . ."

"Warren. That's his name, right?"

She frowned. "Yeah — what's it to you?"

"Nothing, Dayna," he said. "I just thought he might have something to do with you wanting to send the information instead of giving it to me in person. But whatever works best for you will be fine. I appreciate your help."

Brent recited his personal email address and asked her to also send a copy of the information to Tamara. "That way, we're both in the loop."

"Do you have someone who can guide you through the process, or maybe take over this when you're . . . when you're ready to hand it over?" Dayna asked.

"I thought that was going to be you," he

said. "But I'll give it some more thought. Maybe Winston can help."

"Didn't you say last night that he still lives in Jersey?"

"Yep," Brent said. "Still in Jersey, married to Belinda, with five kids. Can you believe it? That brother needs his own foundation to fund college tuition."

They both laughed.

"You may be right," Dayna said.

Of Brent's three siblings, Winston had been her favorite. He was the big brother who mentored them on marriage when they were newlyweds and tried to talk sense into Brent when he asked for a divorce. He was the brother who told her he'd always be her brother, no matter what. She hadn't talked to him in years, but it was nice to know that he was doing okay. She wondered if he'd have time to help with the foundation though, given his busy family life and the fact that he traveled often with his work as a conference planner for a major ministry.

"Can he take this on?"

"Haven't asked him yet, but he won't tell me no," Brent said.

Dayna wanted to feel relieved, but instead felt guilty. "How was Tamara feeling about my possible involvement in this project, by the way?"

His lengthy hesitation told the truth.

"She'll be happy that you're emailing the information instead of hand-delivering it, but don't take it personally," Brent finally said.

"I won't," Dayna said and chuckled. "Look, Brent, I know what you're trying to do, and I commend you. I just think it might cause additional stress for everyone if I'm involved. Whoever helps establish your foundation will probably need to see it all the way through, and I understand why Tamara would be uncomfortable with me being that person. I'd be uncomfortable as well."

There. She had said it. She wished she could see Brent's reaction.

"And?"

Dayna frowned. Did he just dismiss her concerns, and his wife's, with an *and?* Brother man said he wasn't on serious medication for his cancer, but something clearly had him showing contempt. Before she could respond, he continued.

"I'm not trying to disregard how either of you feel," Brent said. "I've put both of you through a lot that you don't deserve. I'm just at a place where I'm trying to look at the greater good, and I wish you two would go there with me."

The greater good? For whom?

If Dayna uttered that question aloud her tone would be bitter. Brent seemed to be cloaking his selfish desires in a pious package. The urge that filled her spirit was to speak the truth in love.

"Brent, you're asking more than a lot. The three of us have a history that isn't so pleasant. I met with you the other night to give you a chance to have your say; now you're trying to guilt me into helping you. So what if it's for a good cause? If it doesn't feel right, it just doesn't, and you have no right to force me or your wife into working together to fulfill your dream. I'm sorry you're dying; I can't tell you how sad that makes me. But it doesn't mean that you have the right to bully the rest of us into doing what you want, just because you want it.

"I will email you the information I spent most of the afternoon researching, and I'll include the phone number and email address of Carmen Vargas, Chesdin Medical Center's foundation director. She's willing to meet with you and help however she can, okay? Beyond that, I wish you the best."

Dayna hung up before Brent could respond.

She raised her head and nearly jumped

129

out of her skin. Audrey stood in the doorway to the office, her arms crossed. She looked like a curvier, taller version of the young Diana Ross, with the full curly hair and star-wattage smile.

"I guess you told him!" She sauntered in and perched on the seat across from Dayna's desk.

"How long were you standing there?" Dayna asked.

"Long enough to know that you did the right thing. All you can do is help; you can't get sucked into a triangle with Brent and his wife. I don't know what he's going through with this death thing, but you can't get caught up in it. He had his chance with you and threw it away."

Dayna smiled at her friend.

"You have been giving a lot of advice lately," Dayna said. "I'm usually the one keeping you in line. Now that I think about it, though, it's been a minute since I've had to help you prepare for a date or recover when Mr. Right turned out to be Mr. 'Run and Hide.' What gives? You on a dating fast?"

Audrey shifted her eyes and turned away from Dayna to peer out of the office window. "Whatever you want to call it. I just don't have time for blind dates and Mr.

Fakes right now," she said, and laughed nervously. "I read that Steve Harvey book and he was right; I have to act like the diva I was born to be, but think strategically like the kind of man I want and need. So yeah, I'm taking it easy for a while. But back to you: you're sending Brent the foundation information, putting him in touch with Carmen, and backing off, right?"

Dayna grinned. "You are such an eavesdropper. Don't you have work to do?"

Audrey shrugged. "It's after five; my workday is over. I came to see if you wanted to go to dinner."

"We haven't gone out together in a while, have we?" Dayna said, shaking her head. "Sorry, can't do it. I gotta catch up on the work I set aside to do the research for Brent. Plus, I've promised Warren a barbecue dinner tonight instead of our regular salsa date."

"You taking him by Bennie's?"

"Yep."

"Enjoy, girl. Guess I'll head home, then."

Dayna recognized the wistfulness in her friend's voice. She hadn't been dating Warren long enough to forget the reality of loneliness. It made you feel like the only single person in the universe.

After grieving the loss of her marriage and

actively seeking ways to love on herself, Dayna had learned to enjoy life on her own terms. She realized that being alone didn't have to equal being lonely. She was certain that's why she had been ready when Warren had shown up. Both of them considered it fate that they'd enrolled in salsa lessons on the same night, at the same location, without knowing they were also colleagues. Warren had been new to town, enjoying a vacation before starting his job at Chesdin Medical. When he became her partner by default in salsa class that evening, she hadn't been looking for a mate. As their friendship blossomed into more, she had chosen to have one.

"Audrey?"

Her friend paused in the doorway.

"Want to join us at Bennie's? We can make it a threesome," Dayna said.

Audrey shook her head. "See you tomorrow, friend. Tell Warren I said hi."

"I will, and let's have lunch tomorrow."

Audrey gave her a thumbs-up and was out of sight in seconds.

Dayna was emailing Brent and Tamara when her boss poked his head into the office.

"Good night, Dayna," Spencer said. "Don't stay here all evening. Work will be here tomorrow."

She paused mid-keyboard stroke and smiled. "I won't be too long. Thanks."

With the email on its way, she dove into the to-do list she'd jotted on a notepad this morning and tackled two major tasks.

Warren startled her with a light tap on her door just after seven.

"Is it time already?"

"Is your work that much fun?" He massaged her neck as she closed her document and began shutting down her computer.

"How is it that this hospital doesn't have a policy against coworkers fraternizing?" she teased.

Warren laughed.

"Are you planning to institute one? If so, let's decide over dinner tonight which one of us will resign."

She giggled and turned to face him.

He peered at the door to make sure no one was coming before he leaned down to kiss her lightly on the lips. They smiled at each other like a pair of high school sweethearts.

"That policy would be a bad idea," she said. "I'd hate for you to have to work somewhere else."

EIGHTEEN

The man sitting across from her, feeding his face a rack of ribs, looked like Warren and talked like Warren, but the Warren she knew didn't eat hot sauce or greens. This man had a plate of both, because they were Bennie's special of the day, and their waitress had convinced him he'd be missing a treat if he didn't give them a try.

"I've been urging you to eat greens for nearly two years and you always politely decline. Our waitress runs down the special of the day once and urges you to 'live a little,' and you give in?"

Warren tugged Dayna's hand away from her hip and kissed her knuckles.

"Ugh!" she said and yanked it back. "Now I have greens juice and hot sauce on my hands!"

"Good — I can take some of it home with me," Warren said.

They fell into a fit of laughter, and Dayna

was certain no one else would have understood what was so funny. She loved that she could be serious with this man one minute and cracking corny jokes the next, and all the while, he had her back.

"Are you real, or did I dream you up?"

"Which version will you marry?" Warren asked.

She frowned. "Please don't tell me you're proposing to me in a rib joint with your hot-sauce breath."

Warren threw back his head and laughed. "Don't worry, that was just a test run. When the time comes, I plan to be a little more romantic than this."

Dayna giggled. "I was about to say, how could I tell this story to our children and grandchildren: 'We were sitting there gazing at each other over sweet and tangy barbecue ribs, potato salad, and mustard greens. He took one last bite of rib and told me he wanted to join my marrow with his.'"

Warren doubled over, and in spite of herself, Dayna succumbed to more laughter. Her joke hadn't been that funny, but if Warren wanted to enjoy it, so would she.

The more the other diners gave them curious glances, the harder they giggled.

"If nothing else, Bennie's will have the honor of catering the rehearsal dinner,"

Warren said when he could talk again. Dayna fell into another fit of giggles.

Their waitress, an older black lady with a silver-gray bun at the nape of her neck, approached with glasses of water for each of them. She set the beverages on the table without uttering a word, but the frown filling her wrinkled forehead spoke volumes.

When she was out of sight, they tried to calm down. Dayna relaxed in the wooden chair and took a gulp of the water. "Stop, Warren. We're making a scene."

"We've been doing that for the past ten minutes and you're just now telling me to stop? Okay, okay," he said, and took a deep breath. "Trust me, babe, when the time is right, I'll make my proposal memorable. It won't happen at Bennie's Rib Shack, as much as I love the food here, okay?"

"And it won't be because you feel a tad bit jealous of another man?"

She'd filled him in on her earlier conversation with Brent, and he had applauded her for doing the right thing and letting her ex remain part of her past.

Warren snorted. "Jealous? Of Brent? He's the one who has reason to be jealous, Dayna. You're with me now."

Her smile softened and she reached for his hand again. "I love you, Warren."

"I know you do, D. Where do we go from here?" he asked.

After eighteen months of dating it wasn't as if he were moving their relationship to the fast track, but the questions were coming when she felt least prepared to answer them. Despite his protests, maybe he did feel threatened by a married, dying man.

"What is it, Warren?"

He looked perplexed. "What do you mean?"

"Why all of this talk about marriage all of a sudden? You know I'm not going anywhere. You make me very happy."

He smiled.

She realized he wasn't going to tell her what had prompted his questions tonight and she decided not to push. Whatever his reasons, they would eventually be revealed.

"How is Michael's thumb healing?"

"It's doing okay, but I've been meaning to tell you, he's scheduled to undergo surgery the day after tomorrow at Chesdin Medical's outpatient clinic. The doctor wants to set the bone right away, before the healing process begins. Fortunately, Michael being a lefty means his schoolwork won't suffer. I'll be taking off work to care for him. Lily is planning to be there too."

Dayna nodded. She wasn't thrilled with

the idea of him spending time with the still-enamored Lily, but Lily had a right to be there for Michael; she always had been.

"Should I take off work as well, in case you need me?"

Warren hesitated, then shook his head. "You can come over to the outpatient clinic and check on us, but you don't have to take off work. We'll be fine. Besides, Michael will be so medicated he won't know whether he's coming or going. You'll be at my place this weekend, won't you? You'll get to spend time with him then."

Dayna nodded a second time. She had grown used to sharing him and his boys with Lily, but sometimes she still felt like he had a life and a family of which she wasn't a part. She looked forward to that changing once they wed. She was ready for a family of her own.

Dayna's ringing cell phone brought her out of her reverie. She looked at the caller ID and raised an eyebrow. "It's Brent."

Warren shrugged and took another bite of rib. "Tell him I said hello."

She smirked and took the call.

Instead of Brent greeting her, it was Tamara. "Why have you been calling my husband? Enough is enough, Dayna. He's no longer yours. Just let it go, so we can

138

move on with whatever time we have left together."

Dayna was stunned. Where had this come from? Was Tamara really bold enough to try and turn the tables? Before she could offer a response, the line went dead. She was left holding the phone and an attitude.

Nineteen

Tamara fingered Brent's cell phone like it was a bomb that could explode if she moved the wrong way.

Had she really just made the crazy-wife call?

She wanted to pinch herself awake, but that wasn't necessary. Yes — in a momentary lapse of judgment she had let her negative thoughts mushroom and conjured up enough anger to replicate what Dayna had once done to her.

Making that "leave my man alone" call was the depth of desperation. Tamara looked toward the bedroom door, wondering when Brent would come through it and what he would say if he found her sitting here looking guilty, holding the evidence in her hand.

God, help me fix this. That call was out of line and I knew it. Tell me what to do.

She bowed her head, closed her eyes, and waited.

Why couldn't God be like those annoying telemarketers who bugged you until you gave in to what they wanted, or at least until you listened to their entire spiel? No, God wasn't demanding or overbearing, and for those very reasons, he wasn't going to give her the guidance she needed on a silver platter. Still, she sensed in her spirit what the good and right thing would be, even though it would cost her more trouble than she cared for.

Tamara slid off the edge of the bed. She tucked the cell phone into the pocket of her bubblegum-pink leisure suit and glanced at herself in the mirror.

She was beautiful and she knew it. Brent told her every day. Other men swooned, and women stole sideways glances when they thought she wasn't aware. So why didn't she feel lovely inside anymore? Why was she so numb, and afraid?

She swallowed the lump in her throat and tried to quiet her thumping heartbeat with a few deep breaths before she faced her husband.

Tamara found Brent in the family room flipping from one ESPN channel to another. She plopped on the sofa and snuggled under his shoulder, like always.

She gazed up at him and fought to keep

the tears at bay. How much longer would this be possible? He felt thinner by the day and seemed to be wasting away before her eyes.

Before more negative thoughts left her speculating the worst, Brent distracted her with a kiss.

"What are you up to, love?"

She wanted to shrink. How was she going to tell him what she'd done? Just how should she broach this subject before Dayna called back and told him herself? The best solution was to stop plotting and get it over with.

Tamara stretched out across his lap and slid the remote from his fingers. She lowered the TV volume and peered into his eyes with a pained smile. "Brent, do I seem like the jealous type?"

He frowned. "Is that a trick question?"

"What if I told you I did something because I was . . . concerned about losing you to someone else?"

"Girl, I've been given less than a year to live and you're worried about fighting another woman for me? Guess a brother still has it."

He cradled her head with his hands, lowered his face to hers, and kissed her.

A tear slid out of the corner of Tamara's eye.

Why are you taking him, Lord? I need him.

Brent grew concerned. "What's wrong, Tami?"

She sat up so she could face him and dabbed at her moist eyes. "I did something stupid just now. When I went into the bedroom and saw your phone on the dresser, it started vibrating, so I picked it up to bring it to you. The call from your friend Tim went to your voicemail, but since I had the phone, I scrolled through your other calls. I got upset when I saw that Dayna contacted you today."

Brent stared at her for what felt like a lifetime.

"And?"

"And so I called her and told her to back off."

Brent shook his head. He slid Tamara off his lap and walked across the room to shut off the TV, though the remote had been next to him on the sofa.

"So what's that about, Tami? I've gone out of my way to be up-front with you about my interactions with Dayna. She called me today to give me some information on setting up a foundation. Have you checked your email? She said she was going to

143

forward the info to you too."

Tamara's heart sank. She had assumed the worst and embarrassed them both. She looked at Brent and apologized with her eyes, but her spirit was still defiant. She couldn't do anything about losing him to cancer, but she wasn't going to willingly give him back to Dayna. Ms. Dayna had had her chance, and while things hadn't been handled the right way, life was different now. Brent was Tamara's husband, and she intended to keep him.

"I thought we agreed that she wouldn't help with the foundation," Tamara said. "What's the email about?"

Brent ran his wide palm across his close-shaven head. Since he was no longer taking chemo and radiation, his hair had slowly started to grow in, and he kept it cut low.

"I haven't had a chance to tell you that she declined to help us with the foundation, in part because of the very attitude you showed today," he said. "She was uncomfortable with the idea and sensed that you were too. She was calling to tell me she had done some online research for us, and she has asked someone with the hospital's foundation to give us some guidance. That's all, baby; that's all."

Brent looked angry, then sad. He spread

his arms and motioned for Tamara to approach him. She let him wrap her in an embrace. Then she rested her head against his chest and wept.

"We've come too far for you not to trust me, Tami. We're in this together."

She nodded and continued to cling to him. She knew she was wrong, but she just wanted Dayna to go away. Why had he felt the need to contact her anyway? Life was complicated enough without his ex-wife's presence. Dayna might no longer be planning to help with the foundation, but now that they had made contact with her after all these years, she was part of their world again.

Look at her and Brent right now, talking about Dayna and thinking about her when she was nowhere around. At least Tamara knew that's what she had been doing — obsessing over the ex-wife. She prayed right now, for the umpteenth time, that Brent wasn't doing the same.

TWENTY

Warren and Dayna steered their vehicles in different directions when they left the rib shack parking lot, but seconds later resumed their conversation.

"Where was I?" Warren said into the cell.

"Telling me that you don't think I should inform Brent about his wife's inappropriate call," Dayna said.

Dayna paused at a stop sign and looked both ways down the dark street before making a right turn.

"Leave it alone," Warren said. "She obviously has some issues with Brent getting back in touch with you, despite her agreeing to his surprise visit to your house and the dinner invitation. Can you blame her? She's got to be going through a lot."

Dayna decided to ignore Warren's sympathetic view of Tamara. "I can't believe her. I made a call just like that to her, years ago, when she was dating Brent while he was married to me. At least I was justified."

"Dayna, you know by now that no good comes from rehashing past wrongs," Warren said. "If you aren't careful, you'll get stuck there. You home yet?"

Dayna turned another corner and this time sat idling at a traffic light. "In another five minutes. How close are you?"

"I'm pulling into the driveway," he said. "I'll stay on the phone with you until you get inside."

"Such a gentleman," Dayna teased. She wondered what it would be like to live with him and have him serve as her protector and her husband.

"Stop kissing up to me," he said, but she knew he was blushing.

When she entered her kitchen, he bid her farewell. "Gotta check on Michael and Mason and make them get to bed," he said. "Then I'm calling it a night. My first meeting is at seven in the morning. Thanks for treating me to the ribs, babe. Delicious as always. And yes, the greens were off the chain."

"You're welcome, sweetie," Dayna said.

She fell into her usual routine of preparing a cup of hot tea.

"Tell the boys I said hello, and tell Michael I'm already praying that all goes well with his surgery."

Dayna ended the call and took her tea into the bedroom, where she rummaged through her dresser in search of sleepwear. It was just 9:20, a good two hours earlier than her bedtime. But no catching up on a novel or watching her favorite sitcom on demand tonight. She felt drained by all of the day's events.

Dayna pressed the speaker on her bedside phone so she could hear her new messages. She sat on the bed and sipped her tea while she listened.

The first voicemail was from her neighbor, Mary, inviting her to a Bunco party over the weekend.

The next message was a surprise.

"Hello, Dayna? This is Mama. Haven't heard from you in a while. Can you give me a call as soon as possible?"

Dayna's stomach grew tense. Great. There went her good night's sleep. She could put off calling Mama until tomorrow, but she'd spend all night wondering what she wanted.

"Let me get it over with now." Alabama's time zone was an hour earlier than central Florida's, so it was just eight-something there — perfect timing for her mother to lead a long evening chat.

Dayna set her mug on the nightstand and

tapped the telephone digits she'd learned in kindergarten.

Daddy answered with a smile in his booming voice. "How's my oldest daughter doing? Haven't heard from you in a while."

"Hi, Daddy. How are you?" Dayna had learned it was safer not to try and explain herself. Daddy always had the last word, and in his world, his word was always right.

"I'm doing fine, just settling in for a cold evening. We might actually get some snow this week, the weatherman says. Gotta get down to the church tomorrow to make sure everything is secured, in case we have to cancel Bible study."

Dayna knew that would be his top priority. The family home might also need "securing," but his beloved church was going to be taken care of first, and whatever energy or resources he had left over may or may not cover the rest.

"Is Mama around? I'm returning her call."

"She's right here," Daddy said. Dayna heard him huff and puff as he pushed himself up from his favorite chair to put the phone in her mother's hand.

"Take care, Daddy. Nice talking to you," Dayna said before he made the transfer.

"You too, young lady. Don't be such a stranger."

Was he actually indicating that he missed her? Dayna wasn't sure if that was the case, or if he was just making small talk.

She heard her mother fumbling the phone to position.

"Well, hello, Dayna," she said in her sing-song Southern drawl. "How you been?"

"Fine, Mama, just busy. How about you?"

"I'm doing good, dear. Been keeping busy with your little nephews running underfoot in the afternoons. Shiloh is teaching piano most evenings now, so I offered to watch the boys."

Dayna smirked. Ah, Shiloh. Ever the perfect daughter, following in Mama's footsteps as a good preacher's wife, mother, and community member.

"So what's up?" Dayna asked.

"Oh, I haven't talked to you in a while, so I was calling to say hello, first of all," Mama said. "Then I started thinking about Easter . . ."

Here it comes, Dayna thought.

"And I realized we didn't see you at Thanksgiving or Christmas," Mama said. "It would be a shame for another major holiday to go by and you not spend it with family."

"I wasn't alone, though, Mama," Dayna said. "Remember I had Thanksgiving here,

150

because Vanora and her parents came to town to visit her great-aunt Duchess. Then Warren and I took his sons on a cruise for Christmas. Remember?"

"I haven't forgotten all of that," Mama said. "But you and Warren aren't married. What kind of example was that setting for his sons? And you know I love Vanora, but she would have understood if you had come home. You've been away so long, the folks at church are starting to talk."

Bingo. Mama's words always had a way of winding to the heart of a matter.

"Mama, I'm nearly forty," Dayna said. "Why on earth would my absence over the holidays be something to talk about? It's not like I'm in college and failing to come home during breaks. And by the way, Warren shared a cabin on the Christmas cruise with the boys. I stayed in my own space, on the other side of the ship. Anyway . . . what do you have in mind for Easter?"

If she didn't cut to the chase, Mama would beat around the bush for the next hour.

"Would you be able to make it home that weekend? It's in late March this year, and we'd all love to have you here. It happens to fall the week of Daddy's pastoral anniversary too, and we might even want you to sing a solo during service."

She rolled her eyes. Was this visit for show, or because they wanted to see her? She hadn't been able to tell for a long, long time. The oldest child in a family was usually the most doted on, from what she'd always heard, but every time she talked with her folks, she wound up feeling like the black sheep. That had been the case since she and Brent split, and all these years later, nothing had changed.

Her hoping was in vain again tonight. Maybe one day Mama and Daddy would call to talk with her just because they wanted to hear her voice or invite her home without expecting a performance. That's what she wanted, but that wasn't reality.

"Can I bring Warren?"

Now it was Mama's turn to pause.

"Well, of course you know we like Warren," she began, "but I don't know how the congregation would handle . . ."

"Why are you worried about the congregation, Mama? Shouldn't you be worried about making sure that as your guest, Warren feels comfortable, especially in the Lord's house?"

Her voice had risen and Dayna knew she was bordering on being disrespectful. She took it down a notch.

"Mama, you and Daddy need to understand how important Warren is to me. We may be getting married."

Mama gasped.

"Why are you so surprised?" Dayna asked. "I've been dating him for eighteen months. What did you think?"

"Has he asked you?"

"Not formally, but we've discussed it," Dayna said.

"Well, it's never formal until he asks," Mama said, with palpable relief. "Why not wait and bring him for a visit when it's official?"

Dayna's heart ached.

"Maybe I need to wait until 'it's official' to visit myself," she said. "I've gotta run, Mama. It's almost ten p.m. here, and I've had a long day."

"So you aren't going to come, Dayna? I really want you to come, it's just that . . ."

Dayna couldn't handle any more excuses right now. Appearances still mattered most to Mama and to Daddy, regardless of the truths that lay behind them. What would they say if she told them their favorite former son-in-law had stopped by out of the blue last week to apologize?

Dayna bet he'd still be welcome at the church, even after abandoning their daugh-

153

ter. In Atchity, Alabama, and especially in the Wilson household, Brent Davidson still held star status, though he'd only played for Alabama U for two years.

Dayna quashed the despair that threatened to engulf her whenever she tried to talk to Mama about something meaningful.

Mama's voice trailed off, so Dayna finished the sentiment for her. "It's just that you and Daddy need to do what's best for the church, right? I understand," Dayna said. "I'm going to run now. Thank you for the invitation to visit at Easter. I'll let you know something soon, maybe by the end of the week. You take care, and kiss the boys for me. And by the way, will Jessica be coming home?"

Mama hesitated. Dayna knew that meant her baby sister was on the fence as well. She'd call Jessica tomorrow and get the scoop. If her fabulously successful sibling couldn't fit a visit home into her busy professional speaking schedule, maybe Dayna needed to be conveniently busy too.

Twenty-One

In the week since Dayna had followed Warren's advice, life seemed to be returning to normal.

She kept her mouth shut about the call from Tamara and moved on. She was stunned then, when just after lunch today, Monica buzzed her office intercom and told her a woman named Tamara was in the lobby, waiting to see her.

Dayna asked Monica to repeat herself.

"Yes," Monica reiterated. "She says her name is Tamara Davidson."

Dayna stood and walked around to the front of the desk. She looked herself up and down, surveying the black pantsuit she had worn today with her three-inch heels. She and Tamara were both ladies, but if she needed to defend herself, she could step out of the shoes and handle her business.

"Send her in," she said to Monica, and folded her arms across her chest.

Seconds later, Monica swung open the door and ushered in Tamara, who was casually glamorous in jeans and a wrap top. The polished makeup, curly hairdo, and over-sized designer purse helped her make an entrance that was also a statement.

Dayna felt dull in comparison. Had this been one of her friends, she would have rewarded Tamara with a "Wow." Instead, she nodded and motioned for her to have a seat.

"This is a surprise," Dayna said from her perch on the front of the desk.

Tamara nodded. "I know, and I apologize for bothering you in the middle of your workday. But I figured having one Davidson show up unexpectedly at your home was probably enough."

Dayna crossed her arms and raised an eyebrow. "True," she said. "So, what brings you here?"

Tamara shrugged. "You're probably tired of us Davidsons apologizing too, but I came to ask you to excuse that phone call I made a week ago, insisting that you not call Brent. I talked with him about it and realized that I was out of line. I had no right to accuse you, especially when Brent sought you out, so I'm sorry."

Dayna wondered what had prompted this

olive branch but decided not to question it. "Apology accepted."

She wondered how Brent was faring, but in light of the reason that Tamara had come, she wasn't sure it was a good idea to even ask about him. Tamara must have sensed the hesitation.

"You're welcome to call him and help him with the foundation, if you want."

Dayna's brows furrowed. "Excuse me? Did you and Brent receive my email with the information I sent? Did he contact Carmen to schedule a lunch meeting?"

Tamara sighed, and her voice wavered. "We got it, and we read it, and to be honest, it took us back to square one," she said. "There's just so much involved in doing this, I know my eyes glazed over. And Brent . . . Brent can fool you when he wants. He can make it through a dinner or a short visit and have you thinking he's okay, but he's been in a lot of pain the past week, so he hasn't felt up to reviewing the information and considering what the next steps should be."

Dayna's spirits sank. "I'm sorry," she said.

Tamara's eyes filled with tears. "Me too," she said. "I don't understand why this is happening." She seemed to remember where she was and to whom she was talking, and with a sniff and a sigh, she pulled herself together and continued. "He hasn't been feeling well lately, but all he can think about and talk about is this darn foundation. In a way, I think . . ."

Dayna could tell she was still struggling with how much to say.

"He wants to be remembered for having done something of value, and he's pinning his hopes on this foundation helping him do that. But with the way he's been feeling this week, I'm not sure how much progress he can make on his own. I do think . . . if you can . . . would you be willing to walk us through the process and help us get an idea of where to start and who can help us long-term? I know you have a career and all, and we don't want to do anything that would take you away from that, but if you could get us started, Brent would . . . we would sincerely appreciate it." Tamara released another big sigh, which seemed to help rein in the tears.

Dayna was surprised at herself — her heart went out to Tamara. It must have taken a lot of courage for Tamara to come to her in the first place, but especially about a project that would require Dayna to work closely with Brent to help fulfill his wishes. But she had to honor her own truths.

"Tamara, I don't know what to tell you," Dayna said. "You and I — and Brent — have some pretty ugly history. I thought you were a friend and all the while I was busy trying to help you settle into our neighborhood and make friends, you were helping yourself to my husband. Why do you and Brent think you have the right to receive my help, just because it's convenient and you need it?"

Tamara nodded. "I understand where you're coming from, Dayna. Believe me, just as hard as it is for you to consider doing this, it's hard for me to ask." She hesitated. "Dayna, would you mind if we pray about this — together?"

Dayna's eyes grew wide. But she acknowledged her consent by bowing her head, and Tamara followed suit.

"Lord, here we are, two sinners saved by grace, trying to figure out how to help one of your children. We don't know what's best for Brent, but you do. We don't even really know what to pray for. We're just praying for him to be healed as you see fit, for him to be given emotional strength, and for guidance on how to launch this foundation he's dreamed of for so long. If it's your will, please give Dayna and me the grace, the strength, and the patience to work together

159

on this project, so that in the end, Brent's wishes are fulfilled and your name is glorified. Amen."

Tamara raised her head and Dayna recognized gratitude in her eyes. Tamara rose from the cushioned office chair as if she wanted to hug Dayna, but thought better of it. She stood there, facing Dayna, looking lovely and lost.

What could Dayna say? She had expected an argument or worse, but Tamara had delivered a knockout punch with prayer.

"I'll follow up with Carmen to see when she's available to meet with you, me, and Brent for lunch, okay?" Dayna said. "We'll get the ball rolling sooner rather than later and try to give Brent some peace of mind." She'd ease her way into this, and see what happened.

Tamara nodded. "Thank you, Dayna. Thank you."

With that, she picked up her purse and turned to leave. She closed the office door behind her without looking back.

Dayna sat transfixed for a while, processing all that had just occurred. Tamara might be camera-ready pretty and may have done some terrible things in the past, but she clearly loved Brent enough to put aside her issues for his sake. As much as Dayna had loved Brent when she was married to him, she didn't know if she would have had the guts to approach her husband's former wife and invite her into their lives. Where was this ride going to take them?

TWENTY-TWO

Seconds after sliding behind the wheel of her GMC, Tamara let go. Her head collapsed in her hands and she wept until she experienced dry heaves.

Her tears were for Brent, who was at home in bed today, writhing in pain and worrying whether he'd finish all of the tasks on his personal to-do list. They were also for the babies she'd never have with her husband. After five years of trying with no success, the discovery of Brent's cancer and the chemo and radiation that followed had snuffed out the dream. The realization hit Tamara again yesterday, when a coworker at the bank announced her pregnancy.

These tears were also a sigh of relief for having done today what she didn't want to do — ask a favor of Dayna, the woman in whose shadow she realized she'd always stand, at least when it came to Brent and his extended family.

162

And finally, she cried for herself and for her dying dreams. Being the good wife, the long-suffering caretaker and companion, and the perfect daughter was taking a toll. She released her frustration through these tears and prayed that God would let them cleanse her.

The sobs subsided and Tamara rested her forehead against the steering wheel. She must look a hot mess, she imagined, with tears and smeared makeup creating trails across her face. She rummaged through her floppy bag until she found a package of tissues and cleaned herself up. Minutes later, Tamara started the car and headed toward Cocoa Beach.

Mom was at home with Brent, but since this morning had been so rough, Tamara didn't feel comfortable leaving him for long. Neither of them knew where she'd gone, and Brent would probably be sleeping when she got home. She couldn't wait to see his face when she told him not to fret; his dream of leaving a legacy for other college athletes was still alive.

TWENTY-THREE

Dayna gave up after reading the critical care nurse's report for the third time without comprehending it.

Tamara's midafternoon visit had thrown her for such a loop that trying to focus on work was like trying to ride a Ferris wheel in a tornado. Her mind flitted from the need to help Brent with his requests, to fretting about getting pulled back into his life, to frustration over Mama's loaded Easter invitation, to wondering whether Warren would be having dinner with Lily and the boys again tonight — and how she was going to tell him about the latest turn of events with Brent and Tamara.

She shut off the computer and pressed Monica's line.

"Yes, Dayna?"

"Believe it or not, I'm gonna leave a little early today. Take messages and let Spencer and the others know I'll respond first thing in the morning."

"Got it."

Dayna spun her chair toward the window and peered at the cloudless sky. It was beautiful and uncomplicated and seemed to offer happiness in the form of a sunny day. Why couldn't life be like that, for 90 percent of the time at least?

She thought about Vanora's sweet aunt Duchess, and what her response would be to a query like that: "Thank God for both the mountains and valleys, baby. They help shape your character. Don't ask him to take them away; you just want the strength to climb them."

Duchess said that quite often, and today, Dayna finally could relate.

She packed up her briefcase, then shot a quick email to Warren and Audrey, canceling their salsa outing tonight. If Brent was doing as badly as Tamara had indicated, she needed to buckle down on the foundation work sooner rather than later. Tonight was one of her free evenings, so she might as well get focused.

She asked the two of them for a rain check 'til next week. Then she privately emailed Warren and told him to call her for details about what she'd be doing instead of dancing. Subconsciously she knew chatting with him through email was a cop-out; it allowed her to delay the inevitable update about what was pulling her away.

While she was online, she searched her sent email file and pulled up the message she had sent Tamara and Brent two weeks earlier, sharing details about different types of foundations. There was a lot of material here. She could see why Tamara and Brent might have felt overwhelmed — reading through it again, she did too. She realized that while she might help guide them in the right direction, they were going to need a team of professionals to really pull this off.

Dayna paused to ponder the next logical step. It seemed to her that the meeting she had suggested with Carmen would make the most sense. She picked up the phone to call Brent and ask when he and Tamara could meet with her and Carmen, but on second thought returned it to its cradle.

"Why didn't I get Tamara's phone number while she was here?" Dayna mused aloud.

That may have eliminated some of the concern Tamara initially had about her and Brent getting too close. Oh well, at this rate email would be best.

She sent a quick note to Tamara asking for the best contact phone numbers for her and also for a few dates in the next week or two when she and Brent could meet for lunch or dinner to discuss the project and decide how to proceed.

Before she could shut down her computer, she received a reply.

Tamara sent both home and cell numbers and indicated that Tuesday evenings or Fridays at lunchtime would be best, because she didn't work on Fridays or have classes on Tuesdays.

Brent has adopted a flexible, work-from-home arrangement with his boss, due to his illness, so he can also manage a meeting on either of those days, as long as he's feeling well. Thanks for doing this, Dayna.

God bless you, Tamara

Tuesday nights? Great — the one regular date night she and Warren fought to keep because it was the best night for salsa in town. She set aside that dilemma for the moment and called Carmen to chat with her about Tamara and Brent's schedules and the need to expedite their meetings.

"I think it's wonderful that he wants to leave this kind of legacy, and I'm happy to help however I can," Carmen said. "If they want to meet next Tuesday evening that works for me. Fridays at lunchtime can be iffy, depending on what I have to do for the hospital."

Dayna quickly relayed the message to Tamara via email. Before she could type another sentence, Monica popped her head into the office.

"Thought you were leaving thirty minutes ago?"

Dayna shrugged. "I thought I was too, but I got on a roll. I'm leaving soon, though."

"Well, Audrey's here to see you. Maybe she can visit while you gather your belongings?"

"That's fine," Dayna said. "Send her in."

She was printing notes from the email to Tamara and Brent when Audrey strode in with her characteristic runway-model sway. "This is the second time you've let me down on salsa night. What gives?"

Audrey settled in the chair Tamara had graced a few hours earlier, and Dayna filled her friend in on Mrs. Davidson's surprise visit.

"Wow. So you're going to do it?"

"I'm going to do it."

"I don't know what to say. That's deep. Have you told Warren?"

Dayna shook her head. "I'm waiting to hear back from him, to give him this latest update, but he'll be fine. He had given me his blessing before, when I pulled back. The only problem is I don't know how much time Brent really has, so I'm feeling like I need to turn this around quickly."

Audrey nodded. "I understand. I'm in too, if you need me."

"Excuse me?" Dayna couldn't hide her surprise.

"Typically when you're setting up or operating a foundation, you need an attorney and an accountant on board. I help Carmen all the time with the work she does for Chesdin Medical's foundation, so if you need me to help you with any of the IRS documents or financial questions that may arise about the proper structure to follow, I'm here for you."

A smile spread across Dayna's face. "I'm blessed with some pretty special friends. Thanks, Audrey. I'll let you know how far along we get, but I'm pretty sure we'll need your help."

Audrey left her seat and approached Dayna with her arms open. "You're doing something special," Audrey said, and embraced her. She stepped back and searched Dayna's eyes. "But don't get so caught up in the sympathy thing that you forget to let them walk their path, so you can walk yours."

Dayna frowned. "What does that mean?"

"Brent is still married to Tamara, and you still have a relationship to maintain with Warren," Audrey said. "Keep that front and center, even as you're doing all you can to help. Me personally, I think you should still go salsa dancing tonight. You need to do something fun and lighthearted with all of this going on, and you need to be having fun with your man. But if you must, go ahead and focus on the foundation stuff tonight; just don't make this pattern a habit."

Dayna smirked, but she secretly was grateful for the advice.

"I hear you, but no salsa for me tonight," Dayna said. "I need to get my bearings and figure out how to fit this into my schedule, with everything else."

Audrey nodded. "Okay, well, I'll see you soon. I'm gonna run and have dinner with my goddaughter, Chastity. She's a high school senior now and doesn't always make time for me like she used to."

Dayna shooed her out of the door. "Enjoy, and thanks again, Audrey."

With the office quiet again, Dayna leaned back in her chair and thought about all Audrey had said. Was there a reason to worry about losing herself in Brent and Tamara's world, even by just helping with the foundation? Thinking of Brent sick and dying made her sad.

Maybe that was the greatest danger — that her heart would get involved as much as her head. Audrey knew her well enough to recognize that threat to her happiness.

TWENTY-FOUR

The doorbell rang and Dayna trotted to it once again, hoping this time it was Warren, and that he had surprised her by coming after all. He hadn't taken her about-face with Brent and Tamara well, and despite Dayna's pleas for him to join the committee so he could be part of the process, he had vowed to stay away.

She tried to mask her disappointment when Carmen's bright smile greeted her.

"Welcome, and thanks for coming!"

Carmen hugged Dayna's neck and stepped into the foyer. Her large brown eyes grew saucer-sized as she surveyed the entrance and the framed African American art lining the walls.

"You've got a beautiful place here, Dayna. I love it."

Carmen had grown up in America, but somehow still managed to possess a slight hint of her parents' lilting Cuban accent.

"Thank you," Dayna said. "Follow me. Everyone is gathering in the dining room."

She led Carmen to an adjacent room where Brent and Tamara were hovering near a credenza, chatting with Audrey.

"Hi, everyone — long time no see!" Carmen joked, before offering a round of hugs.

At just four feet ten, Carmen's offered embrace required that she stand on her tiptoes and that Tamara, Brent, and Audrey bend to receive it. Dayna chuckled at the scene.

Tonight's meeting was a follow-up to their lunchtime discussion four days ago, when everyone had met for the first time in a conference room at Chesdin Medical and Carmen had outlined for Brent and Tamara the various options for creating a foundation. By the end of that hour-long meeting on Friday, Audrey and Carmen's interest in helping Brent had been solidified.

"I don't know what went down between you two," Audrey had confided in Dayna later that day, "and I hope you don't get mad at me for saying this, but Brent is a good guy. I like his spirit."

Dayna hadn't known how to respond. She had once believed that about him too. What had changed, she still didn't really know, but at least she had heard his side, and while

173

his explanation hadn't been fully understandable, she was grateful for it.

Tonight, Brent somehow looked thinner since she had last seen him, but the white polo shirt he wore with his khakis accentuated his still-muscular frame. While he seemed tired, his handsome grin still lit up the room.

"Did you work today?" Audrey asked him.

He shoved his hands in his pockets and nodded. "Yeah, I did. I was moving a little slow last week, but I managed to get back on track yesterday and today. Staying busy helps."

Dayna saw worry sprint through Tamara's eyes, as well as her effort to hide it.

"You guys want to go ahead and start the meeting?" She motioned for everyone to join her at the dining room table and seat themselves wherever they liked. They formed a cluster at one end, with Carmen sitting at the head of the table and Audrey and Tamara choosing seats to her left. Dayna was surprised when Brent plopped in the seat next to her, rather than sitting on the opposite side, next to his wife. Warren would have a field day with this.

She stole a glance at Tamara, who was trying to send a silent message of "What's up with that?" to an oblivious Brent. He had pulled out a notebook and pen and had fixed his gaze on Carmen.

Dayna wrestled with whether to suggest that he move next to Tamara or let it be. Before she could decide what to do, Brent cleared his throat to get everyone's attention. He looked at Dayna.

"I know this is your home, but would you mind if I open the meeting with prayer?"

Dayna was flabbergasted. "Uh, sure."

Brent surveyed the group. "Is everyone okay with that?"

Carmen and Audrey nodded, along with Tamara, whose demeanor still conveyed frustration.

"Dear heavenly Father, thank you for another day," Brent began. "Thank you for giving me enough health and strength to work this week and to spend time creating something beyond myself that I believe you are going to use for good. Thank you for every person around this table, who is taking the time and making sacrifices to help me."

Dayna's mind wandered to Warren during the prayer. Where was he right now? Was this really worth alienating him?

"Lord, let us produce something good here," Brent continued, "and let your name be glorified, even in the midst of my trial. Amen."

"Amen," the rest of the group said in unison.

Dayna left her seat for a few minutes and transferred the snacks from the credenza to the center of the table, within everyone's reach. When she was settled again, the magnitude of what was taking place hit her: two weeks ago, Brent had shown up at her door, a stranger for all intents and purposes, and now here he sat next to her, breaking bread, praying, and collaborating with her on something positive. Was this what it looked like when God created beauty from ashes?

Dayna wished she had a camera to snap the picture, and the courage to post it on Facebook. The scene unfolding before her was a memorable one.

Carmen twisted the cap off a bottle of water and wasted no time in revisiting the discussions from their Friday meeting. "I'm hoping we can decide tonight whether to move forward with the private foundation model that provides more decision-making flexibility, or to place Brent's foundation under the umbrella of a larger public foundation that could offer administrative support and other services.

"As I mentioned last week, I think establishing a supporting organization is going to be your best route," Carmen told Brent and Tamara. "In my experience, it will be less work for you, but you still get the full benefit and support of the overseeing foundation. You can still name it what you want, and it would be treated as a separate charitable entity."

Brent turned to Dayna. "What do you think?"

Dayna looked back and forth from him to Tamara, being careful to include her. "Carmen's the expert at this, of course, but based on all of the research I've done, I agree with her," Dayna said. "As we discussed last week, the private foundation would allow you to maintain more overall control, but you'd have so many more IRS rules and regulations to abide by, and fewer tax benefits.

"If you create a supporting organization, like Carmen is suggesting, you still have the right to select forty-nine percent of the board. You and Tamara could remain as hands-on in the decision making as you'd like to be, your federal reporting and administrative needs would be handled by the overseeing foundation, and you'd get the tax benefits of being an umbrella program under your oversight foundation.

"Carmen and I discussed it and came up with two solid options — there's the Calero Community Foundation, which has an excellent reputation in this region for supporting local philanthropists; or if you wanted to work with an organization on the Space Coast, you might consider working with the Community Foundation of the Beaches."

Brent and Tamara exchanged a glance, and Tamara asked what appeared to be a mutual question. "Which one is better?"

Carmen jumped in. "I'm familiar with most of the community foundations in the state because of the work I do, and both of these have great reputations. The Calero Foundation's greatest strength might be that it has been around the longest — since the 1950s. However, the Beaches foundation is twenty years old and solidly run, so you can't go wrong with either."

Audrey nodded in agreement. "One thing you might want to consider," she said, "is who will serve on your board and where they're located. If it's mostly Brevard residents and they'll have an issue traveling to Calero for quarterly, bimonthly, or monthly meetings, based on how you structure the foundation, that might sway you toward

Beaches. If the travel possibility isn't an issue, then I'd certainly take the time to request a meeting with officials from both foundations to get a sense of which one you're most comfortable with."

Brent smiled. "That's a great idea," he said. "I think that's what we should do — go with the supporting organization option and meet with these two organizations to see which will be the better fit."

Tamara looked skeptical. "How much time will all of this take?"

Carmen shrugged. "The process of forming a charitable giving program takes a nice chunk of time, regardless of the format you use," she told Tamara. "You've got to create a business plan, establish the board of directors, draft bylaws and board policies, and apply to the IRS for tax-exempt status, among other things."

Dayna noticed that Carmen didn't actually answer Tamara's question. She made a note to ask her later what the realistic time frame would be. But Brent was sharper than she was giving him credit for.

"So . . . does all of this work need to be completed before I pass? Or can we get the ball rolling and put the right people in place so that my wishes will be honored after I'm gone?"

Tears welled up in Tamara's eyes. "Why do you have to be so blunt?" she asked Brent.

He sighed and lifted his palms. "Sorry, Tami, but it is what it is. I don't have time to waste. We gotta get on with doing what we need to do."

Tamara turned to Dayna. "Where is your bathroom?"

Dayna jumped up and led her to the foyer, then pointed down the hallway. "Third door on your left. You okay?"

Tamara shook her head. "I don't know, Dayna. I don't know anymore."

She disappeared into the bathroom, and Dayna took her time returning to the table.

"Everything, okay?" Carmen asked.

Dayna wasn't sure, but Brent seemed resolute.

"Keep going, Carmen," he said. "It will be all right."

Carmen shuffled through her papers and reviewed her notes.

"Along with utilizing Audrey's expertise, I recommend hiring a lawyer, or bringing one onto the board, to help you draft and process some of the legal documents you'll need to turn around fairly quickly," she said. "And in light of what Brent was just asking, I'd get an attorney to create a document that outlines all of Brent's wishes for the foundation and for how he'd like to have the fund administered and students chosen to receive the proceeds. That way, in the event that something happens to him before the project is completed, the newbie program won't stall. The documents will guide the board members who have bought into his vision on how to move forward."

Brent sat stone-faced, nodding and jotting notes, as if he were participating in an executive board discussion about employee bonuses rather than how to handle his wishes upon his death. Was he really that okay with it, Dayna wondered, or had he perfected a public façade?

It was obvious that the looming reality was getting harder for Tamara to handle. Dayna wondered whether Brent was giving himself space to grieve too.

Tamara returned, but instead of sitting next to Audrey, she pulled out the chair on the other side of Brent. Everyone pretended not to notice, including Brent.

An hour later, Carmen, Audrey, and Dayna had crafted a to-do list for the creation of the supporting organization, which Brent had decided to name the Injured Collegiate Athlete Fund. He decided to offer the scholarships and accompanying support to any athlete, not just football players, who participated in a sport at the college level and suffered a career-ending injury.

"You don't want your name in the title of the supporting organization?" Carmen asked.

Brent shrugged. "That's not necessary; it's not like I'm a celebrity."

"Except at Alabama U," Dayna said and smiled. "They still give him preferential treatment whenever he visits Atchity, I'm sure."

Brent shrugged and grinned. "What can I say? Seriously, though, I want this to be about the kids who need it, and the name Tamara and I came up with makes it clear. Any athlete who sees this name and gets injured will remember to look to this fund for support."

Dayna nodded. She was sure that if Warren were here to lend his marketing expertise, he would agree that it was an appropriate name with great branding potential.

They wrapped up the meeting by deciding when they'd get together again. Since everyone felt time was of the essence, they agreed to meet a week later, on the next Tuesday evening.

"Evenings are better because we aren't as

rushed as during lunchtime," Carmen said.

Audrey cleared her throat. "But you have a standing commitment most Tuesday evenings, don't you, Dayna?"

She knew Audrey was alluding to her salsa date with Warren, which she was missing for the third time tonight.

"Yes, but —"

Brent raised his palm to interrupt her. "I'm asking you to help with this out of the kindness of your heart, Dayna," he said. "You don't have to do this. But since you are, I'm fine with doing it at a time that's convenient for you. Tami and I can drive up on Wednesday or Thursday evening, if either of those nights is better for everyone else. We'll change whatever we need to in our schedules."

Dayna was about to protest, then hesitated. Audrey was right. Warren's absence from these meetings was evidence that while he would never hold her back from something she believed in, she was skating on thin ice. He deserved to remain her priority.

She fingered her faith, hope, and love charm bracelet, and out of the corner of her eye, saw Brent watching her. He had a faint smile on his face, and she knew he recognized the gift from his mom.

Lord, she prayed suddenly, *please don't let*

this man mention this gift from his mother in front of Tamara.

"Thanks for offering to change the meeting day, Brent," she said aloud. "Thursdays at six-thirty would be great, if that's okay with everyone else."

That would leave the door open for Warren to come if he ever chose. Wednesdays were his Bible study nights, and lately she'd felt the tug to join him and the boys there. It had been an important part of her life before the divorce, because it was the one place where no pomp and circumstance was required, just a Bible and a willingness to read and learn. But it had been among the casualties of her flight from organized church and God. The stronger she felt, however, the more she sensed a longing to reclaim the pieces of her broken past that had actually been good.

The group agreed on the standing Thursday meeting, and half an hour later, Dayna's dining room and house were empty.

Dayna prepared her cup of tea and plopped on her sofa. Instead of turning on the TV or playing a CD, she closed her eyes and processed her day. It was still early, and she pondered how to spend the stretch of evening that lay before her. She thought of several important tasks she could tackle, but she knew what she wanted to do. Minutes later, she followed her heart.

TWENTY-FIVE

Dayna considered calling ahead, but decided to surprise him.

Ten minutes later, she rang Warren's doorbell and heard him trotting down the wood stairs to the front door. He opened it with a breathless sigh and stood there with a question in his eyes. She was tempted to respond with a kiss, but restrained herself.

"Hi, I came to check on you and the boys and to see if you're still speaking to me," Dayna said. "If you'll let me in, I'll practice my salsa moves with you."

Warren remained poker-faced but gently grabbed her wrist and tugged her inside. He closed the door with his foot and pulled her toward him for a kiss.

"How's that for a salsa move?"

"Yuck!"

Dayna peeked up the stairs and saw Mason sitting on the landing.

"Get back in bed, son," Warren said. "If

you hadn't been sneaking and eavesdropping, you wouldn't have been grossed out. Good night!"

Dayna laughed. "Good night, Mason. Smooches to you and to Michael. Tell him I hope his thumb is feeling better."

"Yes, ma'am."

He disappeared, and Dayna laughed again.

She turned to Warren, who was leaning against the wall, watching her. His tender expression reassured her that he wasn't upset with her, and she relaxed.

"Will you give me another chance?"

"Will you stop canceling on me for some other man?"

"But he's —"

Warren pulled her close again and placed his forefinger on her lips. She recalled Brent touching her in the same spot the evening he reappeared in her life, and she had been furious. Tonight, the same gesture from Warren made her heart soar. His face was close enough to hers that she could feel his breath on her cheeks. Moments like this made her wish she were Mrs. Avery, for more reasons than one.

"I know Brent is dying, babe, and I respect how difficult that is," Warren said. "But he's technically part of your past. I am your present and your future, and we need to nurture that. Right?"

She stared at him, wanting to protest — at least the bleeding-heart side of her did. But she heard him: he was echoing the warnings Audrey kept giving her.

"You're right, Warren," she said. "I'm sorry if I've lost sight of that. It's just that I really don't know how much longer Brent has, and I can tell that he's driven to get this thing rolling before he gets any sicker. I wish you had been there tonight; we could have used your help."

Warren didn't respond. He loosened his grip and motioned for her to follow him into the family room. "TV or music?"

She plopped on his sofa. "The usual," she said.

Warren turned on his surround-sound stereo and Lizz Wright's contralto filled the air. Dayna closed her eyes and basked in the singer's throaty voice and thought-provoking lyrics, as the CD rotated from a jazz selection to a gospel one. When Warren returned with a cup of ginger peach tea, the CD was switching to a tune that could almost be classified R&B funk.

"I think she's my favorite singer," Dayna said, and curved her body into Warren's as he settled on the sofa next to her with a book. "Thanks for the tea. What are you reading?"

"Nothing intellectual," he said, and ran his fingers through her hair. "Just the latest James Patterson. Keeps me current with the boys. They love his Maximum Ride series."

"That's cool," she said. "You know you're gonna have to comb my hair before I leave here, right?"

Warren smiled mischievously. "We gotta fix this leaving thing. It's getting harder and harder, you know?"

He kissed her neck, and if she'd been any shade but brown, he'd have known the effect he was having on her before she shoved him away and slid to the opposite end of the sofa.

"Careful, babe," she said. "You're in dangerous territory tonight. We promised each other we'd wait until after our vows . . . remember that?"

Warren gave her a pained smile. "The fact that you remember so well makes me love you and hate you at the same time. What's the plan here again?"

He pulled Dayna close again and instead of protesting, she willed her pulse to stop racing. "Let's see — a preacher, a ring, and a wedding. All in your time, though."

She grinned and shifted in his arms so

that her back rested against his chest. "We slipped that one time, Warren, not long after we met, and you and I both felt guilty. It complicated things between us before we were sure of what we meant to each other. Now that we know, let's stick to our commitment to not cross that line again until we seal our deal before God."

Warren shook his head. "Whether you own up to it or not, some of that preacher's daughter upbringing is still in you. You're honoring God even when you aren't calling it that. And just so you know, I repented about what happened between us, but I don't consider our first 'encounter' a slip-up since God has knit our hearts together. We made the mistake a lot of people make when they're dealing with the 'rebound relationship effect': we jumped in feet first.

"But fortunately, God saw us through that, and what we have now is real, babe."

Dayna was about to speak when he silenced her. "Shh! I know . . . you want to wait until our wedding night, and I do too. Just know that it won't be too much longer. I'm a man, babe. Don't be surprised if I get desperate and whisk you to Vegas one weekend. That will keep us saved until we can book the preacher."

Dayna burst into laughter. "You worry me

sometimes, Warren. I really think you've got some Vegas tickets stashed somewhere, along with that preacher. Silly man. I guess I'll keep you."

He turned her chin upward and kissed her. "Sorry for my attitude about this whole thing with Brent."

Dayna sat back and looked at him. She sighed. "You should be. You are being a little immature, but I hear where you're coming from. The situation is more than a little strange. Besides that, the meeting messed with our salsa nights. I know I have a tendency to get consumed by what I'm working on, sometimes to the detriment of the people in my life. I need to watch that. So let's call it even, okay? And by the way, the meetings have moved to Thursdays, so we can reclaim our salsa date night."

She punched his arm, and he hugged her. They spent the next couple of hours in one another's comfortable company, with Dayna enjoying the rest of the Lizz Wright compilation while Warren read his novel. The silence between them was easy and full.

Suddenly her thoughts turned to her to-do list and her promise to let Mama know whether she'd come home for Easter.

"What do you think about going to Alabama with me next month?"

"I don't think I have anything major planned; I just need to check with Lily about the twins' schedules. Why, what's going on in Atchity?"

"Easter, and the week leading up to my dad's pastoral anniversary at Riverview Baptist." Dayna sighed. "They want me to come so the congregation won't think I'm snubbing the family. Plus, they want me to sing a solo."

"Come again?" Warren sat back so he could look into her eyes.

"I've told you how my parents are. They're all about appearances," she said. "And by the way, I'm inviting you; they're not. It might be 'unsettling' for the congregation to know you've come with me since . . . you're not tan enough."

Warren frowned. "You're serious?"

"As a heart attack," Dayna said.

"I've spent time with your parents on more than one occasion and have gotten to know them. I thought they were cool with me, and now they don't want me to visit? What's this all about?"

Warren sounded like an anxious teenager worried about impressing his prom date's parents instead of a forty-six-year-old seasoned executive with two kids. Dayna sat up so she could tell Warren the real deal. If they were going to be together long-term, he needed to know.

"I keep telling you, you've met the public personas of Rev. Dr. Alston and First Lady Annie Wilson. What I'm describing to you are the parents who raised me. For as long as I can remember, it's been all about the congregation and what the members think or expect or want. My sisters and I had to toe the line. We were expected to look the part and act the part — no rebellious PKs in that household."

Warren looked incredulous, as he always did when she shared details about her childhood, and if it hadn't been her life, Dayna might have considered this tale an exaggeration too.

"The two years of therapy I received after my divorce from Brent helped me heal from my upbringing too," Dayna said. "It still gets to me, for sure, but I'm much stronger than I was. Daddy was always there; but he was really never there. We were his trophies, to show off and brag about and make him look good; but it took too much energy to really love us for who we were and to spend quality time with us. And Mama went right along with it, like the perfect little Stepford wife. Maybe that's all she knew about being a wife: Do what your husband says and make sure your children look nice and behave properly. I think Daddy loves us in his own way, but we never really had him or his heart, if you know what I mean."

As she said it, she doubted that Warren would, or could, understand, since he was so close to his mother, and had been close to his father before his dad's death from cancer, a few months after they'd begun dating.

"You know how when you decided we were getting serious enough that you should tell your parents I was black?"

"Yeah?" Warren said, still looking perplexed.

"You told me they accepted the news without any hesitation or issues; they just wanted you to be happy and loved, right?"

Warren nodded. "Exactly. Your race was an interesting fact, but it didn't change their love for me."

"Well, my divorce from Brent? It was nearly a deal breaker with my parents."

Warren made a funny face. "I'm not understanding that. The man cheated on you, dumped you — sorry for putting it so bluntly, babe — then married the other woman as soon as your divorce was final. How could that be cause for judging or disowning you?"

Dayna shook her head. "It's all about appearances," she said. "To be honest, I think Mama is upset with me to this day for not finding some way to hold onto Brent. It didn't matter that he'd had an affair; from her perspective and generation, men do that all the time, and some have families on the other side of town. I should have been woman enough to keep him and should have been patient while he sowed his oats, because eventually he would settle down and be all mine."

"That's what you were told?"

"That's what I was told — by Mama and by my sister Shiloh, her twin for all intents and purposes. They really hurt me behind all that happened with Brent. You just don't know."

Warren sat back on the sofa, stunned speechless.

"It's a lot to process," Dayna said. "Guess you need to know what you're in for . . . if you're still in."

Warren stared at Dayna and cocked his head to the side. "And why wouldn't I be, babe? I'm not in this relationship with your folks, and who said my family was perfect? We have our issues just like everyone else."

Dayna sat back on the sofa so they were shoulder to shoulder. "I'm talking about major issues, though, issues that left me feeling rejected as a child, and only good enough as an adult if I come home 'on their terms.' To make them proud, I have to sing a solo; to keep them from being embarrassed, I shouldn't bring you along. It's not enough for me to simply show up, happy to see them and wanting to spend time with them, or vice versa."

Warren put his arm around her. "That's good enough for me, Dayna," he said. "I really don't care what your parents think or want. If you decide to go home for Easter, I'm happy to come along regardless of how they'll feel about it. You can stay with them and I'll lodge at a nearby hotel. But if you decide to sing that solo in church on Sunday morning, this white, Presbyterian brother will be there. Bet on it."

Dayna wanted to laugh and cry at the same time. How had she been lucky enough to find herself with this man? She hugged him. "You are something else, Warren Avery. I love you," she said.

"I love when you tell me you love me," he said and smiled. "Don't decide tonight, but if you want me to go, just let me know in enough time to take off work, okay? You probably remember that the boys usually spend Easter weekend with April's parents in West Palm Beach, so they should be squared away during that time. If not, we can bring them along, unless you think it will cause your parents to go into cardiac arrest."

"Deal," Dayna said, and laughed. "I've got to stand up for myself sometime. I think this is it."

"In the meantime," Warren said, "I've added your parents, and your relationship with them, to my prayer list. Put them on yours too."

The look she gave him conveyed her "Yeah, right" attitude. Warren knew she didn't always remember to pray every morning and evening like he did. But maybe this was his not-so-subtle effort to get her back on track, and maybe she'd take him up on it. What could it hurt?

Just so she wouldn't have to fret about confessing her inconsistent prayer life to Warren, she decided to do what he was asking. If she put sticky notes on her bathroom mirror and nightstand, that would help her remember to pray. Along with concentrating on Mama and Daddy, she decided she'd pray for Brent and Tamara too. Wonders never ceased.

Twenty-Six

Dayna left Warren's place a few minutes past 10:30 p.m. and mentally reviewed her schedule for tomorrow's workday. She was in the middle of a long yawn when Audrey's ringtone filled the air.

"What's up?" Dayna asked when she answered.

Instead of receiving a response, she heard what sounded like weeping.

"Audrey? You okay?"

The crying intensified. Dayna made a U-turn on the empty street in front of Warren's house and sped toward Audrey's neighborhood.

"I'm on my way. Do you want to stay on the phone with me until I get there?"

Audrey managed to yelp out a no, so Dayna ended the call and promised to be there in ten minutes. When she reached an intersection where the light was red, she sent a text to Warren, who was expecting her to check in when she made it home safely.

Just got a call from Audrey.
Need to stop by her place on way home.
Will call you in the a.m. Luv u.

Warren replied with an "ok" a few seconds later, but as she had anticipated, he insisted that she text him when she made it home for the night, however late it was.

Dayna rang the doorbell to the side entrance of Audrey's townhouse five times before Audrey answered. When her friend finally opened the door, Dayna was stunned speechless.

Audrey's thick, curly hair was disheveled, and tears streaked her face. She clutched a tissue box and collapsed into Dayna's arms before Dayna could step inside.

"What is it, Audrey? Are your parents okay? Is someone hurt? Let me come in."

Dayna led Audrey into the kitchen and filled a glass with water from the filtered water system next to the kitchen island.

"Here." She handed the glass to Audrey and motioned for her to sit at the kitchen table. A still-emotional Audrey shook her head.

"Follow me into the living room; that's

probably the best place to meet the police."

Dayna paused midstep. "Excuse me?" She took a deep breath and willed herself to calm down. It wouldn't be helpful if she and Audrey both lost it. She joined Audrey in the living room, sat next to her on the red leather sofa, and waited for details.

Audrey took a sip of the water and shed a few more tears before attempting to gain her composure. She set the tissue box she'd been clutching on the coffee table and blew her nose.

"I can't believe this is happening. I want to die."

Dayna reached for her hand. "What on earth could have happened in the three hours since I last saw you?"

Audrey lowered her eyes and her voice. "Enough to make you ashamed to know me."

TWENTY-SEVEN

The doorbell rang just as Audrey launched into an explanation.

"They're here," she said resolutely.

Dayna felt like she had walked into an episode of a Lifetime TV movie. Who would be ringing her friend's doorbell this late on a Tuesday night? Had Audrey been serious about it being the police? She didn't know whether to open the door or run for the side entrance through which she'd entered. She looked to Audrey for guidance.

Audrey stood, and the tissue she'd just used fell from her lap. She stepped over it, squared her shoulders, and walked to the door. Before opening it, she peeked out of a window. Whatever she saw led her to rest her forehead on the door and close her eyes.

When the bell rang twice more, she stood back and unlocked the door, which was still secured by a chain. Dayna had often teased Audrey about using that old-fashioned measure of security, but as she watched this strange scene unfold, fearful that her heart might beat its way loose from her chest, the extra barrier the chain provided gave her some comfort.

Two men dressed in Calero police uniforms stood on the doorstep. The taller one spoke before Audrey could greet them.

"Audrey Hammond?"

"Yes." Her usually firm and in-control voice sounded squeaky and thin.

Both men flashed their badges. "May we come in and speak with you concerning an incident with a Mrs. Evelyn Anderson? We're here about the simple assault she suffered earlier this evening, reportedly at your hands."

Audrey unchained the door with trembling fingers and stepped aside. The officers entered the dim hallway, and Audrey flipped the switch behind the door, filling the area with light.

Dayna couldn't move. Had she heard that stream of conversation correctly? Chesdin Medical Center's top-notch accountant Audrey Hammond was being questioned by police on suspicion of committing assault?

Dayna remained near the sofa while one officer surveyed Audrey's living room and kitchen and the other man assessed her and

Audrey. Dayna knew he must be thinking what she herself was: Why was a good-looking, accomplished professional like Audrey somehow in trouble with the law?

"Ma'am, who are you?"

Dayna had been wondering when her presence would be acknowledged.

"She's my friend," Audrey said before Dayna could find her voice. "She came over to check on me."

"Well," the officer said, "we need to talk to you about something serious. Maybe your friend needs to find her way home."

He spoke to Audrey as if he were reprimanding a teenager for missing curfew. Dayna wasn't sure how to react. Audrey glanced at her, and the fear Dayna read in her friend's eyes translated into "Don't leave me."

Dayna cleared her throat. "Officer, if it's okay with Audrey and with you, I want to stay."

The other officer added his two cents. "I don't know that Ms. Hammond really has any say in the matter. We need to talk to her privately."

"Actually," the shorter policeman said, "we didn't come here to talk to her, so it doesn't matter whether her friend stays or goes."

His partner pulled a yellow sheet of paper from his back pocket. It reminded Dayna of a speeding violation form, but from what little she had fathomed from their comments, and from Audrey's actions in the past half hour, Audrey's troubles were more serious than having a lead foot or running a few lights.

"Ma'am, we need you to come with us, in regard to an assault on Evelyn Anderson, the woman we mentioned earlier. She has filed charges against you, and we are placing you under arrest."

Audrey began to shake and sob.

Dayna sank onto the sofa. What on earth?

The officers watched with mild disinterest and, after a few minutes, suggested that Audrey find shoes to wear down to the station.

"There's no need for us to handcuff you, as long as you come with us willingly," the taller officer said.

With her permission, he followed Audrey to her bedroom to watch as she slid on sneakers. She returned to the living room carrying her designer leather purse, and the other officer searched the bag until he located her wallet, so she could take her ID down to the station. He suggested that she leave her purse with Dayna so there would be less to process at the station.

"The key to the house is on a hook under one of the kitchen cabinets," Audrey said.

She seemed dazed. Dayna wanted to hug her but was afraid to move.

"Come with us, ma'am," the shorter officer told Audrey. He looked toward Dayna. "We're taking her to the downtown precinct, on Eighth Street, if you're planning to bail her out."

Dayna nodded. "Don't worry, Audrey," she said to her friend. "I'm coming for you."

Audrey didn't look her way, but she mumbled a plea. "Please don't tell anyone about this, Dayna. Not even Warren."

She lowered her head and walked out of her house, between the two officers. They led her to their squad car, and she slid into the backseat when one of them opened the door.

Dayna knew Audrey would weep during the entire twenty-minute drive downtown. She wasn't sure what to do next. Should she call Warren, Audrey's parents or sister, or honor her friend's request to keep this quiet?

She sat on the sofa and tried to calm her racing thoughts. She played with the charms on her bracelet and started to pace. Finally, she realized the only helpful thing she could do right now was give this to God.

"Lord, I committed earlier tonight to pray for my mother and father, and for Brent and Tamara," she said. "Right now I'm praying for Audrey. I don't know what exactly she's accused of doing or whether the charges are valid or a mistake; I just know that my friend needs you. So I'm calling on your name on her behalf and asking you to rescue her and give her your peace and comfort. In Jesus's name, amen."

Whatever was being brought to light tonight, suddenly Dayna realized what her daddy meant when he boomed from the pulpit that there were some things only God had the power to fix. In her humble opinion, this situation qualified.

TWENTY-EIGHT

Forty minutes later and five hundred dollars lighter, Dayna sat in the dingy lobby of the police station, anxious for Audrey to be released and give her the answers she craved.

She waited next to an elderly man with watery gray eyes who swore under his breath every few minutes; a pregnant girl who looked no older than fifteen; and a heavyset Hispanic woman who gripped a sleepy, squirming toddler in her arms. *What could have brought this motley crew down here tonight?* she wondered, then realized they were probably sitting there asking the same about her.

When Audrey emerged from the holding cell at close to 1:00 a.m., she was stone-faced, as if she had shut down her emotions to keep from completely losing it. The woman Dayna enjoyed dinner, shopping, and occasional double dates and worship services with didn't look like herself.

Audrey's shame was as transparent as the nonchalance of the officers on duty. Their eyes and attitudes intimated they had seen it all and could care less about what had led to tonight's arrests.

Dayna leapt from her seat to comfort Audrey. "You're going to be okay," she told her friend, and patted her arm.

The officer escorting Audrey from the holding cell interjected. "Ma'am, she needs to fill out some paperwork and claim her belongings before she leaves. Wait over there where you were sitting before."

He guided Audrey to a desk across the room and pulled out a piece of paper, along with the ID she had brought with her and the shoes she had put on during her arrest.

The officer said something to Audrey that Dayna couldn't hear. Audrey signed the paper, then headed in Dayna's direction. They walked out of the precinct shoulder to shoulder, and the minute they were on the other side of the door, Audrey crumbled.

Dayna held her as she sat on the sidewalk in front of the police precinct and wept. After what seemed like eternity, but was really less than five minutes, Dayna managed to lead Audrey to the Lexus. She helped Audrey into the passenger seat then trotted around to the driver's side.

Dayna pulled away, full of questions and concerns. She decided to give Audrey time to calm down before pestering her for answers. After a few minutes, though, she couldn't resist.

"Was this a big mistake, or did you really injure someone?"

Audrey sighed and let her head fall. When she began sobbing again, Dayna patted her on the back and drove on in silence.

"You're coming home with me," she told Audrey. "I'm way taller than you, but I have some jammies you can roll up at the hem and sleep in, and a pair of jeans and a T-shirt for tomorrow. I think you might be calling in sick anyway."

The tears kept flowing, and Audrey didn't protest. Dayna realized she might have to take the day off too, not only to console her friend, but also to get some rest. It was nearly two a.m.

A half hour later, a much calmer, puffy-eyed Audrey emerged from the guest bedroom and joined Dayna in her family room, in front of the TV. She plopped next to Dayna and pulled a blue silk robe tighter around her waist just as Dayna issued a text to Warren, letting him know she was finally home safe and sound.

"You couldn't sleep either, huh?" Dayna asked.

Audrey shook her head. "Not when I've ruined my life."

Dayna pressed the remote to shut off the TV and turned to her friend. "What on earth happened after you left Brent's foundation meeting here?"

Audrey leaned back and laid her head on the sofa. She closed her eyes and sighed. "If I tell you, you may never speak to me again."

"Please, Audrey. We're better than that. So you messed up. Talk to me."

With her eyes still closed, Audrey shook her head. "This isn't just a 'mess up,' Dayna," she said. "This is something I chose to do that represents everything you hate."

She turned her head toward Dayna and pursed her lips. She looked as if she were wrestling with herself about whether to speak, but finally, she did.

"I'm in love with someone else's husband, and tonight, I let her know it in the worst way possible."

TWENTY-NINE

If words could slice, that one sentence uttered by Audrey would have ripped Dayna's flesh.

Did she really just bail someone out of jail for being an unhappy mistress? Had she consoled and offered her spare bedroom to a woman who was intent on making another woman's husband her own?

Dayna felt dizzy. Audrey knew her story and her pain.

"How could you even call me?" she whispered the question and didn't try to mask her shock. "I should have been the last person on your list."

"But you were first," Audrey replied. "You are my friend, and I knew I could trust you."

"You also know my husband left me for another woman."

Dayna slid closer to the farthest end of the sofa and shook her head, as if doing so would distance her from Audrey's revelation.

"How could you do something like that? Here I was, all this time feeling sorry for you because I thought you were lonely and praying that God would send you 'Mr. Right' so you would be happy. And you weren't lonely — you were busy having a good time at someone else's expense. Wow, Audrey."

Audrey moved toward Dayna on the sofa, and Dayna slid backward again.

"I didn't mean for this to happen — really," Audrey said. "It just did. And once I fell in love with Raymond, I couldn't leave. I couldn't, Dayna. I've been hiding this for a year because I felt so guilty. Then Brent came back, and the back-and-forth conversations I had with myself about how to tell you just shut down. How could I let you know that I had become the kind of person you despise?"

Dayna smirked. She was so angry that tears began to form. "So you decided to be selfish and deceitful on top of what you'd already done, huh? What happened tonight? Did your boyfriend's wife show up ready to fight?"

Shame danced across Audrey's face again. She lowered her eyes and wrung her hands.

"Actually, the opposite happened. She and a friend showed up at the restaurant where Raymond and I were having dinner, and she walked over to us, all cool, calm, and collected, and asked him if our date was the reason he had refused to join her for Bible study that night. She told him she wasn't even going to worry about it; God had her back.

"Then she looked at me and told me she pitied any woman whose self-esteem was low enough to allow her to sneak around with a married church deacon. She told me she'd pray for me, and that maybe she and Raymond would do so together when he made it home that night."

Dayna couldn't help but be intrigued and shocked. She wanted to laugh out loud at this woman's unusual boldness — too bad she hadn't had that much guts, and sense, when Brent and Tamara were tripping. Dayna wanted to ask what happened next, but she decided to be patient. Audrey had to get it all out anyway.

"Can you believe she went back to the table with her girlfriend and actually sat down and ordered?" Audrey fumed.

"Raymond made me get up, and I thought we were leaving together, but I noticed as I walked toward the door that he had stopped at her table and was trying to talk to her. I got confused. Was he with me or not? I waited and finally I called his name. He looked at me like he didn't know me and told me he had to take his wife home.

"I flipped out," Audrey said. She hugged herself and rocked back and forth as she remembered how the incident unfolded. "I started yelling and crying and I don't even know what I said. What I do remember is that he escorted his wife and her friend out of the restaurant and left me standing there. When I followed them outside, Raymond got in his car and pulled up alongside the car that his wife's friend was driving. He acted like he didn't see me and motioned for Evelyn to get in the car with him."

Audrey shook her head and looked away as she remembered.

"Something inside me just broke," she said. "I realized I had been used, treated like scum, and all for nothing when the wife showed up. Without even thinking about it, I took off one of the three-inch wedge heels I was wearing and hurled it in their direction. I saw the shoe graze Evelyn's forehead before she ducked into Raymond's car. I could tell by the way she was holding her head as he drove off that it must have hurt. He rolled down his window and told me he was calling the police on me for attacking his wife. Somehow I made it home and called you."

Dayna stared at Audrey.

"So what do you think about all of this?" Dayna asked.

Fresh tears stained Audrey's cheeks. "I think I should be as ashamed of myself as I feel. I was completely wrong and I knew better. Now I'm paying for it with the possibility of losing my job and my reputation for a man who didn't even think enough of me to pay the dinner bill. The restaurant manager brought me the receipt while I stood outside the restaurant, with one shoe on and mascara going every which way."

She doubled over and began sobbing again. When the tears eased, she reached for one of the tissues Dayna set before her and blew her nose. She stared at her hands while she spoke. "Why did I call you, knowing how you feel about cheating spouses and mistresses? I don't know, Dayna. I guess because you're the only real friend I have, the only one with enough integrity not to have my business blasted all over Calero before sunrise. I can't let my parents and siblings know about this, let alone our boss. My career would be over, my family would label me a disgrace for the rest of my life, and I'd never be able to hold my head up in this town again. It made me sick to my stomach when I realized I was going to have to tell you what I had been doing. I knew this revelation would hurt you, but the Dayna I know is also forgiving. I was hoping that you'd help me in a desperate situation."

"So you used me."

Dayna couldn't see straight. Yet this blinding anger helped her understand how Audrey could have been upset enough to hurl her shoe. What struck her to her core too was how Audrey's boyfriend had handled the situation. Unlike Brent, he had chosen his wife over the girlfriend. Audrey's experience was just another reminder of the rejection she had endured. Why hadn't she been worth fighting for, like this man's wife?

She stood and left the room before her own tears escaped.

"Where are you going?" Audrey called after her.

Dayna kept walking and answered without turning to face her. "To bed. It's after three a.m., and I've heard all I can take. Good night, Audrey. See you in the morning."

Dayna switched off the light in the kitchen, but left the hallway light on so Audrey could find her way to the guest room.

She climbed into her bed and snuggled under the silk sheets as the reality of what she'd just been told washed over her again. Did you ever really know another person, or just the façade they presented to the world?

Daddy's voice boomed in her head with one of the messages he routinely delivered from the pulpit: "Know God for yourself. He's the only friend you can ever trust to be real and true, no matter what. He'll stick by you and love you more than your mother, your father, your brother, or your sister. God won't cheat you, mistreat you, fool you, or misguide you. Rest in him always and you'll be okay."

She thought about that tonight as she hugged her pillow and struggled to find some peace in sleep. Could it be that her dad's sermons had given her some solid advice after all? Maybe so, because the brief request for uninterrupted rest that she'd uttered to God just minutes ago was the only thing lulling her to sleep right now.

THIRTY

Dayna awoke hours later to the smell of bacon and pancakes.

She sat up in her queen-sized bed and surveyed her surroundings to make sure she was where she should be — in the home she owned and lived in by herself. Then she remembered. Audrey was here.

How dare she be in the kitchen making breakfast like everything was normal and okay between them? Dayna's stomach betrayed her, though. The smell of the food ignited her hunger.

She strolled into her kitchen and found Audrey trying to start the coffee maker. Along with the pancakes and bacon that had tickled Dayna's nose, she discovered a dish filled with fluffy scrambled eggs on the island countertop.

"What are you doing?"

Audrey peered at her with uncertainty.

Dayna looked away. A meal wasn't going to fix this.

"Just thought I'd prepare breakfast for you, after all you did for me last night. Thank you, Dayna. I know you're angry with me, and I don't blame you."

Dayna plopped into a chair at the cherry table across the room from the stove where Audrey was preparing the food. "Angry" didn't adequately capture what she was feeling; furious was more accurate. But she was also hurt, and she couldn't pinpoint why. She just knew that something inside her had shifted, and it was more than a shift in how she felt about Audrey. She felt as if some of the trust she had in humanity had been lost.

There I go being melodramatic.

She decided not to beat herself up this morning. Her feelings were justified. She had been used and deceived.

Audrey flipped the final pancake out of the pan and carefully placed it atop a stack of perfectly round, golden-brown other ones. She brought the plate of pancakes and the bowl of eggs to the table and set them in front of Dayna. When she retrieved the bacon from the rack where it sat draining its grease, she also grabbed two small juice glasses.

Her final excursion led her to the fridge

and to the pantry, and she trotted back to the table with cranberry-grape juice, syrup, and napkins. She sat across from Dayna and extended her hand so they could join together in blessing the food. Dayna ignored the gesture and settled farther into her seat. She stared at Audrey, silently daring her to speak.

"Look, Dayna —"

"Spare me, Audrey, okay? Thanks for breakfast. Let's just eat and go on with the day."

They consumed the meal in silence, with Audrey focusing on her plate, then on the ruby-throated hummingbird just outside the window, hovering in the air, peering in at them.

Dayna wondered if the bird were an eavesdropper. She wouldn't allow herself to enjoy its presence, but Audrey seemed fascinated. When the bird flew away, she turned her attention back to Dayna.

"I wish I could just let it be," Audrey said. "But we've been friends for too long to let this come between us."

Dayna started to yield, but changed her mind. "You're right — we've been friends too long for me to find out something like this about you, in this way. You're not who I thought you were."

Audrey pursed her lips, as if to keep from saying the wrong thing.

"What makes you think I'm not that person?" she asked. "So I made a bad choice — a really bad one. Are you going to hold that over my head forever? Are you going to tell everyone what happened yesterday?"

"As a matter of fact, I might," Dayna said. "Are you planning to break up with this Raymond person?"

Fear, then defiance, flickered in Audrey's eyes. "Well . . ." Audrey began.

"Well?" Dayna said.

"I haven't heard from him since last night, so I might be dumped anyway."

"But if you hear from him, what's your plan? Are you going to forgive him for how he treated you in front of his wife or use that as a wake-up call?"

Tears formed in Audrey's eyes and she shook her head. "I know what I should do, but I love him, Dayna. I didn't know he was married when we started dating, and by the time I found out, I was in so deep that I believed him when he said it wasn't going to last much longer. He's part of my life now. I love him, and I'm ready to settle down and start a family. I can't start over."

Dayna frowned. "Did you just hear yourself? How can you start a family with someone who already has one? I assume he does have one?" She waited with eyebrow raised.

Audrey looked down and mumbled, "Yes, he has three kids."

"Do you really think he'll cast aside his wife and children to start over again with you? And if he could so easily do that to them, what makes you think he wouldn't someday discard you, Audrey?"

Audrey slammed her fork onto the table. "If I wanted a lecture, I would have shared all of this with my mother and father, thank you."

"You might not have wanted a lecture, but you wanted me to bail you out of jail," Dayna said.

"So the price I'm paying is to sit here and listen to you berate me? You'll be reimbursed before sundown."

"Good, but this isn't about money. What I'm doing is telling you the truth, Audrey. That's what a real friend does."

"Oh, really? Well, maybe I'd rather have Raymond instead of a real 'friend.' "

She stormed out of the kitchen. Seconds later, Dayna heard the bathroom door slam. She also heard sobs.

She half rose from her seat, but then sat

back down. Consoling Audrey seemed like the right thing to do, but Dayna couldn't calm her anger. Plus, in this instance, she had to hold true to her convictions. She meant what she told her friend, and she believed it was a truth she would have declared even if she hadn't been through this with Brent and Tamara. She couldn't make this all better for Audrey, and if she was honest, she didn't believe Audrey was going to be able to fix it either. Raymond had gone off with his wife and had sent police to Audrey's door hours later instead of knocking on it himself. That didn't bode well for their so-called relationship.

Dayna picked over the now-cold fluffy eggs with her fork and then took a bite of pancake. It was good, but it was cold too. It could be reheated of course, but she had no appetite. Such a shame that a good meal was going to go to waste, just like so many other things.

She walked to her kitchen sink and scraped the food into the garbage disposal before gazing out of the window. Watching a small black bird flit from tree to tree, she had a realization: She'd spent the past few hours behaving more judgmentally and holier-than-thou than she ever imagined she could. Whenever Mama treated her, or others, that way, Dayna felt sick to her stomach, and here she was, mimicking the behavior.

Dayna felt burdened and tried to consider what Warren, or her older friend Duchess, would advise her to do. Duchess would urge her to keep telling Audrey the truth, but to temper it with love. Warren would tell her to just love and let that be Audrey's medicine and lesson.

THIRTY-ONE

It was nearly noon when Dayna's ringing cell phone startled her awake.

After the failed attempt to finish breakfast, she had spoken through the bathroom door to Audrey, inviting her to stay as long as she needed. Then she had retreated to her bedroom to get dressed for work, when all of a sudden, the lack of sleep and weight of the emotions coursing through her body hit her. She called Monica to tell her she'd be taking a vacation day. Sleep came as quickly as her head hit the pillow.

Now she scrambled to reach across the night stand, to the other side of the lamp where her cell phone had slid, and pick it up before it stopped ringing. She didn't quite make it and saw that the missed call was from Brent. What did he want this morning?

She also saw that she had three texts from Warren, asking where she was and whether she was okay. She must have slept through the pinging when they came in, and he must have been in meetings all morning since he hadn't followed up with a call.

Dayna sent him a quick text and told him she had taken the day off to help Audrey. Audrey's plea for her not to tell Warren about her arrest rang in Dayna's ears, but no such promise had been given regarding the other circumstances, the ones which Dayna was angrier about anyway.

She climbed out of bed and padded down the hallway in her flip-flops to see if Audrey was still around. Instead of her distraught friend, she found a note on the kitchen island, thanking her for her hospitality and promising to repay her the bail money.

Please keep this to yourself, Dayna. You don't owe me anything, but I beg you to be a friend and let me handle this in my own way — privately.

And I'm really sorry that I hurt you — sorrier than you know.

Thanks for your friendship. Audrey

There. The challenge had been issued after all to keep every shred of Audrey's drama to herself. Dayna wasn't sure what she'd say to Warren, and she decided she'd figure that out later. Right now she needed to sort through her feelings about everything Audrey had revealed.

Could she still be this woman's friend? And could any man be trusted? This Raymond guy was an official in his church and had a wife and three kids at home. Brent had been a good guy too, and look at how he had behaved.

Maybe Warren's too good to be true.

As soon as the thought crossed her mind, Dayna dismissed it. Warren *was* a good guy, pure and simple. She couldn't let her one bad experience, or Audrey's chosen path, distract her or make her believe otherwise.

Dayna walked over to the sink, prepared to load the dishwasher with the breakfast dishes, but Audrey had taken care of all of that before leaving.

She rested her palms on the edge of the sink and peered out of the window for a second time this morning, this time appreciating her lush, green backyard. The blue sky was cloudless today, yet her heart felt heavy. Why was she taking Audrey's confession so hard? Audrey was an adult who had made a choice that other single women made every day. It was natural to be disappointed in her friend, but why did Dayna feel so disillusioned?

She got still and quiet and lifted that question to God.

I know this isn't a prayer, but Warren said I could talk to you about anything. What gives here, Lord?

She was on her way back to her bedroom when what could pass for answers dropped into her spirit. Could this be about more than Audrey? Was her friend bearing the brunt of some leftover anger she hadn't resolved with Brent and Tamara? Those thoughts were too unsettling to grapple with right now, Dayna decided.

She trotted to the bedroom and picked up her cell phone to listen to Brent's message.

"I called your office and your secretary said you were off today. I hope you didn't get worn out from working on my foundation project last night. Just wanted to thank you again. I can't tell you how much your help, and that of your colleagues, means. We're doing something great together. I had a question I wanted to run by you. If you get this message before two, please give me a call, okay?"

The message wasn't flirty or suggestive, but something about Brent's easy, friendly tone didn't sit well with Dayna. It appeared he thought they were becoming friends, which would make sense, given that she was helping him shape his legacy. On the other hand, he was the ex-husband to whom she hadn't spoken in years and who had contributed to her extended season of self-doubt, anguish, and anger. Now he wanted to chitchat with her?

She sat on the edge of her unmade bed and let her mind wander. What did his cute, little wife have to say about this? Dayna hesitated to call him back, because if Tamara checked his phone and saw her number again, she'd flip. Dayna also knew that Brent should be spending this time with Tamara, who seemed more overwhelmed every time she saw her.

Dayna stared at her cell and wrestled with what to do. She poised her thumb over the call-back key, but hesitated. What was she going to say if they talked anyway — ask him all of these questions that were racing through her mind? Meet him as he asked?

She sighed. Life was getting complicated again. Dayna wanted to rewind a few weeks back to when she was contentedly going through the motions at work, dating Warren, enjoying her friends, and living life. These days she felt like a puppet whose strings were being pulled in directions she hadn't planned.

THIRTY-TWO

Dayna listened to Brent's message three more times before deciding to text him instead of calling him back. That way, Tamara could read their exchanges, word for word. Besides, Dayna didn't want him to get in the habit of calling her on a whim, especially during her workday. She'd have to find the right time to make that clear.

Her text message was brief.

Received your message. What's the latest?

She sighed in frustration when he responded by calling. She was tempted to send him straight to voicemail but decided at the last minute to hear him out.

"Hi, Brent."

"Hi, Dayna, guess what? I called the Calero Community Foundation early this morning and spoke to one of the program officers, and she told me I was welcome to come by to get my questions answered in person," he said. "I didn't tell her that 'coming by' meant driving for nearly an hour to get here. It was worth it, though; that is an impressive organization. You mind having lunch with me so I can share what I learned?"

Dayna hesitated. "Is Tamara with you?"

"No — does that make a difference?"

"Of course," Dayna said, thinking of Audrey's predicament. She felt confident that Brent wasn't hitting on her, but he certainly wasn't using good judgment. "How do you think she'd feel about us meeting without her?"

Now it was Brent's turn to process.

"I see what you mean," he said, sounding disappointed. "Can Audrey or Carmen join us too? That would make it better."

"I'm off work today, Brent, so that's not an option." There was no need to tell him just how unavailable Audrey was at the moment, or to bother Carmen when she was already doing so much. He was going to have to be patient.

"What about Warren?"

Now he was really pushing his luck.

"Please, Dayna? We can meet at a public park or the mall café — wherever tons of people are around us and you'll be comfortable."

Dayna closed her eyes. She'd had enough drama for one twenty-four hour period. What was going on? In exasperation, she relented. "I can meet you for one hour, Brent, at 1:30 p.m." She suggested a Thai restaurant in a shopping plaza not far from her home.

She hung up and lay across the bed for a few minutes, staring at the ceiling and pondering the question that nagged at her soul. *What is this all about?*

No ready answers had surfaced by the time she showered and slid into jeans and a dressy T-shirt, but she had rationalized this impromptu meeting enough to feel okay about it. Why *wouldn't* Brent call her if he was in the area researching some information on the foundation? He was excited, and he needed to get everything finalized sooner rather than later. Of course he'd want to process what he learned today and get her feedback. Plus, he was probably grateful that she had been able to forgive him. She had surprised herself by how well that had gone. Then again, her reaction to Audrey's situation was sounding the alarm that she had more work to do than she thought.

Dayna glanced at the iPod charger on her

nightstand that also doubled as an alarm clock. She had five minutes to get out of the door and still be on time.

She reached for her cell phone to chuck it into her purse and paused when she saw she had missed a call from Warren.

"Back-to-back meetings today about the annual report my department is finalizing," Warren said. "Enjoy the rest of your day, babe. Get some rest. See ya soon."

She smiled at his obvious plans to come over later, but suddenly felt guilty. How would he feel about her having lunch with Brent? Should she tell him?

The uncertainty drove her thoughts to all that was going on with Audrey — having an affair, then the alleged assault of her boyfriend's wife, followed by an arrest. She and Warren had promised to always be open and honest. Today's lunch should be no exception.

Dayna slid into a pair of flats and grabbed her floppy purse. The cell phone was at her ear when she climbed into the car and waited for Warren's voicemail beep.

"Hey, babe, thanks for your call. I hope your meetings are going well. Brent decided to drive up today to get more information on the Calero Community Foundation, so we're going to meet for lunch and go over everything together. If by some miracle you get a short break, we're meeting at Thai Today, near my house, from 1:30 to 2:30 p.m. See you there, or later this evening, maybe at the gym."

Brent was waiting in the foyer when Dayna stepped inside the dimly lit restaurant. A slow smiled brightened his wan features, and he approached her with open arms. She didn't resist when he gave her a light hug.

"Hello again," he said, and smiled.

Dayna's heart sank. She'd been worried about how worn and weary she might look when she should have considered how Brent was faring. He looked like she felt — which meant he probably felt worse than he looked.

It was easy to overlook the fact that he was dying when they were busy planning for the future, but in these brief seconds of greeting, with no agenda before them and no one else to watch their interaction, she let down her guard enough to really see Brent as he was today, rather than the strong force to be reckoned with that she had known and loved years earlier. Today, that Brent seemed to be a shadow. What stood before her now appeared to be a man who refused to give in to his illness without a fight, and while he might lose the war, he was determined to do it on his own terms.

"Where's Tamara today?" she asked.

"She's at the bank, and as I said, this was a spur-of-the-moment trip. I'll fill her in on everything when I get home."

The waiter led them to a booth that hosted a window through which a steady stream of sunlight cast a glow across the fake flower centerpiece. They slid into their seats and perused the menu.

Dayna gasped. "I just realized that you may not be able to eat this kind of food. I'm sorry. Can you find something on the menu that won't upset your stomach, or should we go somewhere else?"

Brent scanned the menu. "No worries. I'll find something. Soup and a spring roll will be fine. Maybe some brown rice."

Under different circumstances, Dayna would have enjoyed teasing him about eating like a dieting woman. But this . . . this wasn't funny.

She stared at him as he continued to review the menu with his head slightly bowed. His hair had thinned on top, and she could see his scalp. She wondered if that was just nature taking its course or if it was from the treatments he had received before the most recent diagnosis.

Brent raised his eyes and caught her mid-muse.

"Why so sad?" he asked. "I'm the one who's dying, right?"

He laughed and after a few seconds, Dayna did too. "I see that you can still be silly," she teased.

"And I see that you can still be too serious. Lighten up, lady," he said. "Let's enjoy lunch and treasure the moment. I'm learning to be still and be present more and more these days, instead of fretting over the past or worrying about the future. There's nothing I can do to change either, so I might as well enjoy myself in the here and now."

The waiter returned to take their order before Dayna could respond. Tears filled her eyes and a lump knotted her throat, so rather than verbally give her selection to the waiter, she pointed on the menu to the papaya salad and chicken satay. Those few seconds gave her time to compose herself.

"And Tamara?" she asked.

Brent frowned. "What do you mean?"

"Has she adopted that same attitude?"

Brent sat back and sighed.

"I guess not," he finally said. "She's definitely struggling with my diagnosis and with the fact that I won't just sit still and rest."

He leaned forward again. "Who wants to sit in a corner like an old man and rest? As long as I am able to do for myself and be out and about, why wouldn't I? I don't want to shrivel up and die. If this is all the life I've got left, I'm going to live it. With no regrets."

He extended his hands across the table and opened his palms as an invitation for Dayna to place her hands in his. Dayna hesitated but gingerly complied. What was this all about?

When her palms were resting in his, her heart quivered, like it had the day he'd shown up at her door several weeks earlier. This felt right, believe it or not. But it also scared her.

Brent began speaking before she could further process her feelings. "Who would have thought we would be sitting here like this now, all these years later? No longer married, but still partnering on something important."

He smiled at Dayna and squeezed her hands. She squirmed and tried to smile back.

"This means a lot to me, Dayna," he said. "Thank you for allowing me back in your life. Thank you for helping me fulfill an important goal and for just being here. Now."

"You don't have to thank me, Brent," she said. "I wasn't expecting any of this, but I can't say I regret it. I'm glad that we've had a chance to clear the air between us. I'm just sorry it's under these circumstances."

Brent's eyes told her he had something else to say, but instead, he squeezed her hands again before releasing them. He sat back and gulped down most of his water.

"I'm sorry too, Dayna. More than you know."

Thirty-Three

By the time they'd finished their meal and insisted on no dessert, Dayna and Brent were chatting like the friends they once had been.

"Amazing," Dayna said once Brent ticked off the names of his nine nieces and nephews — about half of whom had been born while Dayna was still part of the family. "I know your parents must love to have you all home at the same time over the holidays, with all those babies to spoil."

Brent laughed and nodded.

Dayna wanted to ask, but was afraid. He must have read the question in her eyes, because he answered what she hadn't uttered. "No, Tami and I tried for several years, but it never happened. Then I got cancer, and the chemo and radiation made it too dangerous. That's one of my biggest regrets. I won't have a son or daughter to continue my legacy after I'm gone."

Dayna felt numb. Her mind traveled back to the months just before she'd learned about his affair, when they had agreed to start a family. Funny now how clear it was that Brent's 'Yes, let's go for it' all those years ago had really been a 'No,' because he started seeing Tamara soon after Dayna stopped using birth control.

She stared at him now and wondered if she should tell him how close he had been to becoming a parent. How close *they* had been.

Tears pooled in her eyes, and she looked away before memories of the miscarriage consumed her. It had taken years, but God had healed her heart regarding the loss of what would have been her firstborn child, soon after she had learned about Brent and Tamara's affair. Dayna had never felt the need to tell him, not even during the divorce proceedings. Why hurt him now?

"You okay?" he asked.

Dayna coughed and took a sip of tea. "Yeah — just got choked up for a minute. I'm fine."

Half an hour later, Dayna and Brent emerged from the restaurant, satiated from the meal and also full from each other's company. They had stayed on safe ground during the rest of their conversation, chatting more about each other's families and eventually getting down to business — reviewing the pros and the cons of working with the Calero Community Foundation.

Now at nearly 4:00 p.m., Brent had to make the drive back to the Space Coast.

"Leave now and you'll just miss the evening traffic," Dayna said.

Brent nodded. "Yep. In forty or so minutes I'll be home, back in the land of retirees, where commuters and traffic don't exist."

They laughed.

"Thanks again for your time and for doing this, Dayna," he said. "You're something else."

"Will you stop with all of the praise, please? I'm heading to the gym now, to work off all of this great food. You drive safely, and tell Tamara I said hello."

She could feel Brent's eyes on her with every step toward her car, and it made her self-conscious. As she started the car and headed toward the street, Brent was still standing at the entrance to the restaurant, watching her with a half smile on his face. Why hadn't he followed her to the parking lot, to his vehicle? She slowed to a stop and lowered the driver's side window. Brent leaned in and rested his elbows on the window ledge.

"I'll call you before the week is over to let you know which foundation I've decided to go with, okay?"

His voice was husky, and she saw something tender in his eyes.

"Um, that's fine . . . but why don't you save your report to share with the entire group when we meet next week Thursday? I don't mind waiting until then."

Brent shifted from one foot to the other, then stood back. "I guess I can do that. Thanks again for today. You take care."

"You have a safe drive home, okay?"

Dayna drove away, feeling like she was leaving behind a jilted boyfriend. Her mind must be playing tricks on her, because that made absolutely no sense at all. And yet, when she turned the corner and Brent was out of view, he was still lodged in her thoughts.

THIRTY-FOUR

Tamara checked the time again and sighed.

Would five o'clock ever come? And why hadn't Brent called? Had he gotten sick?

She forced herself to focus and smiled at Mrs. Chestnut when she slid the cash-filled envelope through the acrylic and glass window separating them.

"Here you go, same amount as usual," she said.

"Thank you, sweetie," Mrs. Chestnut said. "I'll be back next month as usual, when the Social Security arrives. See you then."

The elegant elderly woman gave a light wave before shuffling for the door. She paused halfway there and returned to Tamara's teller window before someone else could take her spot. Mrs. Chestnut leaned close to the opening in the glass and lowered her voice. "I forgot to ask you, dear . . . anything better with your husband this month? I'm still praying for him, you know."

A lump formed in Tamara's throat. She shook her head instead of verbally responding.

Mrs. Chestnut had been asking that same question once a month since bonding with Tamara after a problem with her account had been resolved to her satisfaction. Once Tamara shared Brent's diagnosis with her more than a year ago, Mrs. Chestnut had sustained a hope for his healing that inspired Tamara to keep hoping too. In recent months, though, not even Mrs. Chestnut's unwavering faith could prevent Tamara's spirits from sagging. Tamara hadn't had the heart to tell her customer and friend that Brent was dying. She could hardly accept it herself.

This afternoon, Mrs. Chestnut peered into her eyes for what felt like an eternity.

"You're giving up, aren't you?"

This time Tamara couldn't control herself. Tears slid down her cheeks and dripped onto her hands. She swiped at them, hoping the tellers on either side of her hadn't noticed, all the while realizing that Sasha and Bernice never missed a thing, even when they pretended to be otherwise occupied.

"I can't talk about it right now, Mrs. Chestnut." She managed to release the words without a quiver or sob in her voice. "Things are not good, but your prayers are appreciated."

Compassion filled the woman's eyes, and Tamara wanted to hug her. She knew she couldn't leave her post, though. A line was beginning to form, and she had to help ease the flow of the traffic.

"I understand, dear girl. I understand," Mrs. Chestnut said. "I will keep praying for you, and the next time I come in, I'll bring you a prayer book that might be helpful."

How could anything in a prayer book ease her breaking heart? Or help her accept that soon she would be husbandless and childless, with nothing and no one to live for?

Those questions raced through her mind and heart, but Tamara didn't utter them. Instead she nodded at her sweet friend and took a deep breath to settle her thoughts, so she could focus on serving her other customers.

Mrs. Chestnut ambled away, and in seconds, a distracted construction worker stood before her, checking his watch in the same motion as he handed over his paycheck for cashing.

Tamara switched on an auto-pilot smile and went through the motions of providing excellent customer service. Her mind, however, nursed worries about her husband and how he was doing on this last-minute trip to Calero that he had insisted on making.

He had surprised her with his plans during breakfast, when she had no choice but to go on to work instead of taking the day off to accompany him. Tamara had been tempted to ask him if he had purposely waited until the last minute to share details about the visit so he'd have an excuse to call Dayna and spend time alone with her.

There you go, allowing your mind to play tricks again, she told herself now, as she made a deposit for a friendly Hispanic woman with two small children in tow. *Brent didn't mention plans to see Dayna. Why are you so suspicious?*

But Tamara knew why. Brent also hadn't mentioned his whereabouts years ago, when Dayna was his wife and he was stepping out to see Tamara. Now she couldn't help but fear that the tables were turning, despite how sick he was.

Her heart sank at the thought, and not so much because she suspected that Brent, who was a good and godly man, would do something like that now. What hurt her more was the possibility that even though he might not act on those feelings, he had them in the first place. He hadn't said anything to that effect, but his eyes told Tamara more than she cared to know.

THIRTY-FIVE

Sweat coursed a path down Dayna's forehead as she trotted into a third mile on the treadmill and allowed her mind to jog through alternating thoughts of her lunch with Brent and Audrey's admission that she was someone's mistress.

Dayna had been more comfortable with Brent today than she'd felt since they reconnected, yet their growing familiarity also felt awkward. And Audrey . . . was her self-confidence so low that she chose to settle for someone else's crumbs rather than hold out for her own personal best? As much as they had talked about neither of them going that route, how had this happened?

The rhythmic pounding of her feet against the treadmill's running surface matched the staccato beat of her emotions. What could she say about any of this to Warren without causing unnecessary alarm or telling all of Audrey's business? Better yet, why should she care about Audrey's privacy? She knew how humiliated, angry, and hurt the wife of Audrey's boyfriend must be. How dare Dayna be asked to understand the mistress, no matter who it was?

She ran for ten more minutes, and as the treadmill tempo slowed to a brisk walk, she realized she didn't feel better. Her five-mile run usually eased the tension in her shoulders and centered her. This evening, she was still a ball of pent-up emotions.

The treadmill crawled to a stop and she stepped off. Someone tapped her shoulder as she wiped sweat from her forehead causing her to jump.

Dayna turned and swatted Warren with her towel. "Man — you scared me!"

He chuckled, then frowned. "In this busy gym? I usually meet you here, don't I?"

He was right. Instead of being caught off guard, she should have been looking out for him. They exercised together several days a week in this space reserved for hospital employees.

Dayna shook her head to clear her thoughts. "Yeah, you do — sorry," she said, and patted his chest. "Just have a lot on my mind today."

He pulled her by the hand over to the stationary bikes and motioned for her to climb onto one, before straddling the adjacent one himself. When each had positioned themselves and started pedaling, he resumed the conversation.

"So you took the day off work, and you're distracted . . . what gives?"

Dayna glanced to the left and to the right and saw that the only other person near them was the man three bikes away who wore headphones and bobbed his head to a beat only he could hear.

She shrugged and lowered her voice as much as she could without being drowned out by the sound of the bikes. "When I left your place last night I had to rush over to Audrey's to help her out with a crisis, which she will need to tell you about," she said. "That kept me up most of the night, so I rested until Brent called."

"Yeah? What did he want?"

Warren tried to seem nonchalant, but Dayna recognized the familiar locked jaw.

"He called out of the blue and announced that he had driven up today to check out the Calero Community Foundation," she said. "He's eager to move forward and didn't want to wait until our next meeting."

"I got your voicemail about lunch," Warren said.

Dayna knew he continued to gaze at her

because he wanted to know if there was more.

"Well, he met with foundation officials on his own, but he asked me to join him for lunch afterward to process what he had been told so we could make a recommendation at the next meeting about how to move forward. We grabbed a bite at Thai Today and chatted for a while."

When Warren didn't respond, she followed up. "You okay with that?"

He looked straight ahead and shrugged. "Does it matter? You've already had lunch and digested it."

"Why the attitude?"

His jaw set again and he didn't answer. Dayna sighed. In some ways, his jealousy was flattering, in others it was annoying. "What do you want for dinner?"

"Doesn't matter."

Dayna pressed the electronic key to stop her bike and climbed off when it slowed to a crawl. She moved toward Warren, who was still riding in place and staring at the flatscreen TV on the wall across the room. "Babe, stop tripping. It was just lunch."

"With your ex. Who just happened to drive almost an hour to ask questions he could have received answers to by phone, and who conveniently timed his call around lunchtime, so he wouldn't have to 'process' the details alone. Come on, Dayna. Tell me he didn't try to touch you today."

Dayna was speechless, but she had to acknowledge that what Warren was insinuating was fair. Those same questions had crossed her mind. Even though Brent was sick and dying, she recalled him grasping her hands today at the table and how he'd looked at her in the parking lot when she was leaving.

The feelings weren't mutual, though. Her self-assured, handsome, heart-of-gold boyfriend had no reason to be jealous of another man, one she had released a long time ago.

She put her hands on top of Warren's to reassure him, but he stopped the bike and stepped down. He headed across the gym, past rows of exercise equipment, and into the men's locker room without looking back.

THIRTY-SIX

Chicken and vegetables were roasting in the oven and Tamara had just opened a new novel when Brent walked through the door around 6 p.m.

She was furious, but she had convinced herself not to light into him the minute he arrived. When he strolled into the family room, she kept her eyes glued to the book, pretending to be engrossed in every word. She would sit here and read the same page until eternity before she acknowledged him first.

The thought that had crossed her mind all afternoon, after she realized that he wasn't going to call or text her, surfaced again: *How could someone so sick and so concerned about forgiveness for past mistakes be such a jerk in the here and now?*

Brent paused when he saw her reading. "Hey, baby."

She didn't reply, and he walked past her

to hang his keys on their designated hook under the kitchen cabinet. Tamara heard him open the oven. "Something smells good!" he called out.

She kept her head in the book and didn't respond.

Minutes later he was at her side. He sat next to her on the sofa and rested his chin on her shoulder.

"Whatever you're reading must be good."

Brent kissed her cheek, and Tamara leaned away from him.

"What's wrong, Tami?" He sat up and looked at her, surprised.

She glared at him. "Are you serious?"

He raised his palms upward and shrugged. "What gives?"

Tamara sat back and folded her arms. She stared at him for a few minutes before speaking.

"You mean to tell me you think you can leave here early in the morning, in your condition, and never bother to let me know you arrived or how things are going once you get to your destination? Did you stop to think I might worry? Were you at all concerned about filling me in on what the foundation shared and in what direction you might take the charity that you are leaving me to run? Did you?"

By now she was so mad that hot tears spilled down her cheeks. She hated it when she cried in the midst of an angry outburst. Crying diluted the conviction behind her words.

Brent got the message, though. She saw a flicker of recognition register in his eyes. He slid closer to her and she once again moved in the opposite direction.

"Go on, Brent. Your words and hugs can't fix it now."

He sighed and rubbed the palm of his hand across his head. He sat back on the sofa and stared at the ceiling. "Tami, I'm sorry. You are right. I left here and didn't call, didn't text. I had my mind on one thing only and got caught up in what I was doing. Won't happen again, okay?"

She ignored his conciliatory promise and looked at him. "What were you doing? Why were you so busy that you couldn't touch base?"

He looked at her and shrugged. "I visited the foundation and talked to the vice president of supporting organizations, had lunch, and headed home."

"That took all day?"

She knew she was coming off as paranoid or suspicious, but she didn't care. All of these words would accurately describe her

256

state of mind today. When Brent didn't answer, she continued. "Were you with Dayna today? Did she 'help' you visit the foundation?"

Brent rolled his eyes.

"No, she didn't. I met with the officials on my own, thank you."

She folded her arms and pursed her lips, waiting. Didn't he know that she knew all of his tricks? Had he forgotten that he'd perfected his "say only what's necessary" routine while the two of them were dating? That's why she knew she needed to keep pressing him until the full truth came out.

"Okay, so you went to visit the foundation office alone. What did they say? Were you impressed?"

Brent sat up straight and smiled. Tami saw relief wash across his face and wanted to slap him. He really thought she was stupid.

"I was impressed," he said. "They offer a lot of support when it comes to the administrative duties that come with operating a foundation. They've worked before with people whose foundations were launched with proceeds from their life insurance policies. The key will be to put everything we decide to do in writing, have me sign it, and get it notarized."

Tamara nodded but didn't smile. Had she

not been so furious, she would have celebrated the news that what Brent had in mind for his foundation was actually possible. Now that his defenses were down, though, she went after the information she dreaded.

"What did Dayna have to say about this? And where did you two go for lunch?"

Brent squirmed. "Well, she just happened to have the day off, so I was able to get her feedback," he said. "Her thought is that since the Calero Foundation is larger, we'd have more opportunities to reach and serve a national audience of candidates than we would if we went with a smaller program."

Tamara's heart sank. She noticed that he didn't answer her second question, but where they had lunch was irrelevant.

"And you just happened to make a visit by yourself to Calero when she was off work. Less than twenty-four hours after we were there for a group meeting? Got it."

She rose to leave the room, but Brent grabbed her arm lightly and turned her toward him. "Tami, what are you trying to suggest? That I went back to Calero today to sneak in a visit with Dayna? Baby, you know my situation. I don't want to take any more time than necessary to get everything set up. Who knows how I'll be feeling in another week or two? I'm just trying to get the foundation off to a solid start. But yes, I called Dayna and asked her to join me for lunch so we could discuss what I learned, so I could possibly determine which way to go before the next meeting. We ate at a Thai restaurant and then I came home; that's the truth."

The earnestness in his eyes touched her.

"I'm sorry I didn't call or text you. I got caught up in the excitement of seeing this dream really take off, Tami. I thought about it all the way home and was excited about sharing everything with you over dinner tonight. Really."

He leaned in to kiss her, and Tamara's body stiffened. But when his lips touched hers, she relented. How could she not? She loved him and she loved his kisses, and she couldn't help but be thankful that her worry today had been for naught.

Whatever had led him to Calero and whatever happened while he was there didn't matter right now. He had come home to her, not Dayna. That had to count for something. She'd accept it for all it was worth tonight, because the thought of him not doing this very thing someday soon tore her apart.

THIRTY-SEVEN

Warren was leaning against the wall across from the ladies' locker room when Dayna emerged.

She took a swig from her bottle of water and paused in front of him. She yearned to tell him how cute he was when he was angry but decided to hold that thought for later.

"You finished sulking?" she teased, and poked him in the ribs.

He grabbed her around the waist and pulled her toward him. "Enough, all right? I'm just not sure about Brent's motives, that's all. I saw the way he looked at you when he came over."

Dayna's pulse quickened with guilt. It wasn't so easy to dismiss what she was seeing or feeling herself when someone else held similar sentiments. It was easy to regard Warren's feelings as pure jealousy, but Dayna had to admit his radar wasn't far off target.

Warren sighed and turned her toward the door. "A man knows how guys think, okay? Let's just leave it at that for now and get out of here. Want to eat out or order to-go? Lily is picking the boys up from a friend's house tonight and getting their dinner."

Tamara pulled her cell phone from her purse to check the time as they strolled into the parking lot.

"Looks like it's almost 7:30," she said. "I can try to whip up something for us, but it would probably be 8:30 before we sit down to eat. Let's just grab something quick, if you don't mind. Even though I didn't go to the office, it's been a long day."

Warren hugged her and opened her car door for her after she unlocked it.

"Deal," he said. "Got a taste for anything particular?"

"No, it doesn't matter; anything is good except Thai or Chinese. I've had enough rice for today."

Warren smirked. "I bet you have."

Half an hour later, they were seated in her family room, on the floor in front of the sofa, eating from the coffee table and watching TV.

Since they had polished off the salad and seafood pasta Warren picked up from a local hot spot, Dayna leaned into him and encircled his waist with her arms. She laid her head on his chest and closed her eyes.

"Mmmmm," she said. "This is the best dessert, and it's calorie free."

Warren pinched her side playfully. "You remember that the next time some other man calls to invite you to lunch."

Dayna rolled her eyes. "Yes, dear. How about you fill my dance card with dates and then you don't have to worry?"

He tickled her until she screamed for mercy.

"I'll stop if you say yes," he said, once he had her pinned on the floor.

Dayna tried to catch her breath in between bursts of laugher. She opened her eyes. "Yes to what?" she gasped.

"Yes that you'll marry me."

She stopped mid-laugh, unsure whether he was joking. "This is becoming a habit, you know? Just about every time we share a meal, you seem to sneak in a proposal. Are you seriously talking marriage during a game of tickle, just after we've finished take-out?"

This time he got the giggles. His laughter rang throughout the house. "There's the Dayna I know," he said, and grinned. "No, babe, this isn't a formal proposal — yet.

But I am asking you to consider whether you can spend the rest of your life with me and my boys. I love you, Dayna."

Tears filled her eyes. She stroked his cheek.

It had been a long time coming, and God hadn't delivered in the time frame or chocolate-brown package she had thought would suit her best. But she loved God, and she cared enough about Warren to make this work.

"I love you back, Warren, and yes, I can see myself in your arms like this for the rest of my life."

Dayna took his face into her hands and kissed him deeply enough to cause him discomfort. "Careful, babe," he said. "You're playing with fire."

She grinned. "Don't worry — I'm not going to be your Delilah, sweetie. But the clock is ticking."

She allowed a smile to bloom in her heart and decided that tonight she'd recite something more personal than the Lord's Prayer before closing her eyes. Then she'd fall asleep thinking about her future with a man who loved her deeply, instead of focusing on regrets from the past.

THIRTY-EIGHT

Dayna sat across the boardroom's massive table from Audrey and tried to avert her gaze as Audrey assisted an accounting department colleague with a PowerPoint presentation on projected costs to finish the addition to Chesdin Medical Center's hospice.

She had ignored Audrey's texts and voice-mails over the past ten days, but had been forced to sit in on today's meeting with other members of the executive team, including Warren and Stephanie, a member of his marketing staff.

Even as she avoided looking at her friend, Dayna had to admit that the presentation was compelling. Audrey did her job well.

Yet the questions that had plagued Dayna for the past couple of weeks surfaced again: How could Audrey have been so selfish? So weak?

Spencer Hayes, the hospital's chief executive officer, interrupted her reverie. "This is great, Audrey." His blue eyes danced, and he beamed with approval. "It appears that we're moving forward with lightning speed, in both construction and fundraising efforts."

Robert Rogers, president of the hospice foundation's board of directors, chimed in. "Indeed we are. Kudos to the staff and board for their hard work!"

Spencer turned to Warren and to the hospital's development director. "Can we get word out to the public and to our donors thanking them for the help so far and asking them for one last push to reach our goal?"

Warren and Dean nodded.

"We're on it," Warren responded.

Audrey took her seat, and Warren gave her and her colleague a thumbs-up. She smiled, then glanced at Dayna, who looked away.

Audrey had sent her a text a few hours ago, asking if they could meet for coffee after the meeting, or maybe for lunch. Dayna hadn't responded. She hoped the dismissiveness she displayed this morning would be answer enough.

When the meeting ended with Spencer applauding everyone for a job well done, Dayna quickly gathered her files in hopes of escaping before Audrey could approach her. Before she could tuck everything away, however, Audrey was at her side.

"How are you?"

"I'm busy, but good," Dayna responded without looking her way.

"Got a minute to chat over a cup of coffee?"

Dayna stood and tucked her folders under her arm so she could grab her purse with the other hand. "Actually I have a pretty full day, but thanks for asking."

"I'm sure you can spare fifteen minutes."

The response had come from Warren, who had snuck up behind her. Dayna's eyes widened. Since when had he felt comfortable speaking for her?

She turned and asked him that question with her eyes. He didn't flinch.

Rather than make a scene, she decided to go along. "Okaaay . . . you know what? I've got ten minutes. Good enough?"

Audrey gave Warren a grateful glance, then smiled at Dayna. "Good enough. I'll meet you at the coffee shop down the block, in ten minutes."

Dayna nodded. She wondered why Audrey hadn't chosen to meet on the first floor, in the hospital's café, but figured whatever she wanted to say must require some privacy. Hospital staff frequented the coffee shop too, but it was more of a general public hangout than the on-site restaurant.

When Audrey was gone, Dayna glared at Warren, too afraid that if she spoke here in front of their colleagues, she might say the wrong thing and cost them both their jobs. She pushed past him with a nod.

"Call me later?" Warren asked.

She waved good-bye while walking away and closed the door to the boardroom behind her.

When the elevator opened, she was grateful to have it all to herself. A few seconds alone would help her prepare for this awkward meeting with Audrey. As far as she was concerned, nothing had changed. She was still angry. Audrey was wrong, and there was little that could change that.

When she strolled into the bustling coffee shop minutes later, Audrey sat up and waved her over. She motioned for Dayna to take the seat across from her, where a steaming cup of coffee was waiting.

"I ordered your usual, so you wouldn't have to stand in line."

Dayna nodded but didn't smile. "Thanks."

"Thank you for taking time to meet with me, Dayna."

Dayna stared at Audrey, who looked both

fearful and hopeful as she gripped her coffee cup and waited for Dayna to reply.

"Are you still seeing him?" Dayna asked.

"No," Audrey replied. "He dumped me the night of the incident. I haven't heard from him since he left the restaurant with his wife. I called him repeatedly over the next few days, and by the following week, his number had changed."

"Wow," Dayna said. "Have you heard from his wife again?"

"No — I guess she said all she needed to say the night we met."

"Why did you keep calling him after meeting her?"

Dayna didn't know why she was dousing Audrey with questions. Maybe the interrogation was for herself as well, to purge herself of the questions she wished someone had asked Tamara seven years ago when Tamara was stepping out with Brent. Once again, she clearly saw herself channeling her frustrations with her experience onto Audrey, and she knew it was wrong.

"I have no excuse, Dayna. I've known all along that it was wrong, but I love him." Shame and pain canvassed her face. "I've loved him for more than a year. It's hard to turn off, just like that."

Dayna sat back in her chair and took a sip

of her coffee. Love was hard to turn off, wasn't it? She supposed that after a certain point, when the heart took over, it didn't matter to those involved how they came about falling into it.

"How did you get in so deep? Wasn't there a point when you could have restrained yourself?"

"He confessed to me about six months in because he had to go away with his wife for a summer sabbatical, and he knew I'd be trying to contact him while he was with his family. I was crushed, and I had that six-week period while he was gone to get over him and move on."

Audrey took a deep breath and looked Dayna in the eye. "But you know what I realized during his absence? I was lonelier than ever, dating guys who only wanted one thing. I was sick of making great money and buying everything I wanted or needed but not having anyone to share it with. And with Raymond, I could be myself. He cared about what I thought and what made me sad or afraid. He asked about my parents and my work. He spent time with me, just because. And yes, we did have a full-blown affair; but for me, it wasn't just about that. It was having a meaningful, emotional connection with someone.

269

"He made me feel valuable and beautiful," Audrey said. "And he promised me that he would eventually leave his wife so he could marry me, and so I could have the baby I wanted. I'm thirty-nine, Dayna. I desperately want a child. I want a complete family. And if this was the way it was supposed to happen, so be it."

Dayna sighed. She had never heard this level of desperation before from Audrey. But then again, had she always bared her own soul? Hadn't she had similar fears and longings before she and Warren began dating? It had been easy to let those emotions and fears fade to the background once she had someone to share her life with.

"You know, I hear you, Audrey," Dayna said. "And I'm sorry if I've come across as harsh. But you know my history. You know how devastated I was by a woman deciding that my man was hers, and eventually making that so. You can't ask me to overlook the reality of the pain you've caused just because you and I are friends."

Tears filled Audrey's eyes. "I know," she said. "And to be really honest, I need to tell you something else."

Dayna steeled herself.

"I looked at your history, too, Dayna, and I told myself that if your husband's girlfriend won his heart, maybe I'd be able to do the same with Raymond."

This time tears welled up in Dayna's eyes. She felt the urge to slap Audrey, but instead, she clenched her fists in her lap. She told herself to remember who and where she was and prayed for restraint.

Please, God, help me control myself right now.

The more she took time to pray every day, like she'd promised Warren she would, the easier talking to God was becoming.

"You know, Audrey," Dayna finally said, "I realize now that I never knew you. The person I knew wouldn't think like that. Maybe I was friends with the shell of a person you created, not the real Audrey. Now that I've met her, she isn't someone I want to know."

Dayna rose to leave, but Audrey reached for her arm.

"Wait!" she said. Her trembling voice caught the attention of the other diners, who briefly looked their way before resuming their conversations. "You do know the real Audrey. I guess that's why I've been trying to talk with you for the past two weeks, to let you know that she's still in here, somewhere. And even though I don't deserve it, I need your help to bring her

271

back. Please."

Audrey's pleading eyes touched Dayna, and she sat down.

"Raymond has dumped me to make things work with his wife. I'm facing court in three weeks to answer for a crime I admit to committing, over a man who obviously cares nothing about me, despite what he led me to believe. I understand now that he told me what I needed to hear so he could get what he wanted. I'm the biggest fool this side of China, I know. But I don't want to live in fantasyland anymore. I want the real Audrey back, even if she has to be lonely, because I like that person much better than this one. And you know what? I'm certain God does too."

Dayna felt torn. Her heart went out to Audrey, whose life beneath her crumbling façade was as broken as her own had once been. Yet she resented Audrey's sudden interest in relying on God, when faith clearly hadn't been uppermost in her mind when she was sleeping with another woman's husband.

Dayna sighed. There she went again being self-righteous, like Mama. If God started airing her dirty laundry, she'd never lift her head again.

"Look, Audrey, it may take me a while to

forget about all of this and trust you again, but you won't be alone," Dayna said. "I'll stand with you through this."

Audrey appeared ready to hug Dayna, but clearly didn't want to overstep her bounds. She produced a faint smile instead.

"Thank you, Dayna. I value your friendship. I'll make sure you don't regret this."

THIRTY-NINE

Warren's ringtone filled the air as Dayna and Audrey walked back to the hospital.

Audrey was in the middle of sharing how she had been forced to tell Spencer and her immediate supervisor about her arrest, and Dayna hesitated to interrupt her. She also didn't want to ignore Warren, and her discomfort must have been obvious.

"Go ahead and answer if it's important," Audrey said. "I was just gonna share that Spencer has been very understanding, and he has recommended a top-notch lawyer who hopefully can help me put this behind me without ruining my career. I gotta get back inside. Thank you for forgiving me, Dayna."

With a quick hug, she was gone, and Dayna was able to answer on the fourth ring.

"You still speaking to me, babe?"

Dayna sighed dramatically, so Warren

would know she was contemplating her answer. She wanted to stay mad at him, but after her heart-to-heart talk with Audrey, she was over it.

"How long have you known what was going on?" she asked him.

She'd only told him that Audrey had some personal challenges that had come between them, but his insistence this morning in getting them together had made her wonder if he somehow knew more.

"Audrey called me about a week ago and told me everything," Warren said. "You wouldn't return her calls and she was desperate to apologize to you and talk to you."

"She told you everything?"

"Yes, she did," he said. "I know all about the affair and the arrest. She knew you would feel obligated not to say anything, so she spilled the beans on herself."

Dayna was stunned. If Audrey had gone so far as to tell Warren all of her business, she must be serious about making some changes.

"How did your meeting go?" Warren asked.

Dayna sighed again. "We're okay. I need to work on separating her situation from my past experience so I can stop judging her through that lens, but that's the work on my end," she said. "She's my friend, and I need to help her. All that prayer I've been doing in the mornings is working on me, I guess."

"You're getting closer to being marriage material, girl. I need a solid prayer partner, raising these two middle school boys. Keep it up!" Warren laughed before returning the conversation to Audrey. "She's going to be fine. This is her first offense, so she probably won't get any jail time. It will just be a tough lesson learned, to pair with her broken heart."

Dayna realized she was learning some lessons too. Not just about Audrey, but about herself and the kind of woman she wanted to be.

Before she could respond to Warren's comment, her phone beeped. She glanced at caller ID and was surprised to see Tamara's number. They had met just a week ago as a group and had agreed to establish Brent's foundation under the Calero Community Foundation. What was up?

"Let me call you right back, Warren. Tamara's on the other line."

She clicked over quickly.

"Hi, T—"

Tamara interrupted her before she could

say more. "Dayna, Brent is in the hospital and he's not doing well today."

Her voice shook, and Dayna could tell she had been, or was, crying.

"I'm so sorry, Tamara . . ." She wanted to ask exactly what "not doing well" meant, but she was afraid to upset Tamara further. "What do you need?"

"We're at Holmes Regional Medical Center. Can you come?"

Dayna's eyes widened. Was it that dire?

She looked at the clock and remembered it would take her an hour to drive to Brevard County, where both Cocoa Beach and the medical center in Melbourne were located.

"He's asking for you, Dayna."

Dayna gasped. "Me? But why — I'm. . . . I'm on my way, Tamara. I'll get there as quickly as I can."

Dayna crossed the street at the crosswalk, but instead of heading into the hospital as she had planned, she made a beeline for the parking deck.

She called her secretary, Monica, while she strode toward her car.

"I need you to let Spencer know I won't be in the afternoon meeting because of . . . a family emergency. And can you please reschedule the two telephone conferences I had planned for later in the day?"

Dayna unlocked her car door with the keyless entry device and paused before climbing in. How was she going to tell Warren she was rushing to Brent's bedside?

There was no good way, but texting might be easier.

Tamara said Brent's not doing well. He's at Holmes Regional Medical Center in Melbourne. Need to go check on him. Not sure when I'll be back, but will call. Luv u

She heard a swoosh, indicating his swift reply, as she pulled out of the deck, onto the main road in front of the hospital. The sunlight temporarily blinded her and kept her from reading the text. She laid the phone in the passenger seat and focused on the road, intending to read the message whenever she stopped at a red light.

The phone rang.

"What's this about going to see Brent?"

Dayna heard Warren straining to remain calm.

"I don't have all of the details, Warren," she said, and turned onto Second Avenue, which would lead her onto the interstate. "Tamara was upset, so I didn't ask any questions. She asked me to come, so I'm on my way."

Dayna didn't know how to tell him that Brent had specifically asked for her.

"Okaaay," he said. "Keep me posted. And drive carefully."

"What?"

"What, what?"

"Come on, Warren," Dayna said. "What was the drawn-out 'okay' for?"

"Nothing, babe," he said. "You just get where you're going and call me as soon as you can."

"I will, Warren. Love you."

She cranked up her Kirk Whalum CD and tried to lose herself in the music. The soothing melodies calmed her pounding heart, and when "Dancing on the Shore," a duet with Jonathan Butler, came on, she swayed to the light-hearted beat and felt her spirits rise, despite her concern over what awaited her at the hospital.

The lengthy drive gave her time to ruminate over why she had been summoned. Why had Brent asked for her? And how had that made Tamara feel? Was this the end?

Her thoughts wandered to the special times she had shared with Brent, and for once she didn't fight the memories. Dayna recalled meeting Brent in the campus student union her freshman year after she asked to borrow his pen to jot down another student's number. Brent had given her the pen, then asked for it back so he could write his number on the same piece of paper as the other guy's.

Her mind raced through memories of nursing him back to health after his football injury, of his proposal on Christmas Eve a year after she graduated, and of their fairy-tale wedding officiated by her father.

She recalled the alarm she'd felt the first time in their seven-year marriage he had stayed out all night without calling, and the lame excuse he'd given her when he came home just before noon the next day.

"Ignore that," Mama had advised. "He's a man, and men are gonna do what they want to do. In the end, they know where home is, and they always come home. You just go on about your business and make sure that home is still a clean, warm, and loving place to come home to."

Dayna shook her head now at the memory of that motherly advice. Mama was something else.

Her stomach churned as she remembered the day Brent told her he was in love with Tamara and that their marriage was over. After she'd picked herself up off the floor, she crawled to a phone and called Mama, who accused her of pushing Brent away. Their mother-daughter relationship had never been the same.

The song on the car stereo changed and the new melody jarred Dayna back to the present. She felt a wetness on her cheeks and was startled to find that she had been crying. Before she could react, her cell phone rang with another familiar tone. It was Audrey. Dayna inhaled and tried to compose herself. The last thing she needed was for Audrey to know she'd been shedding tears.

"Warren emailed and told me where you're headed," Audrey said. "You okay? Do you need me to drive down and meet you at the hospital?"

Audrey's concern perplexed her. They had "made up," but things weren't all right between them yet. She was trying too hard.

"I'm okay," Dayna told her. "I needed this quiet time, all to myself. Thanks for calling, though."

"Do you want me to do anything for you here — or call someone — your mother, or anyone else?"

Dayna smirked. Mama was the last person on her list to call, although she would want to know that the former son-in-law she still adored was not in good health.

"I'm good. I'll keep you and Warren posted. Just say a prayer that Brent will get through this."

Audrey was silent.

"You still there?" Dayna asked.

"Yeah, I am," Audrey finally said. "My head is just spinning from all of this. First of all, I'm thinking about the fact that I haven't prayed in a long, long time. And then there's the amazement over what you're doing — going to check on the man who broke your heart. Not to mention the fact that even though he has his wife by his side, he's asking for you."

Dayna had no response.

"Another wake-up call for me, I guess," Audrey said. "And for Brent's wife — Tamara, right?"

"I suppose so," Dayna said, not feeling good about this turn of events at all.

That was the interesting part: Now that Dayna had become reacquainted with Tamara through their foundation meetings, she was seeing her in a different light, and she felt sorry for her. Nothing but love could have led Tamara to make that phone call today.

FORTY

Dayna trotted into the Holmes Regional Medical Center ICU exactly an hour after Tamara's call.

She strode toward the nurse's station, but before she could ask the woman sitting at the desk for help, a petite, freckled brown woman whose hair was graying at the temples sidled up next to her.

"Are you Dayna?"

Dayna hesitated before acknowledging her identity with a smile.

"My, aren't you beautiful," the woman said with surprise. "I'm Tami's mom, Naomi. She told me you'd be tall with short hair, but she didn't mention how striking you are. Let me go get her for you. Only one person can go into the ICU rooms at a time."

A few minutes later, Naomi emerged with Tamara, whose eyes were red and swollen. Dayna wasn't sure whether to hug her, take her hand, or do nothing. She waited for Tamara to lead.

Tamara greeted her with a nod. "Thanks for coming. He's awake. You can go in."

Dayna frowned.

"Can you tell me what's going on? Why is he here in ICU?"

"Sorry about that; it's been a long night," Tamara said. "He's having a bad episode with the bone pain. He couldn't keep any food down yesterday and got dehydrated. This morning, ever since he woke up, he's been asking for you. I'm not sure why, but given his diagnosis, I decided to check and see if you'd be willing to come."

"He asked for me out of the blue?"

Tamara stared at her.

"As far as I know. Out of the blue."

Dayna ignored the insinuation.

"Is he . . . is this . . ."

Tamara shook her head. "The doctor says he's stable. He may not be able to go back to work, though. That's going to crush him."

Dayna's head was spinning. Brent had shown up at her home four weeks ago to ask for forgiveness, and now she had become part of his dying circle?

"Have you called his family?"

"Yes. His parents and his brothers and sister are on their way. He's going to be mad that they've come all this way 'for nothing,' because he's convinced that this is just a bad spell he'll bounce back from. Hopefully he will, but he still needs to spend some time with them. He needs to tell them."

Dayna tried to hide her shock. His family was so close-knit; how could he not have told them? They would be devastated if he died without giving them a chance to be there for him. Was he losing his mind?

She reminded herself she was a guest in this situation. Brent's choices didn't affect her.

Tamara's mother moved to her side. "Guess I need to get back to the house to prepare for your guests. Can't have relatives coming from out of town with nothing to eat and bathrooms that aren't clean."

"They aren't like that," Dayna said, and smiled. "They'll arrive wanting to help you and Tamara and Brent get through this, instead of worrying about how things look and what's available to eat."

Tamara bit her lip. "Seems you have a better handle on them than I do, even after all of these years. You better go in; Brent will be glad to see you."

Dayna reached for Tamara's hand, but Tamara stiffened. "Go on, Dayna," she said, and turned away. "Just go in and see Brent;

that's why you're here. I'll be okay."

Dayna slowly walked toward the room to which she had been directed and knocked on the door before entering. She found a frail Brent lying in the bed with his eyes closed. He appeared to be sleeping, so she tiptoed toward the bed. When she stood next to him, though, he opened his eyes and tried to smile.

"You came," he said, sounding as exhausted as if he'd just run a marathon. "Welcome to the Space Coast. Sorry your first stop is ICU."

Dayna mustered a smile and sat in the chair next to him. She wanted to weep over how unlike himself he looked. Despite his dark-chocolate complexion, he appeared chalky, and his veins were visible through his paper-thin skin. He seemed to have aged enough to be his grandfather's twin. The fact that he looked five pounds thinner than he had just a few days earlier, when she had hosted the foundation planning meeting at her house, frightened her. Had he really shed more weight that quickly? Or had the sweaters he wore during their meetings made him look heavier? Dayna struggled to keep the tears at bay.

"You feeling any better than when you arrived?" she asked, then mentally kicked herself for posing an obviously foolish question.

"Not really, but that's part of the deal, I guess," he said. "Regardless of my issue, I usually come right to ICU every time I'm admitted, because of the cancer. Once I get hydrated and get some food in me, I'll be all right."

Dayna wondered why, if that was all that was wrong, he wanted to see her so badly, and why Tamara felt compelled to call his family. Was he in denial about how aggressively this cancer was attacking him?

"Did you need to see me for a specific reason?"

He reached for her hand, but lowered his when she hesitated.

"Sorry about that. Even in this condition, I'm overstepping my boundaries."

Dayna wasn't sure how to respond. His wife was out in the family waiting room dealing with humiliation and heartbreak, and here he was in a hospital bed, flirting with her. At least, that was what it felt like.

This wasn't the man she remembered loving all those years ago, or the one she was forming a decent friendship with just a few weeks ago. Everyone had two sides, and today Brent's alter ego was present. This man was selfish. She hated to feel that way about someone who was so ill. Yet even with all he was going through, she had to be real with herself, and with him. Audrey's experience had taught her that.

"You realize you've hurt Tamara by asking me to come here, right?" Dayna couldn't believe she was sitting here, sticking up for Tamara, of all people, but Brent seemed unfazed.

"I know it must have been tough for her to have me ask for you, but I'm not going to have too much longer to do the things I feel like I want to do or need to do. She has to understand."

"She doesn't have to," Dayna said. "We all know that your time is limited, and we're all doing our best to help you leave here with dignity, Brent. But you can't step on everyone in the process, especially not your . . . wife."

For the first time, she felt at peace uttering words she knew to be true.

"Tamara loves you, Brent, she really does."

He nodded and turned his head away, toward a small window that offered a sliver of sunlight.

"I know she does," he said, with the volume of his voice rising and falling like the waves of the ocean less than fifteen minutes from the hospital. "She's been a great wife. But loving her hasn't stopped me from loving you. I've told you that before; when are you going to believe me? I never stopped loving you, Dayna, and I never will, and I know that whether you admit it or not, you'll always love me too. I'll always be your first love, won't I?"

Tears formed in Dayna's eyes, and for a while, she fell silent. She was so angry at him, but how could she argue with a dying man?

"Please stop this, Brent," she finally said, as gently as she could. "What does it matter what I believe? I'm not in first place anymore, remember? Tamara was your choice. Don't do this to her, or to yourself, right now."

"If not now, when?"

Dayna paused and peered at him. Was he hallucinating? Or was he reacting this way because he feared death? She wondered if Tamara had told him his family was on the way or if their visit was going to be a surprise. With nothing left to say that felt comfortable, she waited for him to speak again, praying that he would stay on appropriate subjects.

"One of the reasons I wanted to see you so badly was because I think we need to do whatever we can to speed things up with the foundation. I think I'll come out of here okay this time, but I want everything squared away as soon as possible. I want this to really happen."

Dayna sat back in her chair and relaxed. This, she could deal with. She heard his conviction; he was going to do whatever he could to realize this dream.

"Why don't we see if they'll let Tamara come in so the three of us can chat for a few minutes and figure out what we need to do to move things along?"

"Before you do that, there's something else I want to share."

Dayna's heart raced again. "Yeah?"

"I'd like you to serve as president of the foundation board, once it's established."

Dayna's jaw fell. "You're kidding."

This was her confirmation: he was either heavily medicated or losing his mind. Or maybe he just needed some sense knocked into him. There was no way she'd assume this role over Tamara.

"You were with me when the idea for the foundation was born; you're the best one to be the face of the organization after I'm gone. It just makes sense. Why wouldn't you carry through what you helped me imagine?"

"You know what, Brent?" Dayna said.

"Just focus on getting well, and the rest will fall into place."

He shook his head. "Don't have time for that. I have to plan now. Are you with me or not?"

Could he handle an emphatic "no" right now? Dayna wasn't sure, but that was her short and sweet answer. She had no desire to be his other woman, whether he was alive or dead.

FORTY-ONE

Dayna left Brent's bedside as quickly as she could without giving him an answer and nearly fainted when she exited his room into Warren's arms.

"How . . . when . . . what are you doing here?"

She felt disoriented, then realized that Warren must have jumped into his SUV and headed to the hospital as soon as she texted him.

"I didn't want you to be alone, if this was as serious as it appeared," he said. "I arrived shortly after you."

Dayna realized she had sagged in Warren's arms, and he was holding her up, here in the hallway outside of Brent's room. She gathered her bearings and surmised he must have been on the way into Brent's room to join her. Or had he been standing there listening for a while?

She stepped back and looked at him. His

squared jaw told her he was angry.

"How much of our conversation did you hear?"

"Let's just say I didn't hear you deny loving him when he pressed you for an answer, and I didn't hear you turn him down when he offered you the chairmanship of his foundation board."

Dayna could hear the anger simmering beneath Warren's calmly delivered words. Her heart seized. Here she had been worried about Brent's words destroying Tamara, when it looked like they might derail her own life.

She opened her mouth to speak, but nothing came out.

"Were you planning on going back inside?" Warren asked.

"I don't need to see him again," Dayna managed to utter.

She and Warren headed toward the elevators, but they had to pass the waiting room to get there, and inside, Dayna saw Tamara and her mother talking with a doctor.

"Wait, Warren," she said. He shrugged and held open the waiting room door for her. Dayna and Warren approached Tamara, but stood a few feet away so they wouldn't intrude. Tamara noticed them and motioned for them to join her and her mother.

Hearing firsthand from Brent's physician that his current health crisis didn't appear to be life-threatening was reassuring.

"Each time he comes, though, he'll get weaker. Hospice care will become a good alternative," the doctor told Tamara.

She nodded as if she understood, but in Dayna's estimation, Tamara appeared to be a million miles away.

"I hope I'm not prying, but have you two considered counseling to deal with Brent's impending death?" the doctor asked.

Tamara shook her head. "You mentioned it at his last appointment, but Brent insists he's okay. He doesn't want to talk about anything — he just wants to get everything in order."

The doctor didn't seem surprised. "And you?"

Tamara frowned. "Me?"

"It's common not only for patients, but also their closest relatives, to go through the stages of grief after a patient receives a terminal diagnosis. They range from denial to anger to acceptance, with a couple of other steps involved as well. Everyone arrives at the stages in their own way and in their own time, but they will go through each of them, and sometimes you can get stuck in one. It's important as you're preparing for his death that you talk with someone who can help you work through each stage too."

Tamara nodded. "Wonder which one I'm in now?"

The doctor peered at her. "I wouldn't dare try to stand here and tell you for certain, but a good guess with a woman your age and in your circumstances would be that you're spending a significant amount of time in the anger stage. That's quite normal. However, it can be detrimental to your emotional and physical health. Plus, as your husband's caregiver, you've got a lot on your shoulders. It would be wise to get some support for yourself, but also for him, if you can talk him into it."

Tamara nodded. "Thank you, Dr. Grant. I'll take all of that into account."

He patted her arm. "Hang in there, Tamara. I'm so sorry you're having to deal with this, but Brent is stable for now and should be able to go home tomorrow."

Dr. Grant turned toward Dayna. "Hello, are you one of Mr. Davidson's relatives?"

Out of the corner of her eye, she glimpsed a few seconds of pain skip through Tamara's eyes before Tamara's mask fell back into place.

Dayna shook her head. "No, just a concerned friend. I came down from Calero to check on Brent. Glad he's stable. May I . . ." She paused and looked at Tamara. "Is it okay if I ask a question about Brent's health?"

Tamara hesitated, then shrugged. "Go ahead."

"Doctor, is it normal for him to be . . . he seems to be living in a fantasy world, or acting somewhat selfishly, as if only what he wants matters. Does that make sense, especially for a forty-year-old man?"

The question must have struck a chord. Tamara looked at Dr. Grant expectantly. Warren watched with narrowed eyes, but she hoped he had gotten her implied message: *Brent is acting badly, and it's not my fault.*

Dr. Grant nodded. "Absolutely normal. It figures into the stages of grief I mentioned. It sounds like he's in the bargaining stage right now, where he may have in some ways accepted that he's dying, but in another sense feels like if he can just have things his way, he'll feel better and live longer or be able to eventually accept what's coming his way. I can't say for sure without having a long talk with him, but what you're describing is common in terminally ill patients."

Tamara frowned. "So what do we do with

that? Just play along to keep him happy, even though his actions may have a negative impact on everyone around him?"

Dr. Grant cocked his head to the side. "I don't know that you'll have a cut-and-dried solution. You've got to decide circumstance by circumstance, Tamara. Just because he's dying doesn't give him the right to be mean or hurtful, if that's what you're asking. Sure, you may let him have his way on certain things to keep the peace or to make him feel special, but boundaries need to stay in place as much as is realistic."

Tamara seemed to have more questions, but the doctor shifted from one foot to the other, indicating that he needed to move on.

"Get into some counseling, both of you, okay? If you need help finding someone who will be a good fit, call my office, and my receptionist will help you. Take good care."

He patted Tamara's shoulder one last time before leaving.

Tamara hugged herself and walked over to the sofa to sit down. Her mother followed and sat next to her. She put an arm around her daughter and kissed her cheek. "We're going to get through this together, you hear? God is going to see us through."

Tamara's dry laugh sounded empty.

"God's in this? Really? No kids, and soon no husband? What will I have left to live for?"

She looked up at Dayna through the blur of tears. "In fact, my husband already seems to have gone back to the wife of his youth. Is that God's doing too?"

The words pierced Dayna as sharply as if a knife had been thrust in her chest. She was about to protest, but pursed her lips. She knew Warren was standing next to her, likely asking a similar question.

What could she say to change how Brent had made Tamara feel by demanding that she come? And how was Tamara going to handle it if she went into that room and Brent told her of his new plan to leave Dayna in charge of the foundation?

Dayna's heart swam with confusing emotions. Pity for Tamara washed over her one second, followed by a guilty smugness that this woman was recouping some of the pain she had once inflicted on Dayna, followed by a desire to help Tamara get through this as best as she could.

And that was just with Tamara. Concern over what Warren had heard, and possibly misinterpreted, stirred a whole other wave of feelings. What was God doing? And why?

She wanted to leave the hospital this

evening and head home with Warren and make a nice happy life with him and his two sons. Instead, she knew when she got back to Calero, she'd be fighting to keep Warren, while somehow honoring her promise to Brent and Tamara to get the foundation launched and checked off Brent's list.

The sooner that happened, the sooner she could step back into her familiar routine and let Brent and his wife tie up their loose ends.

FORTY-TWO

With no memory of how she'd gotten there, Dayna pulled into her driveway.

Warren had followed her back to Calero to make sure she arrived safely, but he hadn't called her cell to chat while they drove. He was probably still disturbed by the declarations he'd heard from Brent, so small talk and flirting would have felt out of place. But as he'd told her at the hospital before they parted, a serious discussion would have to wait — he was needed at a school function tonight, and tomorrow he was taking the boys sailing.

She remained lost in her thoughts as she prepared her tea and curled up in a chair. Before studying a passage of Scripture, as she'd begun to do at bedtime most nights, she scrolled through caller ID on her cordless phone. Mama had called three times today; she must need an answer about Easter.

Dayna stared at the phone and wrestled with herself. She had so much going on; was she up for an emotionally draining chat with her parents tonight?

She pressed the talk button and dialed Jessica's number instead. Her baby sister picked up on the second ring.

"Well, hello, stranger! Let me guess why you're calling: Mom needs an answer right away about her Easter invitation and you want to know if I'm going before you make your decision?"

Dayna burst into laughter.

"You got it, Miss Motivational Speaker," Dayna said. "So what are we doing?"

Jessica chuckled. "I guess we're going. Keith's coming with me to serve as a buffer. It will be all right for just a weekend. Besides, I haven't been home in eight months; we spent the holidays here in Indianapolis with his family, remember? Are you going to bring your friend, Warren?"

Dayna leaned back in the chair, which reclined. No need to bring today's drama into the conversation; she and Warren were going to work through this.

"I was instructed not to, since his lack of pigmentation might upset the congregation at Daddy's prominent historical African American church," Dayna said.

301

"Stop playing."

"I wish I were. You know Mama. Plus, we're not married, so she'd have to figure out 'appropriate' sleeping arrangements for him."

"If I were you, I'd bring Warren and tell her to deal," Jessica said. "He could stay at the hotel downtown if that's a big issue, but why can't he come to the house of the Lord on Sunday morning, like anybody else? But you decide what's most comfortable."

Dayna raised her eyes to the ceiling. Jessica was right. She was a full-grown woman; why couldn't she bring her beau home? And besides, she and Warren were on the verge of engagement. Mama and Daddy needed to accept this if they wanted her to visit more often.

Dayna grabbed a pillow from the sofa to hug.

"If you're game, I am too. And if Warren can make it, I'll bring him. Have you talked to Shiloh lately?"

"Nah. You know the Second Lady is too busy praying to have a regular conversation with a heathen like me."

They laughed. Dayna knew she and Jessica should be ashamed for the way they teased their middle sister behind her back, but in their minds, Shiloh had somehow forgotten their crazy-making upbringing. She had morphed into a Stepford daughter and wife, all rolled into one.

While her husband Randy sat in the pulpit next to Daddy, waiting for his turn to become senior pastor, she sat next to Mama on Sunday mornings, wearing her hat and practicing the mannerisms of a proper Southern Baptist pastor's wife. Forget that she was barely thirty-five; she carried herself like a woman living in the 1960s. If Randy didn't okay it, she and the children couldn't do it.

Dayna and Jessica's personal disdain for their sister stemmed from different reasons, but it was one of the few things that connected them.

"I saw an article in *O* magazine promoting your speaking engagement at Smith College just before Easter, Miss Lady, so I know you're busy. When will you arrive in Atchity?"

"That was cool, wasn't it?" Jessica, who had just turned thirty, sounded as perky on the phone as she had in the magazine article in which she'd been featured. "I think I'm going to fly in on Good Friday. I have an engagement that week on the West Coast, and Keith may be traveling with me so we can stay over a few days. At least I hope he will."

"Yeah, it was cool seeing your interview," Dayna said. "I'm proud of ya, sis. I'll come in Friday evening after the service, or Saturday morning, depending on whether Warren joins me."

For the first time in a long while, she felt funny about not planning to spend Good Friday in church. Were the morning prayers and Scriptures she'd been meditating on getting to her?

"I hope you bring Warren," Jessica said. "I'd like to get to know him better. And I can't wait to get caught up with you. It's been too long, you know? Our strange family has kept us apart, but we have to do better."

Dayna was surprised. Was baby sister acknowledging that they could have and should have been closer growing up, and now in adulthood?

Jessica was right, though; all three sisters had left home as soon as they could, the best way they knew how. Shiloh's path of marriage and family right after high school had kept her in town, closely connected to the dysfunction, but Dayna and Jessica had gone as far as their skill and talent could take them, neither desiring to ever return long-term.

"We'll see what happens, okay? See you in a few weeks."

They ended the call and Dayna stood up and stretched. Realizing for the first time since getting home that she was hungry, she rummaged through her fridge and decided to make a salad.

Between chopping lettuce and veggies, she texted Warren to let him know she was home, chilling for the night. He promised to call her later, after helping Lily get Michael and Mason squared away with dinner and homework.

Dayna tried to quell the resentment that lately had accompanied his every mention of Lily. Wasn't it her day off? Dayna imagined the four of them sitting down to dinner together, creating the perfect family of Lily's vision.

She felt the urge to call Warren, but knew she was allowing her imagination to run wild. Warren and Lily had worked as a team to care for Michael and Mason long before she entered the picture. If he wanted a relationship with Lily, he wouldn't keep talking marriage with Dayna.

She glanced at her stack of mail while she scarfed down the salad. Soon, she was ready to make The Call.

She dialed her parents' number and began cleaning her dinner dishes while it rang.

Daddy answered. "Hello, my daughter, how are you?"

Dayna rolled her eyes. "Hi, Daddy. I'm fine, and you?"

Kitchen cleaned, she turned off the light and headed toward her bedroom to pick out an outfit for tomorrow while Daddy spent the next ten minutes filling her in on his day, the goings-on at church, and the latest wonderful thing Shiloh and her family had done. She half listened while selecting an ivory sleeveless mock turtleneck and matching slacks, which she would complement with a burnt orange jacket and burnished gold jewelry.

"That's great, Daddy."

Not once did he ask about her day, her health, or her life. Nothing new. Still, each time she called and their one-sided conversation ended with a pass of the phone to Mama without an "I love you" or an inquiry into her concerns, she felt more deflated.

Mama wasted no time addressing her agenda. "Hi, dear, have you made up your mind?"

Dayna couldn't help but laugh. At least Mama wanted her to come home, even if it was for her own motives.

"Yes, Mama, I'll be there for Easter, but I won't arrive until late on Good Friday or early Saturday."

"Aww, so you'll miss the Friday night service? Your daddy and Randy are preaching their traditional joint sermon on the Last Seven Expressions of Christ."

Lord, forgive me, Dayna repented for rolling her eyes heavenward again.

If she heard one more thing about the wonderful Shiloh, Randy, and their four perfect children, she would gag. Dayna had decided that they weren't all that amazing; they were simply obedient to Mama and Daddy's demands, which catapulted them to sainthood in her parents' estimation.

"I'll miss it, but I'm sure I'll have time to see them in full glory on Sunday, Mama."

"You sure will!" Mama said, oblivious to Dayna's sarcasm. "I'm just glad you're coming!"

"Thanks, Mama," Dayna said. "And just to warn you, Warren may be with me. I don't know for sure yet, but I've invited him."

"Well, why would you do that after —"

"After what? After you told me that he wasn't welcome at church?"

"Watch your tone, young lady. I'm still your mother."

Dayna took a deep breath.

"Sorry if I sounded disrespectful, Mama. I hope Warren is welcome, because I won't feel welcome if he isn't. I'm sure he won't mind staying at a hotel if that makes you more comfortable, but he and I are pretty serious, and I think it's important to spend the holiday with him, if he wants to join me. His sons will most likely spend Easter weekend with their grandparents."

"I see."

Mama's disapproving silence lingered in the air between them. Dayna refused to let it wear her down this time. She wasn't going to keep Warren away for reasons that shouldn't be an issue with someone who professed a love for God.

"Anyway, there's something I need to tell you," she said.

Distracting Mama was always the best route to disengage her from an uncomfortable topic, but Dayna hated that this time she would be sharing terrible news about someone who was in part responsible for the strain that existed between them.

"What is it? You're not pregnant, are you?" She whispered the question as if the phone line were tapped.

What if I were? The retort raced to Dayna's lips, but she pursed them before it escaped.

"Mama, just let me talk," Dayna said, ignoring the question. "I need to tell you something sad. Brent and I reconnected a month ago, after he found out that we both were living in Florida."

Mama gasped. "My word! Really?"

She sounded so hopeful. Hadn't she been listening when Dayna mentioned that this involved sad news? Or that she and Warren were serious?

"Is he still married to that . . . that floozy? Or does he want you back?"

Dayna frowned. Who used a word like *floozy* in the twenty-first century?

"I don't know how to say this except to just say it, Mama: Brent has cancer and his doctors say he doesn't have much longer to live. I thought you'd want to know . . . so you could pray for him."

Mama fell silent, and Dayna could imagine just what she was doing: standing in the kitchen with the dainty palm of her hand covering her open mouth.

"Not my Brent!"

The word *my* felt like a jab. Dayna couldn't recall either of her parents using that possessive noun with such warmth in regard to her or her sisters.

"How much longer does he have? How is he doing?"

She should have anticipated the questions, but they made Dayna wish she hadn't said anything.

"He's hanging in there. I'm not sure how much time he has, but his wife Tamara is with him, and he's doing his best to remain optimistic."

Dayna decided not to reveal how often they'd been in touch, or that she was helping him establish a foundation. Armed with that information, Mama would never release her dreams of reconciliation, despite the fact that he was still married to someone else or the reality that Brent was dying. Instead, Dayna steered the conversation back to her upcoming visit.

"I'll let Brent know you're praying for him the next time I talk to him. In the meantime, I'll be in touch when I nail down the specifics of my Easter weekend arrival."

"Oh, yes," Mama said. "And let me know what you decide about Warren. We'll make it work out somehow."

"It will be okay, Mama. Really."

They ended the call with their routine pleasantries and Dayna finally felt free to move into the rest of her evening. Warren had finally texted her that he'd be tied up the rest of the evening with the boys and wished her a good night. She knew they would talk tomorrow and tried not to fret. Had the situation been reversed and she walked in on him with an ex, she would need time to process it all too. Dayna refused to let herself panic.

With Warren unavailable and her thoughts racing too much to do anything productive, she wound up surfing her friends' and colleagues' profiles on Facebook for two hours, and responding to messages on her social network account that had been sent to her weeks earlier.

Bedtime rolled around, and she didn't feel sleepy. Dayna was tempted to dial Warren's cell, but decided against it. She crawled into bed and opened the devotional she had been reading to guide her through the Bible. Tonight's topic was about letting the Lord fight your battles. Dayna read the devotional author's explanations of what that meant, and the accompanying verse, 2 Chronicles 20:17. In the New Living Translation, it read:

But you will not even need to fight. Take your positions; then stand still and watch the LORD's victory. He is with you, O people of Judah and Jerusalem. Do not be afraid or discouraged. Go out against them tomorrow, for the LORD is with you!

Dayna pulled up the verse on her iPad in several other versions, from New King James to *The Message,* to better understand it. She prayed for wisdom to understand how this Old Testament verse could apply to her current situation, and then she uttered the growing list of names for her morning and nightly prayer list. It was long enough now that she had written all of the names down, so she wouldn't forget anyone in the haze of nighttime sleepiness or early morning fogginess.

This verse in particular struck a chord, with all she was facing at work, with her parents, and with Brent, Tamara, and Warren. All very different situations with the need to be worked out by God.

Tomorrow, she'd talk to Warren about what he'd heard in her conversation with Brent, and they'd work through it. She also planned to ask him about the photo of him and April he'd recently posted as his Facebook profile picture. If he hadn't healed from his wife's death, why was he continually hinting at marriage? Dayna wasn't sure what disturbed her more: the photo or the fact that Lily bore such a striking resemblance to April Avery. She wondered for the first time this evening if that's why Warren had kept Lily around for so long. She was determined not to fret, though. 2 Chronicles 20:17 had reassured her it wouldn't be necessary.

FORTY-THREE

A couple days later when the alarm sounded at seven a.m., and for the first Sunday in a long time, Dayna didn't groan.

With all that had been going on in recent weeks, coupled with the promise she had made to Warren and to herself to pray for her parents and for Brent and Tamara, she'd felt a new and fresh yearning to be in God's presence. But Warren was out sailing with the boys again, and she needed something more this morning than a satellite service could provide. Then she thought of Audrey. Maybe she should extend an olive branch and invite her to join her for church.

Dayna couldn't stifle a yawn as she dialed Audrey's number. Her friend heard the last of it and giggled.

"I know how you feel — I stayed up way too late last night for someone who said she was serious about going to church this morning," Audrey said.

"You were planning to go too? Cool — I'll be by to get you at nine-thirty."

They still had a lot of ground to cover before their friendship returned to normal, but this was a good place to start. Calero Community Church held worship service at 9:45 a.m. and was about ten minutes from Audrey's house.

"We haven't been in so long; you think they'll make us sit in sinner's row?" Audrey said, and chuckled at her own joke. "Actually, I was considering attending somewhere other than Calero Community. Chas has been asking me to visit his church, on the north side, and I thought I might surprise him this morning. Want to go with me?"

"Chas who works in my department?" Dayna said.

"Yes, that Chas," Audrey said. "He's not married, is he?"

Dayna doubled over with laughter. "In the two years that I've known him and worked with him, I haven't seen or heard of a wife or significant other, so you should be on safe ground," she said after composing herself. "If you're seriously interested in him though, you'd better ask up front!"

Audrey joined in the laughter. "His church begins worship service at 11 a.m. You game? Or is your heart set on making an appearance at Calero Community?"

Dayna climbed out of bed and padded toward the closet. "It doesn't matter where we go today; I just want to worship in person," she said. "Sounds funny coming from me, huh?"

Audrey grew somber.

"Not funny at all, my friend. You and I must be destined to grow up before we hit the big 4–0, because these past few weeks have been something else for both of us. All I can say is, God has gotten my attention again; I'm just ashamed that it took all of this for me to wake up."

Dayna wondered if she were being taught a lesson too. If so, she needed clearer instruction — it was all so strange. "It doesn't matter how long it took, Audrey," Dayna said. "What matters is that you're open to waking up and to hearing him. I'm trying to get there too. Tell me the attire for Chas's church and I can meet you there or at your place."

Three hours later, she pulled into the parking lot of Haven Church, in northern Calero, and realized she'd never find Audrey's vehicle in this sea of cars. She sent her a text and asked if Audrey wanted to meet near the church entrance.

Seconds later, she looked up to find Audrey standing next to her Lexus, wearing a grin. Dayna stepped out of her car.

"If your father were here, I'm guessing he'd say that God ordained it for us to arrive at the same time and park so close to each other, right?" Audrey laughed and pointed two rows over to where her gray sedan was parked.

Dayna chuckled. "Daddy and Warren would both say that, so I guess that means it's true. You look cute!"

Audrey was wearing a white spaghetti-strapped sundress and matching sandals with a slight heel. The weather was perfect and she looked the part. There was nothing like March in Florida. It rivaled the weather that the rest of the southeast experienced in June.

"Why'd you decide to wear white today?" Dayna couldn't help but tease her friend, now that they had cleared the air between them. She knew Audrey was still hurting, but talking about it, even in a lighthearted manner, seemed to be helpful.

Audrey eyes narrowed. "Very funny. I'm not a member of the *Sister Act* cast by any means, but I can be purified."

"Well, go on with your bad self," said Dayna. They shared a laugh, something

Dayna was grateful for after their recent strain.

"Any word on a court date yet? How do you like the attorney Spencer recommended?"

"He's expensive, but good. The court date is a few weeks away. I'm praying for mercy."

Dayna nodded. "Praying with you."

Audrey smiled at Dayna. "Thank you."

When Dayna raised an eyebrow, as if questioning what for, Audrey had a ready answer. "For being there for me. And forgiving me, even though I was in the wrong."

Dayna reached for Audrey's hand and squeezed it. "Our drama hasn't been the same, but I'm not perfect either, Audrey," she said. "You pray for me today, and I'll pray for you, and we'll both be straight. Deal?"

"Deal," Audrey said. "And with Chas being here, we can be certain he'll be praying for us both."

FORTY-FOUR

Dayna and Audrey strolled to their cars after Sunday morning service and agreed: Chas's pastor was going to need a medicated rubdown when he got home.

"How does that man jump five feet in the air when he's preaching and not break a bone?" Audrey asked, and shook her head. "I know he has to visit a chiropractor or orthopedic doctor at least once or twice a month."

Dayna shrugged.

"God's grace is something else," she said. "I asked Chas about it before he disappeared into an after-service meeting for church leaders. He said when Reverend Miller is flowing in the Spirit, he's all over the place. He was certainly getting his Michael Jordan on today!"

Audrey shook her head. "For a grown woman, you are so corny."

"Whatever." Dayna laughed.

Both grew quiet and retreated to their private thoughts on the rest of the brief walk to their cars. When Dayna paused to find her keys, Audrey stopped alongside her.

"What are you doing the rest of today — spending it with Warren?"

Dayna leaned on her car and peered at Audrey. Without asking why, she knew what had led Audrey to pose the question: Sunday afternoons must have been reserved for her married lover, after he attended church and enjoyed a meal with his family. Now she was at loose ends.

Dayna couldn't quite muster the sympathy she knew Audrey must want and need, yet her heart went out to her friend. She didn't want her to be sad and lonely.

"I may see Warren later, but he's on the boat today for some father-son time with the boys. I'm treating Duchess to lunch — you remember meeting her, right? She's my college friend Vanora's aunt. Want to join us?"

Audrey shook her head. "Nah, I'll pass. I may go to the mall or rent a movie or maybe just spend the afternoon napping. Tell Duchess I said hello, though. She is a sweet lady, and I enjoy seeing her when you bring her around."

"You sure you don't want to come with

me and tell her yourself?"

Audrey shook her head. "You go on and spend that special time with her. She enjoys your company. I'll catch up with you later. Did you decide what you're going to do about Brent?"

Dayna sighed. Before the service, she had filled Audrey in on her hasty visit to the hospital in the Cocoa Beach area and about Brent's behavior toward her and Tamara.

"I know I need to move as fast as I can for two reasons — to get the Injured Collegiate Athlete Fund launched, as Brent wants it to happen before he's too sick to help oversee everything, and to remove myself from his and Tamara's lives. They need some time, just the two of them, to grieve and help each other through this. I've become the third wheel, and it's uncomfortable."

"Warren isn't too pleased either, is he?"

"No, he isn't," Dayna said. She hadn't mentioned that Warren had also come to the hospital or the strain that Brent's comments, and her response to them, had caused between them.

"He can't bring himself to admit that he's jealous of a dying man, but he is. I think he feels like he's in competition with Brent for my attention, which is the farthest thing from the truth."

"Are you sure?"

Audrey's skepticism surprised Dayna. "What are you trying to say?"

Audrey shrugged. "I don't know. You do seem vested in Brent these days. And that means there's less time for Warren. And Warren's got it bad for you."

"He knows I love him."

Audrey looked like she wanted to say more, but didn't.

"At least you're a step closer to having the family we both want — you've got a man who cares and wants to be with you," she finally said. "That's half the battle. I'm all about the name of Jesus now, but you know I grew up as one of the few black Jews in America — according to Jewish tradition my destiny in life is to be a wife and mother. Where did I go wrong?"

Dayna wanted to give her friend a hug, but she knew that would make Audrey feel pitied.

"I say good riddance to Raymond and to your old flame Oscar," Dayna said. "Oscar may have been a jerk, but there are other good guys out there, Audrey. And not all of them ditch their fiancée the week of the wedding."

"You're right," Audrey said. "I must have

a knack for choosing duds, huh? Oscar should be contacting me to apologize for calling it quits three days before our ceremony. It has been four years and I haven't heard a peep from him. Probably somewhere convincing another woman how wonderful he is."

Dayna sighed and stared ahead. "Yeah, he probably is. Just let it go."

The women finally settled into their cars and parted ways. Before she drove off, Dayna sent a text to Warren, knowing she probably wouldn't get a reply since he was out sailing.

Hey, babe. Thinking of you. Attended Chas Carter's church with Audrey today and service was awesome.
Tell Michael and Mason I said hi. Headed to Duchess's place.
Hope to see you later today, as planned.
xoxo

Then Dayna called Duchess to let her special friend know she was on the way. By the time she arrived, Duchess should be ready to eat and share a few stories about her "good church folk."

"Hi, Duchess — almost there!" she said into the answering machine Duchess still insisted on using because it worked well and there was no danger of getting cancer from holding a phone too close to one's ear "tryin' to hear too much."

Dayna called Vanora next and wound up leaving her a message too. "Hey, V, just touching base to say hi. I'm heading over to your aunt's house for a Sunday afternoon visit. Duchess keeps insisting that you're overdue for a visit. Call me when you get a chance, so we can catch up and plan your trip to town."

Dayna placed the cell phone in its holder on her dashboard and cranked up the volume on her radio. Kirk Franklin's latest filled the air, and she bobbed her head to the beat while the lyrics reminded her that fear and faith can't occupy the same space. When would she finally get this, especially when it came to matters of the heart?

Wait until she told Duchess about Brent's surprise visit last month and all that had transpired. Dayna couldn't wait to hear Duchess's perspective. Her spunky, seventy-five-year-old wisdom always rang true, even when it was hard to hear. Dayna wasn't sure what Duchess would say about the responsibilities she had allowed herself to be sucked into in recent weeks, but she was certain she would leave Duchess's presence with a better understanding of what to do going forward and whether that path was pleasing to God. It was actually refreshing to care again.

FORTY-FIVE

Duchess had been hard-headed again.

"Didn't I make it clear when I called yesterday that I was treating you to lunch?" Dayna tried to remain respectful but couldn't hide her annoyance.

The elderly woman, whose beauty defied her age, brushed off Dayna's comments with her customary cackle. "Come on in here, child, and take off your shoes. The dumplings and cornbread will be ready in fifteen minutes. No need for you to go to all of that trouble when my cooking is better than any Calero restaurant you would have taken me to."

She left Dayna standing on the porch and hustled back to the kitchen to check a pot on the stove.

Dayna shook her head in disbelief before relenting and opening the screened door that led to Duchess's cozy living room, which equaled the size of Dayna's master bedroom walk-in closet. The modest rancher was just half an hour away from Dayna's magazine-cover beautiful neighborhood of manicured lawns and mini-mansions, but driving from one section of Calero to the other was like entering a new state. Even so, walking into Duchess's home was like wrapping oneself in a cozy, comfortable blanket.

"It wasn't about the caliber of the food, Duchess," Dayna said. "It was about giving you a break and allowing me to do something nice for you. That's a good thing every once in a while, you know?"

Duchess shuffled into the room in her stockinged feet and bedroom slippers and opened her arms wide for a hug. Dayna bent low so the tiny woman could wrap her thin brown arms around her neck.

"You do something nice for me every time you come and see me, young lady. You could be off on that boat with that handsome man you're dating or spending time with friends your age. When Vanora told me you were moving to the area almost four years ago, I knew I'd meet you, but I didn't know I'd get a chance to love on you."

She cackled again before heading back to the kitchen, which Dayna had decided was the room in the house where Duchess must feel most at home.

Dayna trailed behind her. "You're so sweet, Duchess. I'm glad we've gotten to know each other too. I've loved Vanora since we met at freshman orientation at Alabama U. Having her great-aunt in my life is an extra blessing. But Ms. Mary 'Duchess' Miller was not supposed to be cooking me a meal today. Did you go to church this morning?"

Duchess pulled a pound cake from the oven with two elbow-length pot holders and placed the Bundt pan on top of another pot holder waiting on the kitchen counter. She stood to her full five feet and put her hands on her slender hips.

"You know I did, and that choir sure did sing. I wish you'd visit me on a third Sunday, when the young adults are up there rocking the place. Whenever you come, you always happen to hear the seasoned citizens dragging through their old tunes."

"Duchess!"

"What?" She peered at Dayna with child-like innocence over the rims of her large, round eyeglasses.

If Duchess were one of her own aunts or her grandmother, Dayna would have reminded her that she fit into the "seasoned citizen" category herself. But as much as

Duchess loved her like family, Dayna decided she best not go there. If this little lady believed she was more fly than her peers, so be it.

By the time the two women sat down to eat a few minutes later, they had already traded highlights from the Sunday sermons they'd heard, and Dayna had begun giving Duchess blow-by-blow details of the hospital fundraiser she attended with Warren last month. Duchess loved hearing about Dayna's job and all of the excitement and stress that came with it.

"Now, what did you wear?"

"A stunning red dress, if I say so myself," Dayna said, and laughed. "You would have been proud. Warren was quite happy to be my escort."

Duchess smiled and finished chewing a bite of food.

"Good girl. You keep that up after you marry him, you hear? Don't start letting yourself go just because you get the ring."

Dayna shook her head. "Why is it that every time Warren comes up in a conversation you wind up talking about marriage and a ring?"

"Your eggs are getting old, girl. You better stop playing and move on if that man isn't thinking about giving you a ring. When will you be forty?"

Dayna sighed and took a sip of sweet tea. Usually she drank it unsweetened, but when Duchess took the time to make it special for her, she made sure to oblige.

"In two years, but I'm sure my eggs are fine." She decided not to get into a discussion about how she didn't feel giving birth was necessary for her to become a mom.

Duchess raised an eyebrow and took a bite of cornbread. "So what did Mister Warren have to say when everyone else saw you in that dress?"

Dayna was glad the conversation was shifting; this would be a good time to get Duchess's feedback on everything else that had transpired since that foundation ball.

"Actually, he wasn't too happy with the person who saw me in the dress before he did. My ex-husband showed up at my house that night, just before the ball."

Duchess stopped mid-chew. "What you say?"

Dayna sat back in the chair and folded her arms. When Duchess lapsed into slang, Dayna knew she had her rapt attention.

"Yep. I was stunned too. I hadn't talked to Brent since we left that Alabama courthouse, after the judge declared us divorced. I couldn't believe it. But there he was, in flesh and blood, on my doorstep, bearing a bouquet of roses and an apology."

Duchess shook her head. "You never know what the wind will blow your way, baby; you've just got to be prepared to dance to the music God provides."

Dayna let that wisdom marinate.

"Hmph, I never thought about it like that; that's deep."

Duchess shrugged. "It's the truth, honey. Live long enough and you'll find out just how much. When my first husband left, he came back a year and a half later, but it was much later than he expected. Husband number two was on board, and *he* was prepared to honor the vows he made before God. Those clichés always have some truth to them — you don't miss your water 'til your well run dry! Ha!"

As she often did when she spent time with Duchess, Dayna felt like she was talking to a wiser, more seasoned version of Vanora.

Duchess sat back and folded her arms. With her salt-and-pepper hair pulled back into a bun and her flawless caramel complexion, she could pass for the sister of actress Diahann Carroll. "You mean he lives less than an hour away? Tell me again, how long have you two been divorced?"

"Seven years. And he married his current

wife six months after our divorce."

"My Lawd," Duchess said. "Sounds to me like he's playing with fire. Aren't you two about the same age? He's at that midlife crisis stage where men begin to lose their minds. Don't let him pull you into his fool-ishness."

She pushed her chair away from the table and returned with two dessert plates and the pound cake, which was now cool enough to slice. The aroma tempted Dayna, but she tried not to let it distract her.

"You could be right," she said, and waited for Duchess to settle into her seat again. "It turns out that Brent is dying of cancer. He tracked me down and rang my doorbell that night to ask my forgiveness for cheating on me and divorcing me."

"Oh, my," Duchess said. "Well, bless him."

"There's more."

Duchess peered over her eyeglasses and waited.

"I went to dinner with him and his wife, Tamara — who is the woman he cheated with — and I told him that while it had taken a while, all was forgiven. I didn't mention my years in therapy or the thousands it cost me, but I told him I no longer hold a grudge and haven't for a long time. Well, it should have ended there, but then he kept talking and landed on the topic of a long-held dream to establish a scholarship fund for college athletes who suffer injuries and lose their way. His goal is to hook them up with mentors and with guidance that can help them thrive in school and build a solid career, even if their sports dream has faded."

Duchess nodded. "Sounds like he has a big heart. But what does this have to do with you?"

"Well, when I described to him what I do on staff at Chesdin Medical, as one of the hospital's executives, he got the great idea that I need to be on his planning team, to help establish his foundation before he passes away."

Dayna filled her in on all that had happened with his visits to Calero, with his wife's trepidation, and most recently, with Brent summoning her to his hospital bedside.

"Not only that, he had the nerve to tell me that he loves Tamara but he still loves me too."

"I believe it." Duchess shook her head.

Dayna frowned. "Which part — that he had the nerve to say that, or that he actually loves us both?"

"I believe that he had the nerve to say it,

and that he wants to have his cake and eat it too."

With that, Duchess sliced the pound cake and slid a piece of the still-warm dessert in front of Dayna, who smirked.

"Very funny, Duchess," she said, and picked up her fork to dig in. She took a bite of the melt-in-your-mouth dessert and sighed. "Oh, my goodness. Will you please move in with me and cook like this for me all the time?" She pleaded verbally and with her eyes.

Duchess grinned. "How about I just deliver the meals? You can keep that ritzy part of town for you and those other corporate-type folk. I been here for nearly forty years, and I'm staying in this place until the Lord says otherwise. Now, back to what we were discussing. What are you going to do about this old flame, your former husband . . . what's his name?"

"Brent. Brent Davidson. He was a football star at our alma mater until a serious injury sidelined him. He could have gone pro. Thankfully he was smart too, so he turned his focus to his engineering degree and now he works for NASA.

"Seriously, though, how should I handle this going forward?" Dayna continued. "I mean, I'm committed to helping him get the foundation established, and I have several friends from work helping too, but I'm not sure how fast we can move this along. We already meet weekly, but it's going to require more frequent meetings, and I don't think Brent will be up to traveling.

"Then there's the issue of me traveling to his place to work on the project, even though his wife resents it. And here's the kicker: he told me when I visited him at the hospital that he wants me to lead the foundation board instead of Tamara."

"We're going to have to pray about this one, baby." Duchess shook her head and clasped her palms. "There's no way you can do that to his wife. I know what she did years ago was wrong, but two wrongs don't make a right. This might be his project, but he can't step on people like that, especially the person he's married to. If you can't convince him to give up that idea, you may just have to leave this alone."

That thought startled Dayna. She hadn't considered that completely stepping back from the project was an option. What if she handed the reins to her hospital colleague Carmen and let her work directly with Tamara? That would take Dayna out of the fray and maybe lessen the tension she was feeling between herself, Tamara, and Brent.

"Duchess, you might just be on to something."

She'd call Carmen first thing in the morning to ask if she'd be willing to play a larger role in launching the foundation.

"But what do I do if Brent calls me to come visit him again? Drop everything and get to his bedside?"

"Let me pray about that too," Duchess said. "My first thought is yes, go. Because you don't know why he's calling you and what he needs to tell you to give him peace as he prepares to make this transition. You need to make yourself available to him as much as you feel comfortable, without disrespecting his wife or yourself; that's what forgiving someone is about. But at the same time, you can't let his needs interfere with your job or with your relationship with Warren. Brent is no longer your husband. So while you definitely want to be supportive and caring, you must remember, and possibly remind him, that he made choices that don't give him permission to dictate your comings and goings."

Dayna's head was spinning just thinking about it all. Duchess was right; why had she felt guilty for reaching a similar conclusion on her own? She was so glad she had opened up to her friend. But as usual, that gratitude was tinged with sadness over the fact that she couldn't have talks like this with Mama. In the short time she had known Duchess, this kind lady knew her heart and her life circumstances more intimately than Mama ever would.

Dayna scooted her chair back from the table and gathered the dishes. She carried them to the sink so she could begin rinsing them. "How is Warren handling all of this?"

Dayna shrugged and peered into the backyard through the small window over the sink.

"He doesn't say much. I keep him informed about where I'm going and what I'm doing with regard to Brent, but he's pretty tight-lipped about it."

"That's not a good sign. Be careful."

"What do you mean?"

"It sounds like he may resent all of the attention you're giving Brent, but he isn't going to say anything because Brent is dying. Just be mindful to stay on top of things, and don't neglect Warren if you can help it. He's a good man and he loves you. I can tell from the few times I've met him. Don't let him get away."

Dayna's thoughts turned to the concern she'd a few days ago when Lily was at his house on her day off, helping with the boys, and again today when he'd announced he was going sailing and didn't invite Dayna to join him. Duchess was right; she needed to be more attentive and watchful.

Until recently, Brent had been a tucked-away part of her past. Warren represented her future, and it was one she was looking forward to cultivating.

FORTY-SIX

The warm sand slid through Tamara's toes with an ease that intrigued her. Over and over again, she dipped her bare foot in the warm, grainy sand, and as she pulled it back to the surface, tiny granules slid in between and over her toes like water. The exercise was hypnotizing in its simplicity, and with all of the things going on in her life right now, it was also soothing.

Mom had convinced her to leave the house for just an hour to relax and get her mind off Brent, who was still in the hospital. When Mom had stopped by after church today and found Tamara sitting in a pile of laundry, looking too weary to sort or fold it, she had pushed her out the door.

Tamara kept a beach-ready bag in the trunk of her car, so when she set off from the house, she knew exactly where she'd go. Living in Cocoa Beach had its advantages.

In ten minutes, she had reached her destination.

She sat here now, looking past young and old couples, kids creating sand castles, and women with perfect and imperfect bodies, to take in the beauty of the ocean. The waves and the wind soothed her, slowing her heart to a steady, comforting beat.

Tamara adjusted her shades and pulled her oversized, floppy yellow sunhat lower on her head. Mom would have a fit if she knew she had come to the beach midday when the sun was its hottest and in the best position to tan one's skin. Never mind that Tamara had slathered herself with sunblock, and never mind her honey complexion; if she wanted to keep it that way, Mom, like so many other sisters of color, was convinced that the sun was to be avoided at all times.

Today, Tamara didn't care. Her heart was hurting and she needed to be quiet and feel the ocean breeze speaking to her.

Mrs. Chestnut had once told her if she listened closely, she could hear God speaking in the wind. Tamara thought her bank customer and friend was being eccentric that day, but after Mrs. Chestnut made a surprise visit a week ago to drop off the prayer book she had promised, Tamara believed her.

The book turned out to be a devotional. However, once Tamara began reading the entries, she understood why Mrs. Chestnut referenced prayer. Reading it made Tamara want to deepen her communication with God, curl up in his lap, and give him her problems so she could relax.

Thinking about the book led her to pull *Experiencing God* from her beach bag. She flipped it open to a random passage, since this wasn't her formal prayer and meditation time. Whenever she did this, her eyes landed on a page or passage that made her feel as if God had timed that specific message for that particular moment of need, doubt, or questioning.

Today was no different. She opened the devotional and began reading a paragraph on page 106 that explained how God wants his children to adjust their lives to his will, not the other way around. Did this mean God wanted her to cease her secret prayer that Brent be miraculously healed? Did it mean that he wanted her to live an empty existence once her husband was gone? Was that part of his will? Was it punishment for starting a relationship with Brent when she knew he was married, and she was befriending his wife?

Tamara wept, but she kept reading.

The passage indicated that God's ways are so much better than man's ways — proof to Tamara that if she'd allow herself to fully trust God with this painful and stressful situation, he'd somehow work it out for her good and Brent's as well.

I don't know how to do that, Lord. Show me! Help me! She looked toward the sky and uttered the words aloud just as a strong breeze swept past her. Was the wind carrying her words to her Maker? How she hoped so.

Tamara sat upright for a while, staring at the clouds, wishing a skywriter would fly by in one of those small turbo-engine planes and scrawl God's answers to her.

Knowing that was wishful thinking, she spoke to the Lord again. *Show me your will, in your way, Father. I thought I had forgiven myself for my sins from the past, but maybe I'm still feeling guilty, maybe I'm still worried that Brent's impending death and my infertility are your judgment for my wrong choices. Just so you know, Lord, I am more than sorry. And to make things even worse, now I'm feeling rejected by the man I've loved all these years. What do you want me to do?*

She left her chair and strolled along the beach, near the edge of the ocean where the water occasionally covered her ankles. She was glad her shades somewhat hid the tears streaming down her face as she walked.

She didn't have any answers, but she knew what God wanted her to do in regard to Brent: keep caring for him and encouraging him, even when he hurt her. Keep loving him, even when she sat at his bedside and he called for Dayna.

She might not have known just what she was getting into when she said "for better or worse" on her wedding day, but all these years later, after developing a relationship with God, she knew it meant she had to love her husband, despite his proving her long-held suspicions to be true: after the lust had faded, she registered second place in Brent's lineup of choices. With his life growing dim, he didn't seem to mind letting her know.

FORTY-SEVEN

Seconds after pulling out of Duchess's driveway, Dayna tried Warren's cell to see if he was in close enough range to pick up on the sailboat. The call rolled right into voicemail, and she figured he and the boys were still pretty far out. It was four o'clock, though. They'd be heading back soon.

She decided to stop by the mall and then go to the marina where he kept the boat docked so she could meet him and the twins upon their arrival. He'd be pleasantly surprised, and she would offer to treat all three of them to dinner. Duchess was right; she couldn't get so wrapped up in the man from her past that she failed to nurture the one who held first place in her heart now.

The mall closest to the marina happened to be her favorite shopping spot. It was the perfect day to stroll through its open, outdoor design and flit between shops, and she drove there in anticipation of finding a few bargains.

An hour later, she returned to the boat dock, satisfied with her purchases and eager to share them with Warren. He wouldn't care what had been on sale and what hadn't; he merely liked seeing her wear the new items and enjoy them.

She stood on the pier with her hand shielding her forehead from the sun and watched several boats dock. When Warren's boat, *Water Dancer,* came into view, she grew excited. It finally drew close, and Dayna began waving widely, almost making an arc with her hand and arm.

A grin spread across her face as she saw the boys working in unison with Warren to adjust the masts and slow the boat's speed. Warren loved his time with his boys; she imagined they'd spent the day trading stories and sharing advice in a way that their normal, electronics-filled routine wouldn't allow.

Suddenly though, her heart sank. Before Michael disembarked from the boat, he stretched out his hand to pull someone up behind him. The minute she saw the dainty fingers grasp his, Dayna knew Lily had somehow managed to get invited to the boys-only party.

When she emerged, Lily gave Michael a

big hug, which he returned, and they left the boat hand in hand. Her grin was as wide as Dayna's had been before seeing her nemesis.

Lily's eyes widened in surprise as she and Michael approached, but Dayna knew Lily had to have seen her from afar, if she had been on the boat's stern as they approached land. Why play innocent now? And where was Warren?

Interesting that he hadn't told her that he had invited a guest along — a special guest, her body language seemed to indicate.

Warren surfaced a few minutes later, and he too seemed wonderstruck.

"Hey, babe," he said, and embraced her. "What a nice surprise!"

He didn't seem nervous or awkward, although Dayna felt both for some reason. It was an unsettling feeling she hadn't experienced before in this relationship. Was something shifting? She lingered in Warren's arms and looked over his shoulder at Lily, who was eyeing them intently.

Dayna felt like going sister-girl on the woman and asking her, "You got something to say? What you looking at?" Instead, she focused on Warren. "How were the waves and wind today? Easy sailing or rough?"

"Smooth sailing," Warren said. "It was an

absolutely beautiful day to be on the water. I'm so glad I decided to follow through."

He wrapped his arm around her waist and turned to Lily and the boys.

"Ready to go? Help me tether the boat, boys, and we can be on our way."

Dayna and Lily were left alone while the guys secured *Water Dancer.* They sized each other up without speaking. Lily finally ran her fingers through her shoulder-length blond hair and sighed.

"Warren was right. It was a magical day to be on the ocean. You missed a treat, Dayna."

Dayna counted to ten under her breath and decided not to respond. She surveyed Lily's flawless skin and the lemon-yellow sundress that fit Lily's size-two frame as if it had been tailor-made for her. Her white sandals and coral toenails, which matched the color and tone of her makeup, completed the look.

Dayna felt like a gangly Amazon as she towered over this petite woman. Wasn't anyone's fault but her own that she had left her man open to be pursued by his biggest crush. Dayna didn't blame Lily for trying; Warren was worth it.

But girlfriend better watch out: Dayna wasn't planning to walk away just like that.

"I'm glad you enjoyed your time with my favorite guys," Dayna finally responded. "We'll make sure to invite you again sometime."

The smile Lily plastered on her face didn't reach her eyes. "Warren has already welcomed me back anytime I want. I'm definitely planning to take him up on the offer."

Dayna made a mental note to self: *Ride or die the next time* Water Dancer *hits the water.*

Dayna smiled at Lily and chose not to respond.

Please, Lord, let Warren hurry up.

Time seemed to stand still. The tension between Dayna and Lily had always hovered beneath the surface, but in recent months, it was clear that the more serious Warren grew about Dayna, the more overt Lily grew about expressing her affection for and interest in him.

Dayna had never been the type to go to battle over a guy, but this was different. She and Warren were talking marriage, planning a future together. Even though Lily had been in his life long before Dayna, Lily had no right to try and come between them. If Warren had wanted to build a future with Lily, that would have happened before he showed interest in Dayna.

This time she would follow the guidelines in Nehemiah 4:14 and fight for the family she had already begun treating as if it were hers. She looked toward the pier and was relieved to see Warren strolling in her direction with the boys trotting behind him wrestling with each other.

When he reached the two ladies, who had squared off as if preparing for a boxing match, he looked from one to the other with a curious smile.

"You two okay?"

For a second, Dayna wanted to kick him. He knew how she felt about Lily's constant flirting with him; how dare he take that woman sailing and not even bother to let her know.

She smiled though, hoping the frustration spilling from her eyes wasn't obvious to Lily.

"What are we doing for dinner, Dad?" Michael asked. "We're starving."

"Yeah, and it takes you too long to cook!" Mason chimed in. The boys stood shoulder-to-shoulder in front of him, forming an alliance. They were nearly eye level to Warren and in a few months, might zoom past him.

Warren smirked. "You two always say it takes me too long to cook when you've already decided where we're eating. What's on the menu?"

"It's a pasta night!" Michael said, and grinned.

Warren gave him a playful shove. "Go get in the car, knuckleheads. I'm coming."

The boys pumped their fists in the air and dashed toward Warren's SUV. Mason paused and looked at Dayna. "You coming to Mama Cucina's with us, Dayna?"

She folded her arms and looked at Warren. The real question was whether Lily was coming. Interesting that Mason hadn't asked her.

"Sure, I'll join you," she said. They didn't need to know she was still stuffed from the meal and dessert Duchess had prepared.

Warren nodded. "Great. Lily's coming too, right?"

Lily peered at the two of them, then tucked her hands behind her back. "Actually, Warren, if you don't mind, I'd like to go on home. I'm a little tired from being on the water all day. I think I'll have something at home and go to bed early. If you'll swing by your place so I can get my car, I'll just do that, okay?"

Were her eyes playing tricks on her, or did Warren look relieved? Dayna was getting madder by the minute.

"That will work," Warren told Lily before turning his attention to Dayna. "Want to

350

just meet us there, babe?"

Dayna shook her head. "No, I'll follow you home, and when we get to your place, I'll park my car and hop in with you, okay?"

Warren smiled. "Sounds like a plan; don't know why I didn't think of that."

Dayna, Lily, and Warren left the pier together and she reached her car first. She sat behind the driver's seat and watched from the rearview mirror as Lily and Warren walked side by side to his SUV.

There was appropriate space between them, and nothing that hinted of impropriety. Still, Dayna knew she was in for the fight of her life. Lily had somehow sniffed out Warren's discontent over Dayna's lack of time lately — or maybe he'd even complained to her about it — and she was doing her best to distract him and reel him in.

Dayna sighed. She didn't know if she was up for a fight, and yet she couldn't just hand her future to another woman. Not this time.

FORTY-EIGHT

The twenty-minute drive to Warren's house from the pier felt like two hours to Dayna as she followed his car and watched him laugh and chat with Lily throughout the ride.

She trusted Warren, yet it was all she could do to keep from pulling her car alongside his and honking her horn to distract them at each stop sign and traffic light. When Warren turned into his driveway, she exhaled and parked on the street, behind Lily's white sedan. The two of them sat in his SUV chatting, and Dayna watched as Lily leaned over and gave him a light hug.

Dayna was surprised at her level of worry. Warren and Lily had been friends for years, and Lily was like a member of the family. Why all of this angst now? Even as she questioned herself, though, she knew the answer: the stakes were higher.

Lily saw Warren about to get away, but

little did she know Dayna was facing the same concerns because of his frustration with Brent's reappearance.

While Dayna waited for Lily to emerge from Brent's SUV, she tried to recall the last time she and Warren had gone to salsa lessons or to a movie. They still met at the gym and had dinner together a few nights a week, but she couldn't remember their last authentic date night. She needed to get back in the game.

Warren walked Lily to her car and waved good-bye before walking over to Dayna's. She lowered her driver's-side window and he leaned his elbows against it before taking a finger and tracing her cheek.

"What are you doing?" Dayna asked.

"Wiping off the green stuff," he said.

"Huh?"

He chuckled. "You're cute when you're jealous, you know. But the green-eyed monster conceals your real beauty."

If she hadn't been embarrassed she would have protested.

"I know you better than you think I do, lady." He leaned in and kissed her, then opened her door. "Come on. Roll up your window so we can go. 'Frick' and 'Frack' in the backseat are dying of hunger, so they say."

Dayna closed the window, locked the door, and walked hand in hand with Warren to his SUV. She still had questions — chief among them was why Lily had been on the boat. But that could wait until later. For now, she was glad to be in his presence.

FORTY-NINE

"What do you mean a trip to Alabama is out of the question?" Dayna was floored by Warren's flip-flop on her invitation.

"I gave it some thought. With your parents not really wanting me there, it would be a strained and stressful weekend, and I'd rather spend it here with the boys than deal with that."

Warren squared his jaw, the sign that his mind was made up. Disappointment sapped what little appetite she had left, and she slid the only thing she had ordered tonight, the tiramisu, toward him.

"You aren't going to finish it?"

Dayna shook her head and looked away in hopes that he didn't see the tears forming. What did this about-face mean?

"Aren't the boys spending Easter weekend with their mom's parents, as usual?" Dayna asked, after pulling herself together. "They are welcome to join us in Alabama, of course, but the reason I'd only mentioned it to you, and not to them, was because you told me that's the usual routine."

Warren swallowed a gulp of soda. "They usually do, but it's up in the air this year. Their grandmother is having cataract surgery the week before Easter, so we're deciding whether the boys should still go or stay with me."

"Well, you know as far as I'm concerned, they are welcome. Mama will have an issue either way, so we'll roll in whatever way is best for us."

Warren sat back in his chair and smiled at her.

"What, babe?"

"Why are you trying so hard?" he asked.

"Excuse me?"

"You just don't seem like yourself. You're almost antsy. What's going on?"

Dayna left her seat to sit next to Warren in his booth. The boys were at a table a few feet away, and they scrunched up their faces.

"No PDAs!" Michael hissed.

"Whatever!" Dayna called back to him. Warren looked confused.

"That's 'public display of affection,' babe," she told him and laughed.

Warren shook his head. "I can't keep up with those two. Thanks for translating. And for coming over here to snuggle with me." He kissed her cheek.

Dayna smiled. "Look, Warren, I know I've been spending a lot of time setting up Brent's foundation, and that's an issue. I'm feeling a distance between us, and I guess I just need to know that everything is all right with us. I see how Lily looks at you. I'm not blind. Or stupid."

"I was right about the jealousy, huh?"

"Guess you were. So what?"

Warren grabbed her hands under the table and leaned in toward her.

"It's cute to see you want to fight for me, babe, but where I want to be is with you. I admit I'm a little frustrated by all the time Brent is taking. I mean, Tamara's his wife, not you. On Friday he as much as admitted that he's not over you. You didn't tell him you loved him back, but you didn't deny it either."

Finally, they were getting somewhere. "Warren, I'm sorry that what you heard Brent say to me hurt you. I didn't respond to Brent because I didn't want to hurt him. He was in a precarious place, and I was trying to say as little as possible not to push him over the edge. I hope you know that if I had any feelings for him, I first of all would let you know, and then I'd get as far away from him as possible. I'm not trying to get caught in his web."

Warren's expression didn't reveal what he was thinking.

"I see the way he looks at you," he told Dayna, "and you know what? The same way you looked at Lily today is how Tamara stares at you."

Dayna's eyes widened. This was getting to be too much. "Just so you know, I'm planning to ask Carmen to take over the forming of the foundation so I can step back. I think that's best all the way around."

Dayna was surprised by the relief that washed over Warren's face. He was more troubled by this whole thing than he was letting on. True to form, though, he hadn't said a word.

She took this opportunity to steer the conversation to an issue that concerned her. "So how did Ms. Lily wind up on the boat?" She took a sip of Warren's soda while she waited for his reply.

He shrugged. "She came by to say hello to the boys and make sure they had finished their science projects, and we were heading out. She said her day was free, so I figured I might as well ask if she wanted to come along. It was no big deal."

"Uh huh," Dayna said. *Trust me. It was a*

big deal to Lily.

Dayna kept that opinion to herself. "Well, I'm glad it was a beautiful weekend for sailing, and I'm glad you all had a good time, but when I see Lily with your family in a setting like that, I see her trying to replace April."

She looked at Warren to gauge his reaction, but so far there was none. "Speaking of April . . . I know you'll always love her, Warren, but I was wondering . . . when did you decide to post a picture of you two on Facebook? What does that mean for us?"

"Oh, baby, I'm sorry." He leaned toward her and stroked her face. "I'm on Facebook so rarely that I'd forgotten I did that. I posted the last picture April and I took together on the date of our wedding anniversary. I meant to take it down the next day, but as you know, life gets in the way. April will always have a place in my heart and in my life through these boys we have together, but my loving her doesn't mean I love you any less."

Dayna sighed inwardly, and she asked God to show Warren, when he was ready, how his ability to tuck away his feelings for April in a special, sacred place was not unlike her own as she dealt with Brent.

"I'm so glad we talked this over," she said

instead. "Let's make it a habit to keep this up, okay? It makes a difference."

Warren extended his hand and they shook on it. "Deal," he said.

Dayna grinned and switched subjects again. "Let me know what you decide about going home with me for Easter. I really want you there — you and the boys, if that's how it turns out. Mama and Daddy need to understand that I love you — and your boys."

"No, they don't," Warren countered.

Dayna raised an eyebrow. "Say that again?"

"That's what my mom and dad told me after they met you for the first time: No one needs to understand and appreciate our relationship but the two of us. If others care enough to take the effort to do so or want to be supportive, bless them. But Dayna, you and I are the ones directing this ship. We're the only two that matter, outside of God. My boys respect and care for you, and that's important, along with the need for us to respect and care for each other. The rest is just extra, babe. We can be polite and cordial and know that after a visit of any sort, home is in each other's arms."

If they hadn't been in a public place and if Michael and Mason weren't sitting across the room already rolling their eyes at the two of them, Dayna might have planted a big kiss on Warren's lips. Instead, she rested her head on his shoulder and squeezed his hand.

Subtle yet profound insights like Warren's declaration made her love him all the more. He was right; standing together, they could handle her parents, Lily, and any other obstacles that came their way. She had her armor on, and she was ready.

FIFTY

Helping Carmen take over the establishment and launching of Brent's foundation was the first priority on Dayna's to-do list this morning.

Rather than calling or emailing, she got off on the fourth floor instead of the sixth. But Carmen's secretary greeted her with bad news.

"She's at home today, fighting the flu. I'm not sure she'll be in the office at all this week," Elena said. "Can I help you in some way?"

Dayna's heart sank. This wasn't happening.

"Dayna?"

She remembered where she was and pulled herself back to the present. "Sorry, Elena. No, you're fine. I'll wait to hear from Carmen. If you talk to her this week, please tell her to get well soon and to let me know if there's anything I can do here at the office to help her out."

Dayna was glad she had the elevator to herself. She laid her head against its rear wall and wrestled with what she should do next: find someone on Carmen's staff to help with the process? Contact the Calero Community Foundation to see if they could offer Brent more hands-on guidance as he transitioned into a formal partnership with the organization?

She doubted Brent would go for that before the contracts putting everything in place were signed. She sighed. This meant she was back to where she started — doing the work herself. She couldn't wait for Carmen to feel better so she could ask for her help. Brent's clock was ticking; this needed to be resolved sooner rather than later.

She got off the elevator and headed toward her office, lost in thought. Seconds later, she was fumbling to get the papers that had scattered when her briefcase had somehow flown open.

She looked up into Chas's eyes. Her handsome coworker had accidentally walked into her mess and stepped on some of her documents.

"Sorry, Dayna. Guess I wasn't watching where I was going."

"It's okay, Chas," she said. "I was actually

the one not paying attention; you're okay."

She wondered what had him so nervous. A long-time hospital executive, he had been an associate on the Chesdin staff for about two years. He was usually cool and collected, but not this morning.

Dayna paused to watch him center himself, then straighten his tie and glasses. Funny how his outer actions reflected her inner turmoil. She fingered her charm bracelet and closed the latch on her briefcase before tucking it under her arm.

"Have a good day, Chas. See ya."

Dayna strolled into her department, prepared to ask Monica to hold her calls for at least half an hour while she regrouped and adjusted her morning schedule since she wouldn't be meeting with Carmen. Before she could utter the words Monica told her she had a guest.

"I didn't have an appointment scheduled this morning, did I? Nothing was on my calendar."

Monica shook her head. "No, no, you didn't. It's just Audrey — I don't mean, 'just.' I mean, nothing to worry about."

The tension in Dayna's shoulders dissipated. "Oh, okay. Audrey I can handle this morning."

She stepped inside her office and found

her friend scanning a copy of *The Washington Post* that Monica had placed on her desk this morning.

"Hey, lady, everything okay? You're here early." Dayna shed her jacket and placed it on the back of her leather high-backed seat.

Audrey nodded. "Yeah, I'm fine. Just needed to ask you a huge favor, if you have the time."

Dayna sat at her desk and tried to keep her composure. The last time Audrey had asked an important favor, they had wound up at the police station and lost a night of sleep.

"Ask away," she said.

Audrey cleared her throat and wrung her hands. "Um, my court date for . . . you know . . . got pushed up. It's this Friday at 9 a.m. My lawyer will be there, of course, but I haven't breathed a word of this to anyone else, other than my supervisor and Warren, and I was wondering if you could . . . if you would. . . ."

"I'm there, Audrey. Tell me which courtroom. Or if you want me to pick you up and ride over with you, I can do that too."

Once she set aside her grudge over Audrey's choices, Dayna realized she'd slept like a baby. There was too much drama going on in her life to waste energy being mad over someone else's choices. She needed to be there for Audrey, especially since Audrey had decided not to tell her family in Chicago about the arrest.

Tears mapped a course down Audrey's cheeks.

"Why are you crying?" Dayna asked. "Are you scared?"

Audrey nodded. "Scared and embarrassed. Ashamed."

Dayna nodded. "Nothing we can do to change the past, Audrey. Let's just pray for the best on Friday and try to move forward. That's all you can do."

"Yeah. Move forward is just what I need to do." Audrey wiped her tears.

Dayna pulled her iPhone from her purse and tapped on a particular application before passing the phone to Audrey. The screen featured a Bible verse that read "My grace is sufficient for you."

"Walk in that belief," Dayna told Audrey when Audrey returned the phone. "Has Raymond called you?"

Audrey looked away.

"Audrey?"

Dayna walked around to the front of the desk. She folded her arms and stood in front of her friend. "Please tell me you didn't fall for his foolishness again."

Audrey looked at her. "I didn't. At least I didn't let him come over. He was calling to officially break it off with me, so he said, but he did ask to come over and talk about it. I told him no need; I got the message loud and clear when he sent the police to my place last month."

Dayna released the pensive breath she had been holding. Thank God, this woman was finally coming to her senses.

Audrey laughed through the tears still sitting on the rim of her eyes. "Want to know something even funnier? After I hung up on Raymond last night, I prayed for the first time in a long time without being prompted to do so in a formal worship service. I didn't get on my knees or anything like that. I just sat on the side of my bed and talked to God. I told him the truth: If I had my way, Raymond would have been on his way over to make me feel better and tell me he loved me, and I would have pretended like he meant it. I challenged God to allow me to be approached by a good single man. One that can truly be my own."

Dayna smiled. "Good for you!"

"Then I get here this morning and get off on your floor and guess who I bump into?"

Dayna shrugged.

"Chas Carter. Looking all fine . . . and single."

Dayna and Audrey laughed in unison.

"Do you know he asked me how I was doing in one breath and invited me on a date in the next?"

Dayna's eyes grew wide. "That explains why he was flustered a few minutes ago! I thought it was my looks and charm!"

Audrey attempted a smile.

"He also asked me to join him for coffee on Friday morning, but I had to tell him I have a prior commitment. How sad that a court date might keep me from getting to know a truly good guy better."

"Don't beat yourself up," Dayna said. "And don't be too quick to rush into another relationship. Take some time for you. Your making Chas wait might be a good thing. Men need to do some chasing. Let him ask you again; you'll be worth the wait, and you'll be that much closer to being healed. In the meantime, we've got to get you mentally ready for court on Friday. You need a nice conservative suit — not that flashy stuff you wear around here."

Audrey hugged her, then lightly punched her in the arm. "I should get you for that, but you're right; divas don't do drab. Gotta tone it down for the judge, though."

"Yes, we'll get you through Friday, then I need your help with Brent's foundation. Carmen's out of the picture for a little while it seems, because she's sick. I'm going to need all the help I can get so this thing doesn't overwhelm me."

Audrey gave her a thumbs-up. "Pray me through Friday and I'll do what I can. An accounting background may not provide you with as much help as you need, but I'll be there."

"Thanks. Now get to work."

Audrey left and Dayna turned on her computer to check her weekend messages. She saw a note from Warren and smiled as she read his sweet good-morning pep talk. How was she going to tell him that she was back to square one — in the driver's seat with helping Brent? She'd start, she decided, by proposing salsa dancing tonight, and then go from there.

FIFTY-ONE

"Back and forth; back and forth; come on, people! Shake those groove things!"

Dayna positioned her feet and hands properly in relation to Warren's and moved closer to him. She had missed this. Salsa was relationship medicine. How could she be this close to this man and not long to kiss him?

His eyes told her he was thinking the same thing. Their hips swayed in unison to the up-tempo beat, and they clasped hands in midair while dancing under Footwork Central's bright lights. This was fun. Dayna was glad she'd finally made time to come again.

When the song ended, they took a seat to catch their breath, get something to drink, and watch other student dancers have their turn. They watched with admiration the footwork of some of the more advanced couples and chuckled at others. Either way, being here tonight was magical.

Dayna leaned in her seat so that her back rested on Warren's chest. He leaned into her ear.

"I'm glad you're back, babe; I've missed you."

Dayna frowned and turned toward him. What did that mean? She'd just seen him yesterday.

The loud, fast-paced music resumed before she could ask him, and he swept her up onto the dance floor again. For the next hour, they followed their teacher's instruction to swivel their hips this way and move their feet that way, and worked up a sweat and a fresh affection for each other. When the session ended, they were exhausted.

On the drive home, Warren reached for her hand and squeezed it. "I've missed us," he said.

Dayna shifted in her seat until she was facing him and recalled the curious comment he had made earlier that evening. "What do you mean, Warren? I thought we were okay."

He shrugged. "I don't know, Dayna. This whole thing with Brent has been something else. I mean, it was one thing for you to go to dinner with him to find out why he had returned, but I didn't bargain for this drawn-out drama between you, him, and his wife. If he hadn't found his way back to you, someone else would be helping him get matters squared away before he dies, and that's what I think he should be doing now, not relying on his former wife."

Dayna sighed. "Well, as least you're honest about how you feel. I respect that," she said. "And you're right — someone else could have helped him; it didn't have to be me. I don't know why I didn't just stick to that when he asked and when Tamara showed up in my office to plead his case. Something in me couldn't tell him — them — no."

"Something, huh?"

"What are you insinuating?"

Warren kept his eyes on the road.

"Come on, Warren; we promised from the beginning to put everything on the table. Let me hear it."

He remained silent throughout a stop at a traffic light, and Dayna waited. She wondered if he could hear the fear thumping through her heart. *Faith over fear.* That message from her devotional reading surfaced when she needed it most.

"You still love him, don't you, Dayna?" He looked straight ahead as he asked the question but turned to gaze into Dayna's eyes for the answer.

She stammered. "Where . . . where did that come from? We've been divorced for seven years, Warren!"

"Signing a piece of paper saying something is legally over doesn't mean you turn off your feelings. You just can't seem to let this man go, to live or to die, without you."

"Come on, Warren. You and I have something special. I thought we were planning a future together." She reached for his hand and he pulled away.

"You haven't answered my question."

She reached for the bracelet dangling from her arm and unconsciously began playing with the three charms. The light turned green and Warren drove her home without further questions. Her mind played over the past few months and how she'd handled Brent's declarations of love.

When Warren pulled into her driveway, Dayna used her keychain remote to raise the garage so she could enter through the kitchen. Warren's jaw was set when she turned to him, but she kissed him anyway. "I love *you*. I'm *in love* with you. My feelings for Brent are no different than the love you still have for April."

Warren fixed his eyes on his car's windshield. "Don't try to compare what I feel for my dead wife with your mixed-up emotions about a cheating jerk."

Dayna was taken aback, but she refused to give up. She sighed. "I'm glad we had some time tonight to get back on track. Let's not stop here, okay? You're too important to me."

Warren didn't answer, so she stepped out of the car and trotted into the garage. Before she could lower it, Warren emerged from behind the wheel of the car and called out to her. Dayna approached him, afraid of what he felt the need to share.

When she was face-to-face with him, with his open car door separating them, she waited for him to speak.

"You obviously need to help Brent through this challenging time, and I don't want to be your biggest obstacle," Warren said. "Let's take a break for a while, so you can get through this and figure out what you really want."

Dayna was about to protest and insist that he was overreacting, but Warren silenced her by placing his forefinger on her quivering lips. He looked like he wanted to kiss her, but instead, he settled into the car again and started the engine.

When Dayna was safely inside her home, she dashed to the living room window to watch Warren drive away. But he was still sitting in the driveway, staring at her now-lowered garage door as if he'd lost his best friend.

Dayna wanted to cry too, because he had forced her to face the truth. She loved Warren, but she loved Brent too. Not in the same intense, passionate way she once had, but with the understanding that, like Warren's feelings for April, a piece of her heart would always belong to Brent. Neither time nor distance nor different circumstances could change that, and the fact that Brent wanted her around during his final days meant she had to be there. Even if, she had the terrifying realization, it cost her Warren.

FIFTY-TWO

Dayna didn't think she could possibly have more tears left, but when she awoke the next morning and realized how she and Warren had parted the evening before, her waterworks resumed.

What if she had lost Warren? Over a man who was not only married to someone else, but who also didn't have long to live?

She wanted to roll over and pull the covers over her head and stay in bed, but executive duties called. Some of her back-to-back meetings slated for today couldn't be rescheduled, plus lying in bed and thinking about her woes all day would make them larger than life.

Half an hour later, she finally stood in the shower, letting the water glide over her skin, and prepared to have her morning talk with God.

What have I done, Lord? Warren wanted to marry me! I was finally going to have a family.

And now he thinks I love Brent more than him.
I can't believe this.

Fortunately none of her meetings today included the marketing department, so she wouldn't have to sit across a table from Warren and try to remain composed. She inhaled and exhaled deeply several times to center herself and did what she knew she should have done months ago.

Lord, I surrender this entire situation to you — my relationship with Warren, my friendship with Brent, the tension between Tamara and me, and Lily and me — everything. I don't know what to do with it anymore. Have your way, may your will be done, and may I survive the outcome, knowing that you'll do what's best for me.

The end of her own prayer told her she subconsciously believed it was over with Warren, though that thought terrified her. What if God allowed that nightmare to be true?

That possibility made her weep harder. She wanted him. She needed him. Didn't he know that?

By the time she emerged from the shower and slid into a white linen pantsuit and fuchsia blouse, the redness of her eyes had faded. But her heart was still heavy.

She skipped her usual breakfast of oatmeal and fruit and breezed through the kitchen to grab her cell phone on her way to her car. Once buckled in and backed out of the garage, she paused in the driveway to listen to the message from Carmen. She sounded weak.

"I heard you came by the office yesterday. I'm still home sick, but call me on my cell if you need me. I don't think I'll be in the office at all this week. This flu bug is something else."

Yes, the nurse in Dayna thought, *definitely keep the flu germs out of the office.*

She was tempted to call Carmen right away, but felt bad about disturbing her friend while she was miserably ill. Instead, she dialed Warren's cell. When he didn't answer, she wondered if he was getting the boys off to school, had the phone in another room, or simply didn't want to talk to her.

Can I blame him, Lord?

She maneuvered through the morning traffic and, half an hour later, pulled into her reserved parking space at the hospital.

God, give me the strength to focus, to be productive, and to make it through this day, come what may.

She managed on the elevator ride up to return Carmen's call and briefly filled her in on Brent's rapid decline and the need to turn over the execution of the foundation to her. Even after acknowledging that Warren was right — she still loved Brent and enjoyed being in his company — she knew she had to step back — for the sake of his marriage and to give herself time to sort out the mess her life had become.

"I think it's easier on everyone this way," Dayna told Carmen, without going into detail about Warren's — or Tamara's — concerns. "My only 'Are you sure?' warning is that you will probably have to drive to Cocoa Beach for the meetings, instead of having Brent and Tamara come to Calero. Brent seems to be getting weaker by the day."

Carmen coughed. "That's no problem; I can do that once or twice a week for a few weeks. But keep in mind that it may be a while before I can get down there, with this virus and all. He can't be exposed to me until I'm completely well."

Dayna stepped off the elevator, thankful that her cell phone hadn't dropped the call.

"Yeah, I know. Whatever you can do to speed things along will be appreciated, I'm sure," Dayna said. "Thanks so much, Carmen. I'll inform Brent and Tamara that you'll be taking over as soon as you are well. Get some rest, okay?"

She clicked off the phone and waved to colleagues as she passed their offices on the way to hers. Monica greeted her with coffee, a stack of files, and a pat on the shoulder.

"This will be a busy day, boss. I'll make sure you get through it as smoothly as possible. I've got your back."

Dayna flinched. That was a promise Warren usually made. She wondered if she'd ever hear it again.

She gave Monica a thumbs-up, because she didn't trust herself to speak. Once she settled into her seat, though, she switched into executive mode and managed to shut out the world outside of Chesdin Medical.

Dayna loved what she did, and she was good at it. Helping on the front lines of nursing had been her passion for many years, but this way her service had lasting impact not only on the nursing staff, but also on the patients they helped. Her first meeting of the day was with Spencer regarding some of the general-floor nurses' request to work rotating shifts in the expanding hospice program. She thought it would be an asset to have RNs from general care areas serving hospice patients, even as assistants to the regular hospice nurses. But Spencer was worried about how this would affect their need for nurses to staff the main hospital.

Dayna pulled out the top file Monica had given her and quickly jotted a list of pros and cons in the margins of the first page of the document.

Thank God she wouldn't have much downtime today. Five o'clock would be here before she knew it; she had to get busy. At some point during the day, she'd find time to email Warren to check in and to call Brent and tell him about the plans to have Carmen take over the foundation.

It might be too late to save her relationship with Warren, but maybe she could help salvage Brent's relationship with Tamara while they still had time together. She'd realized as she lay awake in bed last night that she'd never forgive herself if, instead of making sweet memories, Brent and Tamara spent their last days together at odds because of her presence.

She thought about how she would feel if she were in Tamara's shoes and a woman who had once been very important to her husband showed up and infused herself into his life in such a significant way. When her thoughts turned immediately to Warren and Lily, she knew.

The ringing phone brought Dayna back

to the present. She pressed the speaker-phone button on her desktop device.

"Yes?"

"Brent Davidson is on line one. I know you're swamped, but I thought I'd ask if this is an important call, just in case."

Dayna sighed. She had no time for distractions today, but she did need to let him know that Carmen was going to be working with him.

"Put him through, but if I'm not off in five minutes, come in and rescue me."

"Got it," Monica said.

Seconds later, Brent's voice filled her ears. "Good morning, my lady."

"Good morning, Brent. Are you back home? How are you feeling?"

"Yes, I'm back home and feeling pretty strong, so I was just wondering if you could come down today. I thought we might be able to finish writing the executive summary for the foundation."

Dayna paused and tossed her pen from one hand to the other.

"Actually, Brent, I was going to call you about that. First of all, I'm not able to come today because I have so much going on at work that when I leave I'll be exhausted. But I also wanted to tell you Carmen is going to be helping you wrap up things now.

She's the in-house foundation expert anyway, so I'm passing the leadership over to her."

"Why?"

The simple and straightforward question caught her off guard. She shouldn't have been surprised; this was classic Brent.

"It's just best this way, Brent, okay? I'm at work and can't go into a lot of details right now. I'll call you later to check in. Carmen's sick with the flu, so she can't come down today or probably at all this week. But don't worry, she won't drop the ball. I trust her."

The silence that loomed told her Brent wasn't happy. He'd have to get over it this time.

"Gotta run, Brent, okay? I'll talk to you later."

"Yeah. Bet."

He hung up before she could. Dayna shook her head and tried to refocus. Let him be mad; she couldn't fix it this time.

She sat back in her seat and twiddled her pen between her fingers. Maybe that had been one of their issues all along; she had been so busy trying to keep him happy and please him that he'd never realized it should be a mutual effort. Her feelings and needs mattered as much as his.

She'd never told him that, she realized;

she had expected him to know. Maybe if she had been more vocal, he would have been less self-centered.

She put her pen down and massaged her temples to ease the tension forming there. She couldn't psychoanalyze herself or Brent today; she needed to focus on the mountain of work and meetings before her. Her iPhone made a pinging sound, and she saw that today's Scripture had popped up on the phone's display screen:

> Cause me to hear Your loving kindness in
> the morning,
> For in You do I trust;
> Cause me to know the way in which I
> should walk,
> For I lift up my soul to You. (Psalm 143:8
> NKJV)

The verse reminded her she wasn't in control; God had the whole world, including every issue in her life, in his hands. She opened the second folder on the stack that Monica had handed her this morning so she could make notes on its contents. First, however, she bowed her head and closed her eyes and uttered a silent prayer.

Lord, please open Brent's eyes during this difficult season so that he can see the abun-

dant love and support surrounding him and take none of it for granted. Let Carmen be able to help him get the foundation finalized so he can transition to your arms in peace when the time comes. Amen.

Dayna felt at peace with her decision. Now if she could just get some clarity around her relationship with Warren and with her family. The Easter visit was going to be hard without Warren there to support her and make her laugh at Mama and Daddy's quirkiness. Simply put, without Warren, *life* was going to be hard.

FIFTY-THREE

The judge entered the courtroom through a side entrance behind the bench, and Dayna prepared herself for the words she often heard on TV dramas: "All rise!"

The bailiff uttered the phrase, and she and others in the courtroom gallery stood as a thirtyish woman with a short brown bob strode to the bench. The County Court courtroom was full. Defendants prepared to stand before the judge to plead for mercy in traffic cases, petty larceny arrests, and simple assaults.

Audrey's case was called two hours into the court session, and the minute her friend stood to walk to the front of the courtroom with her attorney, Dayna's heart began racing. She felt as if she herself were on trial.

A tall, reed-thin African American woman sat behind the prosecutor's table on the first row of public seating and kept her eyes glued on the defendant's table. The fair-skinned man next to her followed her lead, but Dayna saw him peering at Audrey as if he knew her. This must be the infamous Raymond, Dayna surmised.

Dayna studied the man more closely. He had close-cropped, wavy hair and appeared to have a dimple on his left cheek. When he turned toward his wife, whose perfect posture made her appear regal, and put his arm around the back of her seat, Dayna saw just how handsome he was, a quality he clearly used to his advantage.

The court clerk stood and read the charge against Audrey: one count of simple assault against Evelyn Anderson.

The female judge peered at Audrey over her glasses. "How do you plead?"

Audrey cleared her throat and said, "Guilty," so softly that Dayna almost missed it.

"Could you repeat that loud enough for the clerk to record, please?"

The judge's expression and voice conveyed no emotion.

"Guilty," Audrey said again, this time louder.

Her shoulders were shaking, and Dayna wanted to go over and hug her.

"Judge, Ms. Hammond is pleading guilty to take full responsibility for her actions," her attorney, a dapper silver-haired gentleman in a three-piece suit, said. "However, given that this is her first offense, we are asking for the court to show mercy."

He rummaged through a folder and pulled out several pieces of paper, which he handed to the bailiff to give to the judge. "I'm providing you with documentation of Ms. Hammond's solid work history and a letter of reference from her boss. Her boss has also offered to help place her in an appropriate community service setting if you're in agreement."

Dayna was impressed at how the attorney answered the judge's questions before they were asked, and in doing so, avoided mentioning where Audrey worked or who her boss was. Then again, this was an attorney that Spencer recommended; of course he was the best.

The judge took a few minutes to review the information.

"I see you have been thorough as usual, Mr. Caldwell. To your point, this is Ms. Hammond's first offense, and based on the little testimony I've heard this morning, plus reviewing the case history, I am comfortable with rendering a sentence within your requested parameters.

"Ms. Hammond, will you please stand?"

Audrey stood again and the nervous twitch resumed.

"I hereby accept your guilty plea and sentence you to three hundred hours of community service, to be performed under the direction of your probation officer and the designated supervisor at Hospice of Hope, where you'll undertake and complete whatever tasks they see fit. Understood?"

"Understood, Your Honor," Audrey said. "Thank you for this second chance."

"We appreciate the lenient sentence, Your Honor," her attorney chimed in. "My client has written a letter of apology to the victim, which we'd like to deliver today, and she is looking forward to completing her community service to the best of her ability."

Mr. Caldwell provided the letter Audrey had written Raymond's wife to the judge, who read it before passing it on to the prosecutor to give to the victim, who declined to make a statement during the proceedings.

The judge banged her gavel to quell the murmuring that arose in the courtroom.

Dayna glanced at the woman seated with her husband behind the prosecutor. She didn't seem upset either way, which left Dayna even more curious about her. Her husband leaned over and whispered something in her ear and she nodded without looking in his direction.

Audrey and her attorney filed out of the courtroom, and Dayna was right behind them. Once in the lobby, Audrey hugged her attorney before turning to give Dayna a tight squeeze.

"Thank you — thank you so much, Mr. Caldwell," she said. "What happens next?"

He smiled at Dayna and looked back and forth between her and Audrey.

"The judge will submit your paperwork to the probation team, and in about two weeks you'll be contacted by the probation officer assigned to you," Mr. Caldwell said. "In the meantime, since your boss has connections to the hospice where you'll be volunteering, you two can get the ball rolling with the community service hours by contacting the hospice program to get you started."

"Thank you," Audrey said.

Dayna extended her hand to Mr. Caldwell and thanked him as well. "You were wonderful in there today."

He smiled. "Another client needs me in about fifteen minutes. Good day to you both."

He walked away without looking back, and Audrey shrugged. "He can be as arrogant as he likes; he helped save my life today."

Dayna started to point out that it was a simple assault charge, not murder, but decided to leave it alone. She hadn't walked in Audrey's shoes, so she didn't know what this public embarrassment or a conviction of any kind felt like.

She looped her arm through Audrey's and pulled her along toward the courthouse exit. "Come on — let's grab some lunch and do a little retail therapy. One of your favorite stores is having a blowout sale today."

Audrey smirked. "You're acting as if we have something to celebrate."

"You do — the fact that God has given you a second chance, my friend."

Audrey smiled. "Hadn't thought about it like that; you're right."

They exited the courthouse and were greeted by the sun-filled Florida sky. When they were near Dayna's car, Audrey stopped and followed a dark blue Mercedes with her eyes as it cruised past them and out of the courthouse's winding driveway.

"He acted like I didn't exist today," Audrey said.

Dayna frowned. "Come on, Audrey. Did you expect any different with his wife right beside him?"

Audrey sighed and shrugged. "I don't know what I expected. More than that, after a year of devoting my life to him. Guess I'm a bigger fool than you thought, huh?"

"It doesn't matter what I think, friend; what matters is what you know," Dayna said. "You know he's married to someone else, so he can never fully give himself to you. You know he's selfish and self-centered by the way he treated his wife *and* you. And I hope you know that you deserve way more than that."

Dayna and Audrey hugged, and Audrey wiped away a few tears before settling into Dayna's car.

"I'm beginning to understand that, as old as I am," Audrey said, and laughed. "Let's hit this sale you mentioned."

FIFTY-FOUR

An hour later, each of them had a couple of outfits priced 40 to 50 percent off, and they were now rummaging through designer purses.

Dayna stood nearby as Audrey struck up a conversation with a petite blond woman who had her grandson in tow.

"I need a new bag, but it needs to fit my body type," the woman told Audrey. "You and I are about the same height and size — those big hobo bags swallow us!"

Audrey nodded and grinned at Dayna, who was holding her oversized tan purse while she searched for a new one. The woman asked Audrey to "try on" each of the bags she liked for herself, so she could see if they worked on a petite frame.

Dayna wandered away to the jewelry department and left the two ladies to their adventure.

She found a tie clip that would be perfect

for Daddy's pastoral anniversary gift and added that to her basket. By the time she strolled back to the purse section, a crowd had gathered.

"I had the bag first, so why should I hand it over to you?"

Dayna recognized Audrey's high-pitched indignation before she saw her friend squared off in the middle of the crowd, exchanging words with the purse-shopping stranger.

"Well, you can go to another store location. They have one down in the city, you know? I live near here; this is best for me."

"Look," Audrey said, then lowered the register of her voice. "This is ridiculous. I found the purse, I handed it to you to try on so I could see how it looked, like you've been doing with me for the past twenty minutes. I did not hand over the purse for you to keep; it is mine, and I'd like to go ahead and pay for it so my friend and I can leave."

The woman continued to clutch the purse while her grandson clung to her leg, watching her every move.

"My grandson and I need to go, okay?"

Dayna envisioned fumes unfurling from Audrey's eyes and nostrils. Girlfriend was doing a great job of containing her anger.

Since they'd just left the courthouse, she decided to intervene before a return visit was warranted. She stepped through the crowd and pulled Audrey away by the hand.

"You know what?" Audrey yelled at the woman while being led away, "keep my purse; keep it! And every time you use it, I hope you'll feel guilty and materialistic for stooping so low in getting it!"

Dayna led Audrey to a register where there was no line. The customers were all in the purse section now, anticipating what would happen next. But the purse-shopping stranger and her grandson went deeper into the store to shop more now that she had the black Calvin Klein purse slung over her shoulder.

Dayna stood back as Audrey slapped the other items she had selected to purchase onto the counter to pay for them. She was muttering under her breath and rolling her eyes at no one in particular.

When they were in the car again, Dayna turned to her friend, who was in the passenger seat pouting. "Will you calm down? It was just a purse," Dayna told her.

"That's not the point," Audrey said. "She took something that was mine. I had it first; I was only showing it to her, and she took it and kept it!"

The depth of meaning in Audrey's words struck Dayna to the core. She had to be real with her friend.

"Do you understand what you just said?"

Audrey looked confused.

"You said she took something that wasn't hers; she took it and kept it when she had no right to it. Wouldn't you say that's how Raymond's wife feels — like you took something that wasn't yours, because you wanted it?"

Audrey lowered her gaze. She sat in silence, staring through the windshield, and soon, she was crying.

Dayna patted her back to comfort her. Wasn't it amazing how God could speak to a person in whatever way and through whomever he wanted? The woman who "took" the purse was irrelevant; God was trying to teach Audrey a lesson today, and since material things spoke to her, that's what he used to get her to listen.

What lessons do you have in store for me, God?

Dayna was sure hers wouldn't be easy to accept, either.

FIFTY-FIVE

Dayna parked in front of Brent's house but made no effort to get out of the car.

"You are coming in, right?" Carmen asked.

Dayna chuckled. "Of course. I'm just lost in thought today, that's all."

This was supposed to be her final meeting with the team for a while, but it all seemed for naught, since she and Warren's relationship had been so strained for the past two weeks. He'd text in the mornings to say hello, but didn't call in the evenings or join her for lunch or dinner.

Dayna's heart ached whenever she thought about him, but she hadn't pushed him. She pictured him and the boys having dinner with Lily or hanging out with her on the boat. She missed curling up with Warren on his sofa and scolding the boys for leaving their sports equipment on the kitchen floor. She wondered if they asked about her or missed her as much as she missed them. Part of her wanted to stop by and invite herself in, but she always talked herself out of it. Warren knew where she was if he wanted to see her.

Dayna opened the car door and grabbed the shoulder bag that contained her notes and documents related to the creation of the foundation. She ran down a mental checklist for what felt like the hundredth time to make sure nothing critical had been missed: funds had been set aside or allocated, a board of directors had been formed, and the application for oversight by the Calero Community Foundation had been signed by Brent and submitted. The team felt pretty confident that there'd be no problem.

Dayna rang the doorbell and waited for Tamara to answer. She and Carmen were surprised when Brent greeted them instead.

He smiled broadly, then stepped aside so they could enter. "Hi, ladies, come on in."

Once inside, Dayna tried to hide her dismay over the disheveled state of the living room. She was embarrassed for Carmen to see Brent's house like this, when Tamara usually kept it so neat.

"How are things going, Brent?" she asked, dreading the answer.

"Come in and have a seat," he said. "Excuse the clutter; I've got to do better."

Dayna and Carmen glanced at each other in silent agreement and perched on the edge of the sofa.

Brent cleared a newspaper from the chair across from them so he could sit, then began removing food cartons and juice bottles from the coffee table. He looked like a war refugee who hadn't eaten for days; had he really consumed enough to amass this much trash? He also looked too weak to be trying to clean.

"Brent, what's going on?"

He collapsed in a chair and lifted his chin. "Seems that Tamara got overwhelmed by my illness and decided to take a break."

"Excuse me?" Dayna leaned forward to make sure she wasn't hearing him wrong.

"She left me a note two days ago indicating that she was tired and that she wasn't sure I loved her anymore. So rather than stay here and watch a man die who had his heart in another place, she has chosen to give me space to do what I need, without regrets."

Fear coursed through Dayna. "What does that mean, Brent? What was she trying to say?"

Brent shrugged and wrapped himself in a

blanket. Watching him made Dayna break out in a sweat.

"She's trying to say what she's been saying since that first night we all had dinner — that she believes I'm still in love with you, Dayna, because I've spent so much time lately working with you on the foundation," he said, and gazed out of a window. "She flipped through a notebook that I've been using to journal my thoughts and read my plans to ask you to serve as president of the foundation. That did it. She just got fed up with me, I guess."

His eyes darted from Dayna to Carmen, and he looked frail and defeated.

"So you let her go? You didn't go after her?" Carmen asked.

Brent slumped further into the seat. "I didn't because, in part, she was telling the truth." He looked at Dayna. "The reason I tracked you down six weeks ago was because when I realized I was dying, I knew I couldn't leave this earth without seeing you again, Dayna. I knew without a doubt that I still loved you. I never told Tamara that, but she wasn't blind."

Dayna shook her head, as if that would dislodge her disbelief. Had she really been naive in thinking this had been about his need to seek forgiveness? Had it been about rekindling a lost romance all along?

"But, Brent, she is your wife. Has been for nearly seven years. Has that all been a lie?"

"No, of course not," he said. "I tried to tell her that. But she said she has always lived in your shadow, with me and with my family. And now that you're back, there's no place for her in my life — what's left of my life."

"Do you love her, Brent?"

He paused for so long that Dayna questioned whether he had dozed off.

"I do, Dayna, I do," he said. "But I don't know that I'm willing to lose you again to have her back."

Dayna felt sucker punched. Had she led him to believe he actually *had* her back? This felt like déjà vu, except she was certain that he must have spoken those words to Tamara all those years ago about her.

She didn't feel flattered. If anything, she was angry. "Brent, you can't keep doing this."

He frowned. "Doing what? Being honest?"

Dayna wished her colleague wasn't sitting here to witness such a personal exchange, but it couldn't be helped. When someone needed a "Come to Jesus" meeting, they needed it, right then and there.

"Do you realize what you just said to me?" she asked Brent. "You acknowledged that you are willing to lose your wife, who has cared for you throughout your illness and who loves you desperately, because you've had a sudden change of heart, or a desire to go back in time. We can't go back in time. And truth be told, if we did, you'd realize that back then you were head over heels for Tamara, not me. I'm not sure what's going on with you; I just know you don't want to leave your marriage like this or be the kind of person who toys with other's feelings. You've done that once, and it's not becoming at all. You need to grow up, Brent. I'm not going along with your fantasy. I am in love with Warren Avery, and if he'll have me, that's who I intend to be with."

Dayna felt like storming out and driving off, leaving him to figure it out. But since Carmen had taken the time to come, she needed to honor her commitment.

"Carmen is here today to take over the process to get your foundation up and running, and like we discussed, she's the best woman for the job."

Brent stared at Dayna for a while before turning to Carmen. "Well, thank you, Carmen, for agreeing to lead the charge," he said. "I really appreciate it." He addressed

Dayna again. "Does this mean you won't be on the board in any capacity?"

She shook her head.

"Probably not, Brent. That wouldn't be for the best. I'm moving on with my life, and you need to . . ."

"I need to end mine with dignity, right?"

"You need to find your wife and ask God to help you work things out with her."

Brent lowered his head for a long time. When he looked up, he seemed defeated. "Tamara's been gone for two days. Her mother comes by to make sure I'm eating, but she doesn't stay long or clean up or any of that. I'm alone in this now."

"You don't have to be," Carmen chimed in. "Go find Tamara. Talk to her. I don't know her well, but when I've chatted with her at these board meetings, I can tell that she loves you and she wants the best for you, and with that combination, you can heal a lot."

Brent delivered a strained smile. "I don't even know where she is."

"Did you ask your mother-in-law?" Dayna asked.

He sheepishly looked away, and Dayna knew the answer was no.

"She's probably waiting to spill the beans the second you ask the question, Brent. I guarantee it," Dayna said. "If Tamara doesn't come home tonight, why don't you call her or go find her?"

Carmen nodded. "I'm all up in your business where I haven't been invited, but I agree," she said. "Let's chat about what needs to happen next to get the foundation established, then you can go work things out with Tamara, okay?"

Brent looked from Carmen to Dayna, where his gaze lingered. Dayna could tell he wasn't ready to let go just yet. What would wake him up, before it was too late? She knew she was treading where she shouldn't, but Brent clearly needed someone to take care of him.

"Where's your cell phone?"

Brent frowned. "Excuse me?"

"Just give me your brother Winston's number, then," Dayna said. "That's why I'm asking. You don't need to be here alone."

Brent shook his head. "No worries; Tamara took care of that before she took off. Winston and my mother called this morning to let me know they've booked a flight and will be here in the morning. Let's just do what you two came to do, okay?"

By eight p.m., Dayna and Carmen were on the road, en route back to Calero.

"Can you believe that?" Dayna asked once they were zooming along on the interstate. "I can't tell you what I would have paid just a few short years ago to hear that man come to me like he did tonight, telling me he had made a mistake in leaving me. But I realize now that God's word is true; earth has no sorrow that heaven can't heal. Part of me will always love him, but when I looked at him tonight, I didn't see the Brent I adored seven years ago; I saw Tamara's husband, a dying man in desperate need to find himself before it's too late."

"Wow, Dayna," Carmen said. "Neither of us know what he or Tamara is going through with death at their doorstep. It has to make them both do and think strange things. I'll keep them in prayer."

They settled into a companionable silence, and half an hour later, Dayna dropped Carmen off at her home. Pausing in the driveway, Dayna quickly called Tamara before she lost her nerve and was relieved to get her voicemail. She spoke quickly but carefully, hoping her words could make a difference.

Brent hadn't promised to do what Dayna and Carmen had asked regarding Tamara, but Dayna felt like he finally had grasped that he had no chance with her. She hoped that Tamara wouldn't let Brent die alone. If that happened, Tamara would never forgive herself.

FIFTY-SIX

A clap of thunder jolted Tamara out of a brief after-dinner nap.

Neither sleep nor rest had come easily since she had left home and encouraged Brent to figure things out on his own, and the storm that was brewing fit her mood. She wasn't ready to go back home though. She needed to take care of herself and her spirit right now, or she'd be no good to Brent at all.

Mrs. Chestnut had been telling her that by phone for the past week, during early morning prayer calls she had initiated with Tamara after giving her the prayer book. Still, even Mrs. Chestnut had been stunned when Tamara had called her in tears, frustrated and ready to give up because of Brent's selfish behavior.

"Come to my home, and let me pray with you in person," Mrs. Chestnut had urged.

While Brent was out running errands,

Tamara left a note on the kitchen table telling him she was going away and a voicemail for her mom asking her to check on him while she was away. She knew her mother would fume because she hadn't shared her destination. She also called the bank to let them know she'd be taking some vacation time.

Tamara had driven the half hour to her client's palatial home and had arrived at seven in the evening, two days ago. Mrs. Chestnut had opened the door and welcomed her with a long and meaningful hug, but she had been stunned to see Tamara with an overnight bag.

"I told you to come for prayer, child, not to leave your husband."

Tamara assured Mrs. Chestnut that her mother lived nearby and would make sure Brent ate sufficiently and took his medicine. Plus, she had sent an email and a text to her mother-in-law and one of Brent's brothers encouraging them to visit while she was away, so they could have some time with him. Tamara hadn't talked to her mom or her in-laws, but she prayed that they were on their way or already caring for Brent.

Mrs. Chestnut had offered her either a guest bedroom or the guest house, which was detached from the main house and featured a winding path that led to a tree house.

"I'm here all alone now, since my husband went on to glory and my children and grandchildren are too busy to stop by," she told Tamara. "Make yourself comfortable, my special friend. You are welcome here anytime, but please know that I also want you to be there for your husband. Let's take your concerns before the Lord and leave them there, shall we?'"

Tamara had taken the older woman's hand minutes after her arrival and knelt in prayer in the living room. When they got up off their knees later, Tamara felt lighter and decided she could best help Brent right now from her current location, serving as a prayer warrior on his behalf. Going home to resume her wifely duties would signal to Brent, and to everyone around him, that whispering a few apologies or sweet nothings would make everything okay. But it wouldn't.

Now approaching the third day of her retreat, she desperately missed Brent and was trying not to worry about him. She wanted to call, but she had to let him be.

God's got this, she repeated whenever her concerns engulfed her. No one was forcing her to stay away, but maybe this was a trial run for what life would be like without him. She pondered that notion, but more importantly, she wanted to give him whatever space he needed to clear his head and get honest about his feelings.

As uncaring as this method seemed, it had been the easiest way for Tamara to step back. If Brent didn't want her around, or needed Dayna around more, she would deal with that; but first he had to own that truth.

Tamara sat in the guest house this evening eating popcorn and wondering whether Dayna was at her and Brent's house, enjoying her time with Brent as they held their routine foundation meeting. Dayna had claimed tonight would be her last meeting, but maybe that would change when she realized Tamara was gone.

Before her imagination took her further down a path she didn't want to travel, Tamara picked up the book Mrs. Chestnut had placed on the kitchen table for her this morning after breakfast. Its subject was how to live through grief.

A mystery or suspense novel would have suited her better right about now, but she supposed Mrs. C. was wise — the book on grief was what she needed. The passages she read tonight affirmed the self-care journey she was on. Maybe not her method, but certainly the importance of doing so was encouraged. The author's message left Tamara feeling validated, and she wished more of the text related to her particularly unusual circumstances. With Dayna in the picture, her situation was more complicated than the issues this book addressed.

She glanced at the clock and realized two hours had passed. For months now, her life seemed to be moving in slow motion. The fact that she'd actually been able to lose herself in the pages of a book, even one on such a difficult topic, was comforting.

She stood up to stretch and decided to turn on her cell phone. She had missed three calls — from Winston, Brent, and Dayna. Seeing the names on the phone's flat screen filled her with tension. Her reflex was to ignore them, but common sense told her to pick whom to call back first. Instead, she chose a third option: she sent a text to her mother-in-law, asking if she was coming to Florida and if Brent was okay. As long as she received a positive message, the voice-mails could wait.

Right now, she needed to give it all to God. Only he could soothe her aching heart and soul, so that when she returned home, she could shower Brent with all of the attention and love he needed, despite his attitude or actions.

FIFTY-SEVEN

Dayna was still reeling from Tamara's disappearing act when she received a call from Audrey just as she reached home, asking if she could come over. It was after nine-thirty and Dayna was weary, but if Audrey needed her, Audrey needed her.

Audrey arrived twenty minutes later with a grateful smile and a hug. "Just need to talk through some things with you."

Dayna nodded and ushered her inside. She made her customary cup of tea and gave Audrey the diet soda she requested before they settled on the sofa in the family room.

Dayna was eager to share with her how tonight's foundation meeting with Brent had gone, but she knew Audrey's needs must be pressing.

"What's going on?" she asked and took a sip of tea.

"I saw someone die today during my community service shift at the hospice," Audrey said. "I finally understood what you've been trying to tell me all along, about the dead-end life I was creating for myself with the cheating."

Dayna wasn't sure how to respond. Audrey continued. "My trial and conviction last week shattered my pretense that all was well in my black urban yuppie world, but not until this morning, when Mrs. Cooper died, did I accept how hollow my life has become."

Dayna could feel Audrey's pain. She reached for her friend's hands and let her keep talking.

"Since my court-ordered community service began, I've helped with everything from answering the phones to escorting family members to a relative's room. Believe it or not, the place isn't as gloomy as I expected. People are dying, but most of the ones I've met, and their families, are so Spirit-filled that the place seems more like a residential physical therapy facility instead of a place where people come to die — I can't explain it.

"Today, I happened to be standing in the doorway of a bedroom occupied by a sweet old lady named Mrs. Cooper when she died."

"Oh, Audrey, I'm sorry; that must have been hard," Dayna said.

Tears filled Audrey's eyes and she shook her head. "Watching her die was difficult, but you know what really tore me up, Dayna?"

Dayna waited for her to continue.

"It wasn't the death; it was the jealousy that seeped into my soul."

Dayna frowned.

Audrey hugged herself and continued. "Mrs. Cooper slipped from life with a hint of a smile on her face, not the mark of fear or grimace of pain you always see in those made-for-TV deathbed scenes. Maybe it was because in a fog-free moment, Mrs. Cooper had recognized her husband when he leaned close to gaze into her eyes and kiss her lips. Maybe her children and teenage grandchildren's soft humming of her favorite hymn had helped — I don't know.

"Whatever the reason, Mrs. Cooper made death look like a welcome nap, the kind of resting place everyone should curl up and embrace, and I stood there in the doorway, Dayna, watching like a guilty intruder, stealing the sweetness from this family's private moment, but unable to lift my feet and back away.

"I had expected to get physically ill or to

cry the first time someone died on my watch, you know? Especially if it was a patient and family I had come to know," Audrey continued. "But envy? That caught me off guard."

Dayna was stunned. It made her wonder how she was going to feel when she got the final word about Brent's demise.

"That is powerful, Audrey. Are you okay?"

Audrey shook her head. "Not really. I mean, I've spent the day asking myself what could I possibly want that a dying woman had, and you know what answer I came up with? Authentic love. I watched as Mrs. Cooper's husband, children, grandchildren, and siblings surrounded her and shed tears after she died, caressing her arms and kissing her forehead. They didn't seem to care that she couldn't respond; they wanted to be in her presence for as long as they could.

"That's the kind of devotion and commitment I long for, Dayna. I want to be loved and eventually missed — right now, not someday."

Dayna squeezed Audrey's hand. Her friend had experienced some truths, and right now, it looked like they might once again be in the sea of longing together.

Audrey eked out a laugh. "One of Mrs. Cooper's brothers turned toward the door and saw me standing there, crying," she said. "Do you know he came over and tried to console me? He told me the family was crying tears of joy, because they knew Mrs. Cooper was heaven-bound; he wanted to make sure my tears were for the same reason.

"It would have been rude to tell that kind older gentleman that while Mrs. Cooper had been one of my favorite hospice patients, the woman's journey to heaven was the last thing on my mind. I was crying because I wanted what she left behind — the husband, the children, the love. Am I sick or what?"

Dayna hugged Audrey and they held the embrace for a while.

"You're not sick," Dayna finally responded. "You're finally coming out of the coma Raymond seduced you into. It's not easy to look at your life and realize you've been living it on someone else's terms. I've been there, friend. Just today I've had some revelations myself about who and whose I want to be. I've got some more growing to do too, but we're both going to be okay."

Audrey wiped her tears and smiled. "You're right — we will. Now that I know better, I can do better. Mrs. Cooper's death was a gift of sorts to me, today. I guess I don't have to have exactly what she has, but I definitely want the good God has for me, and I know that means a life rich in all the right things, obtained the right way."

Dayna wiped her moist eyes and nodded in agreement. Audrey had unwittingly taught her a lesson she needed to learn too. "Saying it is easy, isn't it?" Audrey said and smiled. "It's the *doing* that requires courage and commitment. Mrs. Cooper was a wonderful example, and you know what? So are you, Dayna. If you would be my accountability partner, I would be grateful."

"What do you mean?" Dayna asked, thinking about how she had messed up her own relationship with Warren and allowed herself to get so embedded in Brent's life that now his marriage appeared to be in jeopardy, in part due to her. "I don't know that I have any wisdom to share."

Audrey squeezed her hand. "I don't need you to be perfect; I just need more of the encouragement you've already given me to work harder at being my best self. You haven't been a 'yes' friend, allowing me to take the easy way out to do what's most convenient. You've challenged me to stretch myself in every area of life, and for that, I appreciate you."

FIFTY-EIGHT

After stalling by watching the evening news and some Letterman, Tamara finally listened to her messages.

Three voicemails made all the difference. She was still a wanted woman.

Tamara cried as those truths, delivered in messages from her brother-in-law Winston, Brent, and Dayna, tickled her ears.

Winston's call had been first. "Tamara, first I want to let you know that Brent is okay. The second big piece of news is that he has officially been knighted 'Jerk of the Year.'"

Tamara laughed out loud through her tears and had to start Winston's message over four times before she could get past that part. "I know all about what's been going on with Dayna and the foundation — Brent has spent the past few hours filling me in and answering my questions. Just know that your husband loves you, and he wants you to come home. But if you need to rest awhile yet, don't worry; Mom and I plan to fly in and will be there tomorrow morning."

The second voicemail was from Brent, who spoke in a shaky voice. "Take whatever time you need to rest, Tami, and when you get back, I owe you an apology. I'm so sorry, Tami. I guess I've been so caught up with what I had done in the past, I didn't realize what I had in my present and how I was wasting the precious time you and I have together. I love you, baby, and I want to spend the rest of whatever time I have left with you."

Tamara wanted to pack her bags, but the storm was still rattling windows and pelting the guesthouse roof with raindrops. The noises had initially made her uneasy, but now she was lost in joy.

Dayna had called sometime after the foundation meeting to apologize.

"I got caught up in trying to be Brent's savior when he asked me to help set up the foundation," Dayna said in the voicemail message. "It stroked my ego and made me feel like something. Here he was, groveling for my help after all. It was wrong, Tamara; I was wrong.

"My friend Duchess always says, 'If you

do the right thing for the wrong reason, it becomes the wrong thing to do.' I'm just calling to let you know that Carmen has officially taken over the foundation work. I wrapped up my part of the project tonight. Brent was doing okay when we left. He needs a maid service, but mostly, he needs you."

There was a long pause before Dayna continued, but by now, Tamara was smiling into the phone.

"One more thing, Tamara — you and I will never be best buddies; there's too much 'stuff' between us for that. But we can get along; we've proven that. If you ever need me — for something related to the foundation or just to talk — please keep my number."

Tamara curled up on the king-sized bed and stared at the ceiling, letting the power of what had just occurred marinate in her spirit. Then, the truths about how she had become Brent's girlfriend, and then his wife, struck her hard.

She remembered renting a room from a cousin who owned a house in Dayna and Brent's neighborhood because she was between jobs and romances. She saw herself at the neighborhood cookout, meeting Dayna for the first time and eventually accepting invitations to movie night and dinner at Dayna and Brent's house. Dayna had helped her revise her résumé and had called her the minute she learned that the company Brent worked for needed administrative assistants.

Tamara recalled riding to work with Brent a few times when her car wouldn't start and enjoying his company and his jokes. She couldn't recall when or how she'd decided that Brent was her type, or when she'd begun flirting with him; but she remembered him flirting back, especially when she listened to his hopes and dreams and repeated them back to him in his own words.

Tamara lay here tonight, revisiting her life choices in slow motion, and asked herself a tough question: Had she purposely set out to steal her friend's man?

If she was honest and acknowledged the kind of person she was eight years ago, the truthful answer would be yes; if he would allow himself to be "stolen," she'd do the taking. Living a better life, with all the trappings of the American dream, was icing on the cake.

Tamara sat up in bed and thanked God for allowing her to see her flaws and sins for what they were. When she had gathered her bearings, she bowed her head and repented anew. She had sought and received forgiveness from God a long time ago for her role in breaking up Brent and Dayna's marriage. Tonight, she realized the missing link was Dayna. Tamara needed to apologize to her too.

FIFTY-NINE

The following afternoon Dayna drove herself to the airport for the first time in a long time, and it broke her heart.

Usually Warren dropped her off and wished her well. Or if they were traveling together, they'd park the car and walk into the terminal together. Today, however, she was preparing to catch a late afternoon flight into Birmingham, Alabama, all by herself. She'd land around six p.m. and get a rental car to drive the rest of the way to Atchity. The timing would allow her to miss Good Friday services as she had initially planned, but truthfully, after all that had transpired, she wouldn't have minded sitting through the service, even if Daddy and her brother-in-law Randy stood in the pulpit grandstanding. More and more, she was learning to peek behind the pomp and circumstance of organized church and see God's essence, in word, in song, in dance, and in relationships. Warren had been nudging her in that direction for a long time, and in the time since they'd last talked, his admonitions seemed to be sinking in.

Dayna parked the car, checked her bag, and cleared security before she realized her cell phone was buzzing like crazy. She grabbed a spiced chai tea from an airport coffee vendor and settled into a seat near her flight's gate. With at least an hour to spare before boarding, she could catch up on phone calls, emails, and maybe even a nap.

She checked her phone and found that in the twenty-minute drive from her house to the airport, she had received two calls and several text messages.

Tamara had texted to let Dayna know she was back home and that Brent's mom and brother Winston were in town, if she wanted to come by. Dayna wasn't sure what had prompted the olive branch, but she informed Tamara that she was en route to Alabama for Easter and wished her well.

There was a text from her sister Jessica, letting her know she'd be thrilled to see her in a few hours.

It's been too long, sis. We've got to do better about staying connected. Looking forward to a mini-reunion, and even to seeing our folks. Guess there's nothing like family — in small doses. LOL

Dayna chuckled. She hoped she would leave their Easter visit with that same positive sentiment. She was going home out of obedience, but she looked forward to the day when she returned joyfully and expectantly, having forgiven Mama for taking Brent's side, having accepted that Daddy was giving all the affection he was capable of, and having appreciated Shiloh for being a devoted daughter, wife, and mother. Her family was flawed, but they were still her family, and just as she wanted to be loved unconditionally, she had to extend unconditional love.

All of this sounded wonderful in theory. She had begun praying days ago for God to help her put it into practice once she made it home.

The final text came from Monica, reminding her of a final business call Dayna needed to make before officially declaring herself on vacation. Then she switched to pick up voicemail.

Brent had left a message, thanking Dayna for working so hard on his vision and for connecting him with Carmen. "I got an official letter in the mail informing me that the Calero Community Foundation was impressed with my plans and with the organization of my application. My foundation is under careful consideration, and we should have an answer in a week or so.

"I also want to apologize, Dayna," Brent said, in a tired, raspy voice she almost didn't recognize. "My brother Winston and I have been sitting here talking about old times, and at one point I brought you up so much that he stopped me and asked me to share details with him about some of the memories I've formed with Tamara. You know Winston loves you like the brother he once was to you, but he was right; somewhere along the way I developed a bad habit of focusing only on the good memories of which you were a part; in essence, dismissing all of the beautiful seasons I've shared with my wife. I called Tamara last night after you left Cocoa Beach and asked for *her* forgiveness. She's back home now."

Dayna's spirit swelled with joy at the news. This message explained Tamara's text.

"So, I'm calling you to acknowledge that I've been a jerk and to thank you for loving me anyway," Brent said. " 'Cause I know you had to love me to put up with me and help me get this foundation in good enough shape to present to the Calero Community Foundation. Just want you to know I appreciate you. And I called Warren to thank him for sharing you with me. He didn't say much, but he suggested that you might be heading to Alabama for Easter. If you're en route now, travel safely, my friend, and thanks for all you've done for me and for Tamara."

The next message was short and sweet, but it made Dayna's heart leap.

"Hey, this is Warren. All is well with me and the boys. Just wanted to call and say hello and wish you a nice Easter with your family. Don't let them get to you; it's just for a few days. Take care."

Dayna's heart melted. Was it wishful thinking, or had he sounded like he missed her?

Before she talked herself out of it, she dialed Warren's cell number and was stunned when he picked up on the first ring.

"Hey."

That one word sounded like music.

"Hey," she responded. "It's been too long."

"Tell me about it," Warren said. "I thought it was good to hear your voice on your cell phone message; live is even better."

A hug and kiss would be much, much better.

Dayna didn't utter those sentiments, but oh, how she longed to. An airline attendant came over the airport speakerphone and announced that her plane would be boarding soon, and Dayna listened to her heart.

"I know it's been a while since we talked," she said. "I . . . I just want to tell you I'm sorry for taking you for granted. You've probably moved on and all, but I miss you, and I love you, Warren. This time we've been apart has confirmed for me that what we have is real. We can't give up on us . . . can we?"

She hadn't had the strength, or maybe the determination, to fight for Brent, and by the time she had a say in the matter, he was already emotionally gone. With Warren, she just needed to find the courage to dwell in his love, whatever may come.

The plane began boarding her section, and Dayna knew she needed to sign off quickly. She waited for Warren's reply and was surprised by his silence.

"Warren?"

Her heart sank when she realized she had somehow dropped the call. There was no time to call him back; she needed to board the plane. Hopefully when she reached her destination there'd be another message from him, and hopefully it would make everything right with the world.

SIXTY

Returning to Atchity was like stepping back in time for Dayna.

Within minutes of leaving the Birmingham airport in a four-door rental car, she was breezing down a two-lane highway that served as a straight shot to her parents' home. Passing through one small town after another meant waving at porch-sitting strangers who might be offended if she didn't and watching clothes wave in the wind on outdoor clotheslines. Cows still grazed in fields just off the busy road, and some farms still grew cotton.

Atchity was considered one of the more important little cities in the state because it was home to a respected university. As an elite college town that served as home to what some considered the greatest football team this side of the Mississippi, its beautiful brick buildings and expansive sidewalks gave the place a fairy-tale feel.

Dayna's parents lived near the church in the downtown section of Atchity. When she pulled into their driveway just after nightfall, streetlights flickered on and helped her get her bearings.

She was surprised to see a light on in her parents' kitchen, since it wasn't yet eight p.m. and Good Friday service was still underway. She was stunned speechless when the front door opened and out stepped her sister Shiloh.

"You're missing a church service?"

Shiloh came down the steps and stood next to Dayna's rental car. "Well, hello to you, too, sister! Welcome home."

Dayna blushed at her rudeness and climed out of the car.

"Sorry about that, Shiloh," she said, and hugged her sister. "That was rude, wasn't it? What I meant was, what a nice surprise. I hadn't expected anyone to be home. I was going to use the key under the doormat to let myself in."

Shiloh beamed. "Greeting guests is ministry work too. I volunteered to stay home and welcome you. I'm so glad you came, Dayna."

Her sister, three years her junior, was taller, heavier, and older looking than Dayna, but, if Dayna was honest with herself, Shiloh had the biggest, kindest heart Dayna had ever encountered, and her enthusiasm this evening was obviously sincere.

Dayna brought her bag inside and spent the next half hour getting updates on the neighbors, her three nieces and nephew, and anything else Shiloh could remember to tell her about their birthplace.

Dayna relaxed. As long as they stayed on safe, neutral topics, all was well. When Mama and Daddy came home and ventured into why she wasn't remarried yet or whether she'd be able to produce some beautiful grandchildren like Shiloh, things might get sticky.

Dayna decided then and there to do her part to keep her visit light and fun. What good would it serve to bring up old resentments or issues from the past that hadn't changed for decades and wouldn't now? And since Warren hadn't accompanied her, she didn't even have to fight the battle of where he would stay and how they would "present" him to the congregation. Daddy could have his moment in the spotlight without anything detracting from it.

Jessica and Keith would arrive in the morning and offer another distraction. In the meantime, Dayna decided to appreciate the good things about being home — the slower pace, the wonderful meals, the Southern hospitality. Of course Calero was a Southern city too, but as a Florida tourist spot, it lacked the quaint charm of a college town like Atchity.

Shiloh took a break from their chatter to check on the dumplings Mama had left simmering on the stove. Dayna pulled her cell phone from her purse to see if Warren had left her a message after their call had dropped in the airport. He had not, which led her to believe that he would wait till after her visit home to talk with her again.

She tried to turn her thoughts back to Shiloh, who was asking whether she wanted water or tea. Looked like nursing a broken heart was destined to be routine. Might as well put on her mask and hide behind her smile.

SIXTY-ONE

Tamara had sent Dayna a text just yesterday in an attempt to make peace; now it was time to call.

She made that decision as she sat next to Brent's bed, watching the heart monitor beep, the blood pressure machine swoosh and pump, and her husband's chest rise and fall to the rhythm created by a drug-induced sleep. Seeing him in this state was like watching the center of her soul wither; yet she was thankful she *was* here. After enjoying a day at home with Tamara, his mom, and his brother Winston, Brent had taken a turn for the worse only this morning, and he'd been admitted to the hospital by noon. Grasping the seriousness of his condition, Brent's mother called the rest of the family and told them to come as soon as they could.

Tamara and Brent hadn't been to church much since he fell ill, for reasons that ranged from not feeling well to anger at God; but whatever their excuse or state of mind, Pastor Stephenson never failed to be there for them. Today was no exception. He waited just outside Brent's door, prepared to join the family in prayer around Brent's bed when they were ready. Mrs. Chestnut was on her way too.

Brent's eyes flickered open, and Tamara caressed his cheek.

"Baby? Can you hear me?"

He nodded and tried to lift his hand, but when he couldn't, Tamara leaned toward him, to see if he was trying to speak.

"What do you need, baby? Water? Pain medicine?"

Brent shook his head, and she struggled to understand his whispers. Finally she made out the words "Psalm" and "Kiss."

"Psalm and kiss?"

Brent's mother had been watching from the doorway, so nurses wouldn't chide them for breaking the one-visitor-at-a-time rule. She walked over and kissed her son.

"When he was a little boy and came running to me because he was angry or afraid or facing a challenge, I would lead him through the twenty-third Psalm," Mama Davidson told Tamara. She too leaned closer to Brent. "Is that what you're asking for, son? Someone to recite Psalm 23?"

Brent fixed his eyes on his mother's face and nodded once. The request sent a streak of panic through Tamara. She closed her eyes and reminded herself that God's strength was perfect when her own was weak; she needed to keep her composure for Brent's sake.

God, help me.

Tamara motioned for Brent's mother to do the honors, but Mrs. Davidson shook her head.

"No, sweetheart," she told Tamara. "I had that privilege when he was my little boy. You are his beloved wife, and he is in your care now. You recite the Scripture to him. I'll get my Bible out of my purse."

Tears spilled down Tamara's cheeks. "No need. It's one of my favorite passages too. I know it by heart."

Tamara tenderly kissed Brent's parched lips and was rewarded with a smile. He gripped her hand as firmly as he could while she uttered the six verses of the Psalm in a shaky voice.

Minutes later, he dozed off, and she stepped out so his mother could sit with him. Tamara strolled to the exit door at the end of the fifth-floor hallway and stepped into the stairwell. She pulled her cell phone from her pocket and, despite her trembling fingers, managed to dial the number scrawled on a piece of paper. This was the right thing to do, even if it gave her heartburn.

SIXTY-TWO

The Sunday morning routine in the Wilson household hadn't changed since Dayna's childhood; it had merely expanded to include grandchildren. Daddy — and now her brother-in-law Randy — didn't eat breakfast with the family or speak to them. Each delivered a slight nod hello when they strode past everyone in the kitchen on their way to church, clear in heart, mind, and belly, ready to deliver the Lord's Word for the day.

Dayna and Jessica exchanged glances between bites of Mama's pancakes, bacon, and eggs. How was it possible that Shiloh had married Daddy's clone? Or had Randy been a nice guy before getting to know their father and emulating him? Either way, it disheartened Dayna to see her sister living her mother's life. She worried that her nieces and nephew were suffering from the same emotional abandonment she and her siblings had experienced because of their father's singular devotion to the church.

The few times she broached the subject with Shiloh, her sister grew defensive or mustered a high-wattage grin to prove her family's happiness. Dayna wanted to shake Shiloh and remind her that the "smile mask" didn't work on the person who had developed it. Eventually, she'd decided to let it be. She couldn't live Shiloh's life, and who knew — maybe someday they'd be the kind of sisters who trusted and supported each other unconditionally, through fantastic and difficult circumstances, and everything in between.

Just hours into her stay, Dayna's plans to go-along-to-get-along changed. After tossing and turning all night Friday with thoughts of Warren, Brent, and Tamara racing through her mind, she'd realized that the truth was priceless. She decided not to spend this visit painting a sugarcoated picture of her life just to put her family at ease. It was what it was, warts and all. Maybe walking in that truth would help everyone else do the same. Yesterday during an outing to the mall with her mother and sisters, she'd admitted over lunch that she was sad because of her recent estrangement from Warren and how close she'd come to finding happiness with a good man. Without sharing specifics, she acknowledged her efforts to stop being judgmental and help a friend who'd made some bad choices survive a difficult time. She told her mother and sisters about Duchess and how she loved this woman's honesty and spunk.

"She's not afraid to live life and have an opinion about it, and she loves the Lord too," Dayna said and smiled. Her praise of her elderly friend seemed to offend Mama, and Dayna was surprised. Maybe Mama wasn't as satisfied with the life she'd carved out for herself as she portrayed. Perhaps she'd had to set aside some of her own goals and desires for her husband's benefit.

Dayna wished she and Mama and her sisters could talk about those things comfortably, instead of whispering about who was wearing what, who sat where in church, and who had the audacity not to speak to whom. The meaningful stuff would help her — in fact, all of them — grow into being better people.

This morning, though, after the kids were shooed away to brush teeth and finish grooming themselves for church, Jessica returned to Dayna's revelations.

"About what you shared yesterday . . . what happened with Warren?"

441

Dayna shrugged. She wondered whether the sorrow engulfing her spirit at the mention of his name was visible in her eyes.

"I took him for granted and let him slip through my fingers, and probably into the arms of another woman."

Mama frowned. "That sounds a bit . . . like déjà vu."

"It's also inaccurate."

The baritone uttering that statement caused a temporary hiccup in Dayna's breathing. It couldn't be . . . but it was. She turned away from the kitchen table and saw Warren standing in the doorway, with Daddy and Randy on his heels looking concerned and puzzled.

"We were pulling out when he showed up in a taxi," Randy said. "We thought your boyfriend wasn't coming!"

Dayna ignored him and flew from her seat to the place she most wanted to be: in Warren Avery's arms.

Thank you, God.

He kissed her, in front of her entire family, until he needed to come up for air. "I missed my salsa partner," he said, and grinned.

With Dayna secure in his arms, Warren turned toward the frowning Reverend Wilson.

"Sir, this is not how I planned to do this, but this is long overdue. Since we're all here together now, and I honestly don't want to wait any longer, I'd like to respectfully ask for your daughter's hand in marriage."

Daddy seemed frozen. When he didn't respond, Jessica jumped in. "Don't worry, Daddy — you don't have to marry them at Riverview Baptist; we know this might be too progressive for the congregation."

Shiloh swatted Jessica's arm, but Dayna buried her face in Warren's shoulder to muffle her laughter.

"I love her, sir," Warren said to Dayna's father, "and it's taken some minor drama on both of our parts for me to realize what we have is worth the challenges we'll experience as a couple. If we can work together, we can overcome anything. I will love Dayna, serve as her spiritual leader and partner, and do my best to make her happy."

Mama left her seat at the table and stood next to Daddy. She peered up at him, awaiting his reply. Dayna would have given her firstborn to know what excuses, prayers, or pleas were rattling through his mind.

Daddy cleared his throat and looked at Dayna, whose head still rested on Warren's shoulder. His eyes softened more than she'd ever noticed before, even when Brent had gone through this process.

"If you'll do all those things you promise, plus keep God first in your life and in your marriage, you have my blessing — and my wife's — to marry our daughter," Daddy said. "You've got to take good care of her. She's tough, but she's still our baby girl."

Dayna was speechless. This was the man the church members knew and loved. Maybe if she kept at it, she'd see more of this side of him.

Daddy cleared his throat. "I, uh, do have some questions about how this different race thing might cause trouble for you two, but we can talk that over later. Love can triumph. I believe that."

Warren nodded. "We do too, sir. Thank you, and you too, Mrs. Wilson, for your blessing. I'm looking forward to taking care of her."

Dayna hugged him. "Please don't tell me that was your formal proposal."

Warren shook his head and chuckled. "Not hardly, babe. I will take care of that later. I figured I'd get the preliminaries out of the way while your parents are both here. I actually came bearing some sad news. I need to get you back to Florida as quickly as possible. Tamara called last night; things aren't looking good."

Dayna gasped. "Let me grab my things. Are we driving or flying? How will we get there in time?"

"John is helping us out. He's waiting at the airport on a private runway."

She remembered that one of Warren's golf buddies flew planes as a weekend hobby and owned a small four-seater. She had purposely avoided riding in that crop-duster, but today, it appeared she would have to endure the bumpy ride for Brent's sake.

"You're leaving now? What about your Easter Sunday solo?" Mama asked. "You two can't stay for a few hours, at least through the first half of the worship service?"

Dayna's lack of frustration surprised her. She hugged Mama and took her hand. "If Tamara made the effort to call Warren, this is serious, Mama. Brent must be nearing the end, and one or both of them want me there. I need to go."

"Brent?" her sisters screeched his name at the same time. Dayna tried not to glare at Mama. Any other news she would have spilled within seconds of receiving it, but somehow she had forgotten to tell the family that Brent was terminally ill and that he and Dayna had reconnected.

"Mama will fill you all in; I've got to get

there." Dayna trotted to her childhood bedroom and tossed her toiletries and clothing into her suitcase. She shed her bathrobe and slid into the jeans she'd worn the day before and a T-shirt she had planned to wear after church.

Minutes later, she clutched her suitcase and paused in the doorway, remembering how the last time she'd slept in this room before becoming a wife, she'd been full of optimism and unshakable certainty that she was leaving to flourish with her life partner. This time, that same sentiment filled her, but it was accompanied by an unfamiliar peace she hadn't manufactured herself. This time, she knew God was pleased with two mature people making a decision to dance hand in hand through life's peaks and valleys.

The last time she'd left this room with marriage on her mind, she'd been eager to get away from the façade of a happy family so she could create an authentic one. This time, she was leaving with the understanding that God was the true source of joy, no matter her marital status, and that regardless of how far she went or how long she stayed away, her family was so integral to who she was, she'd always take a piece of home with her.

Dayna returned to the kitchen and kissed Mama good-bye. Daddy had already left with Randy to open the church for Sunday school, and her sisters must have retired to their rooms to dress.

"Tell Daddy I love him," Dayna told Mama. "I'm sorry about missing service today."

Mama hugged Dayna and looked into her eyes. "It's okay; you're doing the right thing. I'm proud of you, Dayna. We'll say a prayer for Brent at church, and as a family when we get home."

"Say one for Brent and for Tamara, Mama," Dayna said. "She's going to need it as much as he does."

SIXTY-THREE

Dayna and Warren began the private seventy-five minute flight from Atchity's tiny airstrip into Melbourne's central Florida regional hub with each of them uttering a prayer for Brent and Tamara.

"What did she say when she called?" Dayna asked.

"What struck me most was what she didn't say." Warren sighed. "She confirmed that you were in Alabama and said if I had any ideas about how to get you home quickly and safely, she'd like my help. The fact that she called me instead of you let me know that Brent's time might be waning. She knew you were out of town and didn't want you upset and trying to travel, I guess."

Dayna sat next to Warren in the rear of the small plane, straining to hear him over the hum of the engine. They wore seat belts and sat in close proximity to John as he concentrated on the flight path. She was thankful he wasn't trying to banter with them; she wasn't in the mood for small talk. The priority was to get them where they needed to be in a hurry.

Her thoughts turned to Warren's surprise appearance at her parents' home this morning.

"What a sense of timing," she said. "Couldn't have planned it better myself. You just wanted to hear how wonderful I think you are."

"You got that right!" Warren grinned and reached for her hand. "It's ironic that Brent and Tamara got me there just in time to hear what I needed to hear most."

Dayna wasn't sure what he meant. She stared at him, awaiting an explanation.

"I wouldn't have asked for your hand in marriage if I doubted your love for me, Dayna," he said. "But the past few weeks left me questioning how deep and serious our relationship was. You seemed unsure sometimes whether to honor your past ties to Brent or your current ones with me."

Dayna nodded. "Did you hear the end of my call to you in the airport?"

Warren shook his head. "Your phone cut off while you were still talking. I figured if it was important, you'd call back."

"It was important, but I couldn't call back

because the flight was taking off," Dayna said. "I thought you may have heard but would rather talk later. Or maybe you wanted something different. It's not like you don't have options."

"Speaking of that, Miss 'Déjà vu,' " he said, referring to her mother's comment, "that option you were referring to over breakfast this morning has exercised her right to leave."

Dayna frowned. "Come again?"

"I've been playing Mr. Innocent with you, mostly because I resented what seemed to be happening between you and Brent. I guess it was my way of passively getting revenge, especially after I overheard his hospital-bed declarations of love, but I've known for a while that Lily was interested in me," Warren said.

Dayna smirked. "You're kidding."

"When she realized that you and I had cooled off, she ramped up her efforts to date me, and frankly, it made me uncomfortable."

"Am I going to have to give a beat down?" Dayna was joking, but she was itching to know what Ms. Lily had been up to.

"Not necessary," Warren said over the hum of the plane's engine. "When I caught her throwing one of your pictures in the trash, I pulled it out and told her she could put the ones that featured her there instead. A few days later she told me she would be leaving to help her brother operate his restaurant franchise in Washington, DC."

Dayna didn't believe it. "She'd never leave Michael and Mason that suddenly. Do you think she's calling your bluff?"

Warren shrugged. "May have been. But I took her up on it. I gave her a month's pay and told her she could consider our arrangement immediately terminated. She stopped working for me two days ago.

"The boys will always love her, and she'll always be their Aunt Lily. Truthfully, she's been a tremendous blessing to our family in the four years that April's been gone; we wouldn't have made it through that first year without her.

"But Michael and Mason are old enough now to help out more around the house and care for themselves. I've hired a retired lady from church to prepare dinner each evening and to pick them up after school when they have practices that cause them to miss the bus. Otherwise, we're managing okay on our own, and when you join the family, we'll be even better."

"Wow," Dayna said. "But wait a minute — this thing about me joining the family . . .

I just want you to know we're keeping the cook and driver. You may have made a mistake by sending Lily away if that's what will make you happy."

She raised an eyebrow to feign seriousness over her joke. During the time they'd dated, Warren had tasted and applauded her cooking, but he knew her domestic skills, and interest in acquiring more, were nil.

Warren lifted her chin with the crook of his forefinger so he could search her eyes. The love Dayna saw there made her swoon.

"I never looked at Lily like I'm looking at you. I never felt in danger of losing control when she touched me, and the sound of her voice never made my heart race," he said. "You shimmied your way into my heart the night I met you on the salsa dance floor, and the deal was sealed when we met again a few days later at the hospital staff meeting. I hadn't planned on dating someone at my new job, but I also hadn't planned on meeting you, Dayna Wilson. God knows what he's doing. Lily's season with our family was perfectly timed; and if we had been meant to be more than friends, that would have happened. Instead, he sent you, and I almost let my jealousy keep us apart."

Dayna shook her head.

"I've had a lot of time to think this

through too, Warren. You had every right to feel resentful. I skipped our date nights, and I have to admit that I wavered sometimes between whom to prioritize more — you or Brent. I was wrong for that, and I'm sorry. As far as I've come since my divorce, this experience with Brent and Tamara showed me I still have a lot of growing to do. Sometimes it's safer to cling to familiar dysfunction rather than pursue a healthier, unknown reward. I'm excited to become your wife, but I'd like us to go through some intensive couples counseling before we take the plunge, if you're willing; I want to get this right this time."

John interrupted them by shouting a flight update.

"Landing in ten minutes! Sit back and prepare!"

Dayna and Warren complied. As the plane descended, Warren laced his fingers with hers and mouthed the words she'd feared she'd never hear from him again: *I love you.*

Whatever they were about to face at Holmes Regional Medical Center with Brent and Tamara, this time they'd do it together.

Sixty-Four

We r here.

Dayna sent that text to Tamara when the taxi pulled in front of Holmes Regional Medical Center. Seconds later she received a text with Brent's floor number and room number.

She and Warren rode the elevator to the fifth floor and dashed down the hallway, hand in hand, toward Brent's private hospice room. When they rounded the corner and saw Tamara waiting for them outside one of the patient rooms, Dayna knew.

She and Warren slowed to a walk, and Warren squeezed her hand.

Tamara's eyes were red, and her hands were trembling, but her voice was strong.

"He's gone."

She said the words as if they hurt, and Dayna gripped her in a hug. The two women clung to each other and wept. When they were spent, Tamara wiped her eyes and reached for Dayna's hand.

"You want to see him?"

Dayna hesitated. If he had passed, what was the point?

Then she recalled the Scripture that Audrey's friend and Dayna's coworker Chas had recited to them recently: "Absent from the body means present with the Lord."

Brent's spirit had gone heavenward, but maybe from that place on high, he could witness her paying respect to his earthly remains, and maybe he could hear her say one last time that she loved him.

"Okay," Dayna said, and placed her hand in Tamara's. "Let's go in."

Warren joined Dayna and Tamara in the room and led them in prayer over Brent's breathless body. Then he and Tamara left Dayna alone to say good-bye however she chose.

Dayna was at a loss. What did you say to a first love whose gift had been both loving you and leaving you? If he hadn't left, she may never have dealt with her personal issues and overcome as many of them as she had; and she certainly wouldn't have found the courage to go to a salsa club alone and meet her future husband.

"So you won after all, huh?" she said, and

smiled, oblivious to her own tears. "You wound up with both of your wives at your bedside. And the beauty of it is, we both loved you, Brent, and we'll continue to love you. Carmen will do an excellent job with the foundation, and so will Tamara. Hundreds of injured athletes across this nation will know your name and your story. You done good, Brent, very good."

Dayna kissed his cheek. It was cool and clammy, which both unnerved her and reassured her that his spirit was in a safe and warm place with the Lord.

"Thank you for gracing my life, Brent — both times. I learned a lot from you about love and forgiveness and living one's truth both times around. I'll do my best to honor you in the way I live every tomorrow. I love you, forever."

She emerged from the room and walked into Warren's waiting embrace. He held her tight, until she stepped back, indicating she was okay. Warren escorted Dayna to the waiting room, where she found Tamara and Brent's mother sitting side by side, clinging to each other as they wept, with Winston and Tamara's mother standing nearby. Dayna approached them, and Mrs. Davidson stood and hugged her. Dayna took a seat next to Tamara and whispered, "Thank you."

With her head bowed, Tamara extended an open palm to Dayna. Dayna grasped the hand of Brent Davidson's wife, but extended her other toward Warren. She had not wavered: This was where her future lay.

A CeCe Winan song she'd been listening to recently during her morning meditations surfaced in her spirit. "Blessed, Broken and Given" was about real life. God had broken each of them to bless them, hadn't he?

Out of something evil had come some good. She saw it as clearly as if Brent had written instructions in his foundation plans: Tamara would manage the foundation board, scholarship applications, and media needs, and Dayna would assist her as much or as little as Tamara desired. Together, they'd tell athletes and anyone else who cared about a remarkable man who lived his faith more than he talked about it, and maybe, if and when the time was right, these two strong and beautiful sisters would share how they learned to love one man, and respect each other, despite the odds.

ACKNOWLEDGMENTS

No book that focuses on love and forgiveness is written without the divine hand of God as puppeteer. My first and utmost thanks goes to him for allowing me to speak through the written word.

I'm sincerely grateful to my immediate and extended family for your never-ending support and for gracing my life with yours. To Syd and Jay in particular, may you always know that I love you unconditionally and joyfully. Thank you for being my biggest cheerleaders. Utmost thanks to my siblings for having my back; Dr. Barbara Grayson, Henry Haney, Sandra Williams, and Patsy Scott. Thanks to a supportive crew of friends who are like family — Muriel Miller Branch, Sharon Shahid, Bobbie Walker Trussell, Carol Jackson, Gwendolyn Richard, Barbara Rascoe, Lori Willis, Charmaine Spain, Jeff and Tracy Street, Everett and Danita Cannon, Connie and Ernest

Lambert, Joe and Gloria Murphy, Comfort Anderson-Miller, Robin Farmer, Ursula Murdaugh, Maya Payne Smart, Lissette Pratt, Bonnie Newman Davis, Johanna Schuchert, LaVera Williams, Nancy Lucy, Joyce P. Jones, and many more heroes and "sheroes" this limited space won't permit me to name.

I thank my editors, Sue Brower, Becky Philpott, Leslie Peterson, Tonya Osterhouse, and Lori Vanden Bosch, for challenging me to give my best to every book. Sincere thanks to Steve Sammons, Alicia Mey, Jennifer VerHage, and others on the Zondervan marketing, sales, and publicity team for helping bring this book to life.

Thanks to my agent, Steve Laube, for your encouragement and support, and to one of my first readers, Teresa L. Coleman, for your helpful insight.

I also extend deep gratitude to readers, booksellers, book club members, women's ministry groups, editors, bloggers, radio hosts, and conference organizers for continuing to spread the word about my books and for inviting me to share my stories in your circles. Special thanks for your encouragement to my author friends Carol Mackey, Dee Stuart, Michelle Sutton, Vanessa Easter, Rhonda McKnight, Tia McCollors,

Linda Beed, Booker Mattison, Kendra Norman-Bellamy, Tiffany L. Warren, Victoria Christopher Murray, Fritz Kling, and Adriana Trigiani.

I also thank my church family for your prayers and enthusiasm; members of the Midlothian Chapter of Jack and Jill; and specifically you, the person reading (or listening to) this book now. Thank you for spending time in my fictional world. I hope you have been, or will be, entertained, inspired, and blessed beyond measure.

All My Best,
Stacy

The employees of Thorndike Press hope you have enjoyed this Large Print book. All our Thorndike, Wheeler, and Kennebec Large Print titles are designed for easy reading, and all our books are made to last. Other Thorndike Press Large Print books are available at your library, through selected bookstores, or directly from us.

For information about titles, please call:
  (800) 223-1244

or visit our Web site at:
  http://gale.cengage.com/thorndike

To share your comments, please write:
  Publisher
  Thorndike Press
  10 Water St., Suite 310
  Waterville, ME 04901